ALL THE DEAD HEROES

ALL THE DEAD HEROES

A T.S.W. Sheridan Mystery

STEPHEN F. WILCOX

ST. MARTIN'S PRESS
NEW YORK

This novel is a work of fiction. All of the events, characters, names, and places depicted in this novel are entirely fictitious or are used fictitiously.

ALL THE DEAD HEROES. Copyright © 1992 by Stephen F. Wilcox. All rights reserved. Printed in the United States of America. No part of this book may be used or reproduced in any manner whatsoever without written permission except in the case of brief quotations embodied in critical articles or reviews. For information, address St. Martin's Press, 175 Fifth Avenue, New York, NY 10010.

Production Editor: David Stanford Burr

Library of Congress Cataloging-in-Publication Data
Wilcox, Stephen F.
     All the dead heroes / Stephen F. Wilcox.
        p. cm.
     ISBN 0-312-06896-4
     I. Title.
     PS3573.I419A34 1992
     813'.54—dc20   91-33462
                                        CIP

First Edition: May 1992

10 9 8 7 6 5 4 3 2 1

In memory of Miss K.

Of the character in question, the writer has no more to say, than that he represents a man of native goodness, removed from the temptations of civilised life, though not entirely forgetful of its prejudices and lessons . . . and betraying the weaknesses as well as the virtues of his situation and of his birth.

—James Fenimore Cooper, from the introduction to
The Last of the Mohicans

ALL THE DEAD HEROES

CHAPTER 1

SNOWFLAKES large as drink coasters fell at forty-five-degree angles past the kitchen window while the logs in the great room's fieldstone fireplace crackled and hissed and fought back the icy downdraught that whistled in the chimney. A fresh gust of arctic air caused the cottage to shiver on its foundations and chased William of Orange to a safe haven under the old morris chair. At four-thirty in the afternoon, it was as dark as December outside.

But this was early April, and Mother Nature was merely playing another practical joke on western New York. A major cold front sliding down from Ontario, the irritatingly cheerful TV weatherman had warned the night before, and anyone with a few years' experience in the Finger Lakes, and a modicum of sense, nodded stoically and made sure the wood box was full and muttered an automatic if irrational curse on our neighbor to the north. Upstaters blame all bad weather on Canada; everything else is pinned on Washington or the Japanese.

"Pre-ten-ding."

Eric Clapton's voice poured like single-malt from the stereo's big speakers, and I gamely harmonized while my hands dug through the junk drawer for the corkscrew. A bottle of Bully Hill Seyval Blanc waited on the pass-through counter. I looked out across the great room to the span of double-glazed glass—purposely avoiding eye contact with the stack of work notes I'd left

1

piled on the coffee table—and tried to make out the lake through the gloom and the thickening carpet of snow out on the deck. There'd been a rumor of spring earlier in the week, when the crocuses along the driveway had bloomed and the tiny spearlike leaves of the daffodils had forced their way up through the softening soil beside the front stoop. Now the flowers would have to wait, as would the fly fishermen who'd come to town for the opening of trout season and the grape growers who were eager to inspect their vines for freeze damage. A couple more days, the weatherman had said, until the freakish storm had worn itself out and seasonal temperatures returned.

Two more days cooped up in the cottage, staring out at the rolling gray surface of Seneca Lake, I reflected as my fingers found the corkscrew. Two more days of applewood splits snapping in the fire grate, the fruity bouquet mingling with the smell of fresh-ground coffee. Two more days of deferring that research trip to the library and ignoring the word processor and making no decisions weightier than which music to cue up next on the compact disc player or what wine goes best with broiled lamb chops.

I couldn't help but grin.

Especially when the giant penguin padded out from the back bedroom.

The cat reacted first, letting out a distressed mew and darting from under the morris chair to more substantial fortifications behind the vintage leather sofa. I decided to play it casual myself, taking down a pair of wine glasses from the overhead cabinet and leaning on the pass-through countertop before asking, "Does this mean you'll be wanting krill for dinner?"

"You promised you wouldn't laugh." The voice, half petulant and half chagrined, came from a patch of black gauze just below the penguin's yellow felt beak.

"I'm not laughing, I'm smiling," I said. "Besides, you didn't warn me you'd be impersonating a *Bloom County* cartoon. I was expecting . . . I don't know, an Indian maiden or something. Sexy little buckskin skirt, long black wig, stuff like that. I mean, the 'mohaca' in Mohaca Springs does come from an Iroquois word."

"We're not selling fire water, Sheridan," she said with asperity. "The product is wine coolers. Mohaca Springs Sparkling

Wine Coolers, with the emphasis on cool, like at the North Pole, get it?''

"There aren't any penguins at the North Pole, just polar bears and seals, I think.''

"Well, maybe so," she said, her stubby black wings flailing, "but another wine cooler company is already using a polar bear, and seals aren't cute enough.''

"So you came up with the idea of using that little penguin character in the cartoon strip.''

"Opus," she supplied. "But this is different, a sort of generic penguin. Otherwise we'd have a problem with trademark infringement.'' She raised the wings up and fussed with the folds around the neck of the outfit. There was the ripping sound of Velcro stays giving way as she tugged off the suit's wobbly round head. "Opus has a humongous nose, for one thing, and this guy's is much smaller and pointier, more like a real penguin.'' She held the head out for my inspection, but I was more interested in studying her nose. And mouth and eyes, and the way the deep brown of her shoulder-length hair gave off red highlights when she shook it back into place.

Kate Sumner was in her late twenties. She had dropped out of college in her junior year to get married and, a year later, have a baby. The marriage had ended a couple of years ago, leaving Kate with a six-year-old daughter to support. She had gone back to college to complete her degree in communications/journalism and was now working at her first real job outside the home, as an associate publicist with a Rochester advertising agency. The only difference between advertising and publicity, she told me, was that you had to pay for ad space whereas publicity was something the media gave you for free if you knew how to pull their strings.

Which is where the penguin suit—and I—came into the picture.

Kate and I had met a month earlier at a cocktail party at the Humbert Winery tasting room. I'd been invited by Allison Humbert, who had taken over management duties at the family-owned winery following the death of her uncle some twenty months earlier. The purpose of the event was to announce that Humbert and four other local vintners had joined forces on a new product, to be called Mohaca Springs Sparkling Wine Coolers.

3

The party was an excuse to announce the new venture to the local press. Although I technically qualify, Allison had invited me merely as a courtesy. I'm a freelance reporter, but I specialize in crime stories. And while some folks may consider wine coolers to be a crime against the palate, there was nothing illegal about the stuff and therefore nothing to attract my professional interest. But it had been a long winter and cabin fever alone was enough to convince me to abandon my writing desk for an afternoon of free nibblies and drinks in town.

Kate Sumner's agency had been hired to handle advertising and promotion for the new wine cooler. The attraction, at least on my part, was immediate and visceral when Allison—always the matchmaker—maneuvered the two of us into the same corner of the tasting room. Kate was beautiful and personable, possessed of a quick wit and a ready smile.

She had accepted my invitation to join me for an early dinner after the cocktail party, and things had progressed—albeit slowly—from there. She was rebounding from a bad relationship and an aborted career and wasn't in a hurry to repeat the process. We saw each other sporadically, whenever our itineraries placed us both in Mohaca Springs or Rochester. On our third date, parked at a secluded overlook alongside the Genesee River Gorge we made love in the back seat, furtive and awkward as a couple of teenagers. Kate had been tentative, then voracious, and finally a bit embarrassed by her enthusiasm; it had been a long time, she told me quietly. Now we were on our fourth date and our first overnighter.

"You think it's asinine," she accused me as she rolled up the bird head and tucked it under her arm like an overstuffed handbag. "My first important campaign and you think it's stupid."

"No." I stripped the seal off the seyval blanc and moved the corkscrew into place. "It's a cute idea."

"Cute?" The little black penguin wings found her hips.

"Not cute, no; that isn't the word I want. High concept is what I meant. And hot. Very hot."

"Now you're patronizing me."

"No, I'm not." I gave the handle on the corkscrew several turns, then pushed down the side levers and watched the cork rise out of the bottle. "Teasing you a little maybe," I said as I filled the glasses. "How do you think this will go with lamb chops? I don't have a decent red. . . . "

"Lamb chops! Who gives a good goddamn about the lamb chops? This is only my whole career we're talking about here, and all you can do is smirk at me."

I lifted my glass and took a taste and sighed. "You're right, Kate, I apologize. Here it is a late Friday afternoon, a blizzard blowing outside, a roaring fire inside, a romantic weekend for two in the offing, and I kill the mood by breaking out the wine and smiling too much."

Her brown eyes opened wide and she blinked once. Then the corners crinkled and a small grin crept reluctantly forth. "I promised not to blab about business matters, didn't I," she said.

"Words to that effect."

"And to relax, not to let agency accounts and office politics creep into the conversation."

"I'm thinking of tacking up a sign over the front door," I said. "YE WHO ENTER HERE, NO SHOP TALK."

She waddled the length of the pass-through counter and back. "You're right, you're right; I'm making too much out of this. If I'm going to make it in this business, I have to learn to maintain." Now she stopped and faced me across the counter. "Make a decision and then stay with it, right?"

"Right."

"It's just . . . this *is* pretty important and I *do* value your opinion, your having a media background and all."

"Kate, all I know about advertising is that there are too many damn commercial interruptions for adjustable beds and weight-loss gimmicks when I'm trying to watch the late show." I set down my glass. "As for promoting a new product by paying an actor to stand outside supermarkets in a penguin suit—my honest opinion?—it sounds a little silly to me, but then I never understood why Spuds MacKenzie enticed people to buy a particular brand of beer either. Which means your bird will probably become a cult hero, and you'll sell wine coolers as fast as you can bottle the stuff."

To my surprise the anxious look surrendered to a satisfied smile. "That's almost exactly what my boss said. 'Silly but memorable, Kate, and that's the name of the game.' I think Mr. Penguin and I are going to do just fine." She made a try for her glass, but couldn't negotiate it with the clumsy mittens sewn in under the suit's wing tips. "I think I'd better save the celebratory drink until I change into something more . . . comfortable." I watched her walk awkwardly toward the short hallway leading to the back bedroom, and realized that I knew even less about women than I did about advertising.

I scooped up the glasses and the wine bottle and adjourned to the old sofa facing the fireplace. The sofa—along with most of the rest of the furnishings and the cottage itself—had been left to me by my uncle, Charlie Dugan. Charlie was fond of telling his old card-playing cronies he could read a female's mood simple as reading a newspaper. It was a conceit he'd clung to right up until a woman of his acquaintance stuck a knife in him.

I shook my head and leaned back and watched the logs spit orange flames up toward the flue. Clapton was into a blues rocker now, trading guitar licks with Robert Cray and growling about a woman who'd done him wrong. I tried to empathize but the fire was too warm, the wine too good, the promise of things to come too pleasing. My eyes were half closed when the phone rang.

It took a few moments to track the buzzing to a mound of magazine clippings on the scarred oak coffee table. Cordless phones have their virtues, but staying put isn't one of them. I excavated the thing out from under the clips and punched the little red button on the grip.

"Peter Calvett calling for T.S.W. Sheridan."

"This is Sheridan."

The voice on the other end was female and nasal, and Manhattan with a slight Latin slur. "Please hold for Mr. Calvett," she said automatically. There was a click, followed by a string arrangement of "Blue Bayou." Curiosity was all that kept me from hanging up.

Pete Calvett was special assignments editor for *The Sporting Life*, a biweekly sports magazine aimed at capturing "the people behind the stats," as Pete liked to say; profiles on the personal lives of professional athletes and where-are-they-now pieces were standard fare. Sports aren't my normal beat, but Pete had been good enough to send a couple of assignments my way when the stories had crime hooks. The most recent piece I'd done for the magazine was an investigation into recruiting scandals in Division-One college basketball.

"Sheridan! What's the weather doing up there in the boonies?" Calvett's booming voice came over the line as suddenly as a thunderclap. "It's raining like a son of a bitch here."

"Count your blessings," I said. "It's snowing like a son of a bitch here."

"Blessings, hell. I gotta try to hail a cab in an hour or so, man. You ever try to get a cab at five-thirty in midtown when it's pouring?"

"At least you don't have to shovel it."

"There's that," he agreed. "Anyway, the reason I called, Sheridan, I want you to profile an ex-ballplayer for me—something with depth but lean, like around two K, two and a half tops. You get the byline and the standard rate plus reasonable itemized expenses."

Two K was Calvett's way of saying he wanted the piece to be about two thousand words. That meant it wasn't a lead feature, but it wasn't filler either.

"Who's the subject, Pete?"

"You're a Yankees' fan, right? So who's the best second sacker ever to make the pivot in the pinstripes?"

"Frank Wooley."

"Bingo. The Bronx Black Sheep himself."

It was one of those names that jumped out of the past carrying a suitcase of emotions under each arm. As a boy in the sixties, I'd had my share of idols. Like a good Irish Catholic, I handed out campaign literature for Bobby Kennedy's senate campaign long before I was old enough to vote. My first electric guitar, bought with two years' worth of lawn mowing and paper-route earnings, had to be a Rickenbacker because that's what John Lennon played. And when I was a second baseman in little league I wore a Frank Wooley signature glove. I still looked on voting as a civic duty, but I'd long since given up on the guitar, and the glove was just a tattered remnant tucked away in a trunk in my mother's attic. I wasn't sure which was more tragic—a hero who dies young, or one whose reputation dies first from self-inflicted wounds.

"Hey, Sheridan," Calvett broke into my reverie, "you still there or what?"

"Yeah, I'm here."

"Geez, I thought you'd jump at this assignment. You do realize Wooley's finally going to Cooperstown this year?"

"We get newspapers up here in the boonies, too, Pete." This year's selections to the hall of fame had been announced about two months earlier by the Baseball Writers Association. As expected, former Cincinnati star Joe Morgan and Baltimore pitching ace Jim Palmer had made it in their first year of eligibility. The surprise selection was Frank Wooley.

"So show me a little enthusiasm, Timothy me boy," Pete said, taking a shot at an Irish brogue and missing wide. "Okay, the Wooley profile isn't featured—Palmer and Morgan are gonna get most of the space—but this is a solid assignment here, Sheridan, and you're perfect for it."

"How do you figure that?"

" 'Cause you're good at finding out stuff that people are reluctant to talk about, and with Wooley's background that's gonna come in handy. The other thing is, we've got to locate him first." Calvett lowered his voice to a normal conversational level. "Look, I tried giving this assignment to one of my staff writers last month. A real good wordsmith this guy, but he couldn't find New Jersey if you spotted him the Lincoln Tunnel. Besides, we're ninety-nine percent sure that Wooley's living in the Finger Lakes someplace—his monthly baseball pension checks go to a P.O. box up there. All you have to do is figure out where he is and get him to talk to you."

"I don't know, Pete," I hedged. "I appreciate your sending some work my way, but . . . I'm sort of backed up."

"Hey, take all the time you need. We're not even gonna run the hall stuff until our July 15 issue, the week before the induction ceremonies. Long as I know you've pinned Wooley down, I can wait on your copy until the end of June if necessary."

"I don't know," I repeated.

Calvett sighed. "Listen, I've already Fed-Exed you our file on Wooley—it oughta be there by tomorrow. Read it over, call me back on Monday. If you still don't want the assignment, I'll pay you whatever's fair just to find the guy for me, then I'll send out one my staff writers to do the profile. Good enough? I mean, you do think you can at least locate Wooley?"

"Of course."

"Fine. That's how we'll leave it. Call me Monday."

I frowned at the dead phone for a moment, then I tossed it onto the pile of debris on the coffee table and returned my gaze to the fire. It was a good assignment; a very good assignment. So why was I reluctant?

"I hope that wasn't a business call, Sheridan."

I turned my head ninety degrees. Kate was standing on the great room side of the pass-through counter, still wearing a tentative smile. What she was no longer wearing was the clumsy penguin suit; it had been exchanged for a thigh-length red silk robe and a matching pair of heels. Her legs were long and lean and winter white.

"Call? What call?" I said, through a brand new grin.

CHAPTER 2

THE weatherman blew it again.

The storm that was supposed to peter out by Sunday morning was still hanging in there on Tuesday afternoon. The temperature had risen just enough to make the snowflakes wetter and heavier and to batter the secondary roads into a nervous mix of potholes and slick macadam.

The voice on the radio was doing its damnedest to sustain the optimism of opening day, but the weather wasn't much better in Cleveland and the Yanks were already down five runs in the sixth and I wasn't really listening anyway.

I turned off the radio, flicked on the Bronco's wipers to clear the watery film from the windshield, and let my attention wander momentarily from the building that sat across the road. I was parked in the shadow of a boarded-up general store with a faded FOR SALE sign nailed to its weathered clapboard siding. To my left and behind me were three other buildings, each with rustic cedar shingles: the Snack Shack, a mom-and-pop grocery, and The Friendly Tavern. The only other public building was the one I was watching, and it was really only half public at that.

U.S. POST OFFICE, STEWART, N.Y. read the sign affixed to a boxy one-story addition on the side of a white farmhouse. The house sat close to the road and managed to look both neat and lived-in, with a plastic-covered glider resting in one corner of the porch and a chainlink fence running around the front yard. The fence helped to differentiate between the family's private space and a patch of blacktop that provided parking for the little post office. A picture window dominated the façade of the twenty-foot-square office and through it I could see the working side of the service counter, including the open pigeonhole backs of about two dozen lock boxes. I could also see the middle-aged postmistress sorting the mail, tending to the counter traffic, and, every so often, glancing out the window in the direction of my idling Bronco.

The tiny hamlet of Stewart straddled State Route 230 in northern Schuyler County, some twenty-five miles southwest of Mohaca Springs. One of a score of crossroads communities that dotted the hilly swath of farmland and pine woods that lay between the southern ends of Keuka and Seneca lakes, Stewart was the sort of place you might happen through if you were lost or on a Sunday drive, which often amounted to the same thing.

I watched the woman check on me again, her glance quick and neutral, as if she were merely keeping tabs on the snowfall. I'd stopped into the overheated post office first thing that morning and asked her for an address to go with the P.O. box number I had for Frank Wooley. She told me politely that she couldn't help me and when I pressed a little harder, she turned curt.

"It's against U.S. Postal Service regulations to give out that sort of information, sir," she said firmly.

End of discussion. She gave her attention to an old woman who wanted a letter weighed, and I retreated to the graveled lot outside the shuttered general store. That had been eight hours ago and now, as the afternoon shadows lengthened and the needle on my Ford's gas gauge inched closer toward the red, I had plenty of time to reconsider the easy assurances I'd given Pete Calvett.

The photocopies of the Wooley file arrived Saturday afternoon in a padded red-white-and-purple envelope. I barely glanced at it before tossing it on the kitchen counter, where it stayed until late Sunday afternoon. Kate left the cottage just after a midday brunch of French toast and Canadian bacon and All-American orange juice. I tried to convince her to stay awhile longer, but the snowplow had just gone through, and she decided to take advantage of a break in the storm to begin the seventy-mile drive back to her home and young daughter in Rochester. I carried her bags to her car through drifts of fresh white powder, the warmth of our goodbye kiss more than compensating for the chill in the air.

After she'd gone, I put on some music and took care of a few household chores, moving mechanically around the cottage's first floor, stacking dirty plates in the dishwasher, running a dust cloth over places that didn't require me to bend too far or move anything; doggedly attempting to hold onto the momentum of a quiet weekend and to avoid slipping prematurely into the weekday grind of paperwork and bookkeeping and the amber-on-black glare of a computer screen.

One of the disadvantages of living and working in the same place is that you're never out of earshot of the stacks of unfinished business that call out from your littered desktop. I had two half-written articles in the works already and I'd just started researching a third. But they were all pretty straightforward pieces, nothing I couldn't handle with a few calls and a trip to the library. So I did what all freelancers do when they don't want to do anything but feel compelled to do something. I decided to get a start on the least pressing assignment I had.

I carried a mug of steaming tea and the bundle of photocopies to the chair by the fire and tore open the envelope's end flap, dumping the contents onto the coffee table. Then I began to read.

The statistical life of Franklin George Wooley was readily available to anyone strong enough to lift a copy of the Baseball Encyclopedia down from a library shelf. He'd made his major-league debut with the Yankees in 1958—the second black player to make the team—and had finished up with the Philadelphia Phillies in 1970, after thirteen mostly distinguished seasons. The numbers that had belatedly sent him to Cooperstown included a lifetime batting average of .283, more than twenty-one hundred hits and four hundred steals, and nearly twelve hundred runs scored. He'd won five gold gloves for his gritty play at second base and had led the American League in stolen bases on the odd years that Luis Aparicio hadn't managed to do it for the White Sox or the Orioles. In nine seasons with the Yankees, Wooley played for six pennant winners and three World Series champions.

But I didn't need the Baseball Encyclopedia to remind me of Frank Wooley's accomplishments. I knew the man's career statistics as surely as I could recite the ID number on my old dog tags or name both of the Righteous Brothers. Some things stay with you long after you've forgotten which Spaniard discovered the Pacific Ocean or what distinguishes a trapezoid from a parallelogram. I also knew the numbers alone couldn't explain Wooley's importance to his team—or the fascination he'd held for a kid who lived and died with the Yankees' pennant hopes.

Frank Wooley had been the sparkplug of the great Yankee teams of the late fifties and early sixties, the little man who set the table for the big sticks—Maris and Mantle and Berra. A switch hitter with occasional power, Wooley's greatest offensive virtue was his ability to get on base, whether by a line drive or a bunt or a walk, and then to steal his way into scoring position. His finest single season came in 1961 when he compiled a .313 batting average with 37 stolen bases and 131 runs scored, tossing in 15 homers and 70 runs batted in for good measure. It might've meant most valuable player honors any other year, but this was the season when teammate Roger Maris hammered 61 balls into the seats —the first of many occasions when timing and circumstance seemed to conspire against Frank Wooley.

I took another sip of tea, then started sifting through the photocopies again, this time culling out the stories of his baseball triumphs and concentrating instead on the off-field controversies that eventually drove him into exile.

An old *New York Daily News* item recorded the first time that Wooley, for all the right reasons, got his name in the papers for something other than his ballplaying skills. It was 1964, and while Congress was up in Washington debating the Voting Rights Act, the Yankees were at spring training in St. Petersburg. As the newspaper account revealed, most of the team was staying at a hotel, but the black players had been housed with local black families. A sportswriter had cornered Wooley after an exhibition game and asked his opinion on the civil-rights movement.

"I've been a major leaguer for six seasons now and I've always done my job and kept my mouth zipped and left the politics to the politicians," he was quoted in the article. "But I'm a little g--d--- tired of giving my team a first-class effort on the field and then getting treated like a second-class citizen on the street."

He went on to say that discrimination had cost him the sort of salary and endorsement opportunities that would've gone to any white player with his record.

The day after Wooley's outburst appeared, Yankees' general manager Gus Oldham issued his own statement, lauding the Yankees' "proven commitment to equal justice for all" and calling Wooley "a selfish prima donna more interested in lining his pockets than in being a good team player."

And it didn't end there. Among the clips from 1964, I found half a dozen more discussing the club's "racial tensions." It didn't seem to bother the Yanks—they went on to win ninety-nine games and the pennant that year. But when they lost the World Series to St. Louis in seven games, Oldham, in a post-game tirade, inexplicably blamed the loss on "disruptions by clubhouse lawyers."

For his part, Wooley refused to back away from the civil-rights issue or any other subject he thought needed airing, from the players' pension plan to America's escalating involvement in Vietnam. His positions gained him admiration in some quarters: among activists in the civil-rights and the antiwar movements, and teenage boys with one eye on their favorite team and the other on the draft board. But his candor endeared him not at all to the average blue-collared, white-skinned baseball fan. As a result, over the next two years his relationship with management continued to deteriorate and Gus Oldham hinted broadly and often that he'd get rid of his star second baseman as soon as the right offer came along.

In midseason in 1966, an incident occurred that gave the Yankees' general manager the excuse he needed. Wooley was arrested following a two A.M. fistfight at a Manhattan nightclub. The photo that ran with the story showed an angry Frank Wooley walking out of a police precinct house arm in arm with one of the club's dancers, identified in the article as Evie March. Even the grainy old newspaper photo couldn't hide the fact that she was young and gorgeous—and white. The day after Wooley's arrest the charges were dropped, but the story wasn't finished. Oldham fined Wooley for breaking the team's curfew and "embarrassing the ballclub." Then a news story appeared in which a prominent black civil-rights activist criticized Wooley for "boozing and brawling and chasing white women." A month later, in what some interpreted as an act of defiance, Wooley married Evie March in a civil ceremony at a New Jersey courthouse. During the off-season, Oldham traded Wooley to the Philadelphia Phillies for an over-the-hill catcher.

In Philadelphia, Wooley continued to perform brilliantly on the field and to stir controversy off it. A clip from April, 1968, noted that he had been fined an undisclosed amount by Phillies' management for refusing to suit up for an exhibition game the day after Martin Luther King's assassination. In November of 1969, during a huge antiwar march in Washington, Wooley was teargassed and arrested along with a group that included Yippie Abbie Hoffman.

Then, in 1970, Frank Wooley became entangled in a series of problems that would push him into a premature retirement. In May, the commissioner's office announced that Wooley had been under investigation for consorting with a professional gambler named Harry Lundquist. Although no wrongdoing was proved, Wooley, who admitted knowing Lundquist, was suspended for one month without pay and ordered never again to associate with Lundquist or "any other known gambling figures."

Wooley went on to have what was for him a lackluster season and, at the winter meetings in December, the Philadelphia club traded him to the Kansas City Royals. Two days after the trade was made, Wooley told reporters he wasn't "a slave who can be bought and sold with no say-so." He refused to go to Kansas City, declared himself a free agent, and announced his intention to challenge baseball's reserve clause. The suit took a year and a half and ended up in the Supreme Court, where the justices narrowly sided with major league baseball and upheld the Phillies' right to trade Wooley or any other player. By the time the decision came down, Wooley had been inactive for two seasons. He was thirty-six years old and his once-great skills had atrophied. He had played his last game. Things couldn't get any worse.

But then they did.

Just after the Supreme Court ruling, Wooley was arrested for injuring his wife Evie and their four-year-old daughter in what one paper called "a drunken domestic rampage" at their New Jersey home. To make matters worse, a story in the *Newark*

Ledger included a photo that showed Wooley slipping out the back door of the Bergen County Civic Center accompanied by his lawyer and a second man, later identified as Harry Lundquist. The abuse charges were dismissed a few days later, but few took notice. By then, the commissioner of baseball had stepped in again. The photo proved that Wooley had not ended his association with Lundquist, as he had been ordered to do two years before. As a result, the commissioner told a packed press conference, he had decided to permanently ban Frank Wooley. Wooley could not play, coach, scout, or hold any other job in professional baseball, the commissioner decreed.

Frank Wooley's name all but disappeared from the papers for the next thirteen years—until 1985, when a new commissioner pardoned the former star and ended his banishment. Wooley was free to work in organized baseball again, but it would be another three years before a team was willing to take a chance. In 1988, an old teammate from Wooley's Philadelphia days was named manager of the Geneva Cubs of the New York-Penn League, and one of his first official acts was to hire Wooley as a coach and batting instructor. Wooley lasted two months into the season, then was fired for climbing into the stands to punch out a fan who'd been heckling him. He took his leave with a "no comment" to reporters and shuffled off into oblivion, not to be heard of again until his unexpected election to the hall of fame in January.

"Well, William," I said to the cat, who was rubbing up against my leg, "if nothing else, he's consistent. One screwup after another."

I left the photocopies piled haphazardly on the coffee table and went to bed early, half convinced I could forget about Frank Wooley, push him to the back recesses of my mind where I store all the bittersweet memories of boyhood. But when I got up on Monday morning, the stack of clips was still there and so was Wooley.

I made two phone calls that morning. The second was to Pete Calvett, telling him I'd take the assignment.

I flicked the wipers again and watched the woman in the post office wait on someone. From where I was parked, I couldn't see the customer, only the right profile of the postmistress as she stood at the counter. But that didn't matter. There was only one door into the tiny office, and I had a clear view of anyone passing through it. So far that hadn't included any stocky middle-aged black men.

I glanced at my watch—a half hour until closing time—and listened to my stomach growl. Maybe the weather had discouraged him, I told myself, or maybe he doesn't get enough mail to bother coming in more than once a week. I grimaced at the idea of spending even one more day staring out the Bronco's windshield.

Before talking to Pete Calvett Monday morning, I had placed a call to the office of the Major League Baseball Players Pension Fund in New York. A friendly information officer named Campbell had verified the mailing address on Wooley that Calvett had supplied. I also learned that pension checks were posted on the first Monday of every month.

I perked up a little as a late-model Chevrolet Caprice pulled into the post office lot, but returned to my sulk as soon as the driver slipped out from behind the wheel. A woman. I couldn't see the face hidden inside the scarf and floppy hat, but the long quilted coat and the short heels on the boots and the rolling motion of the hips gave her away.

I turned on the radio again and let my eyes drift up to the rearview mirror. The warm glow of a LABATT'S BLUE sign taunted me from the side window of the Friendly Tavern while the guy on the radio informed me that the Yanks were now down seven runs to the Indians in the eighth. I cursed life in general and searched the glove compartment for a cassette I hadn't already played twice that day. When I couldn't find one, I slapped shut the glove compartment and reluctantly returned to the task at hand.

The owner of the maroon Caprice was behind the wheel again, her business with the U.S. Postal Service concluded. Despite the heavy scarf and broad-brimmed hat she wore, I caught a glimpse of the woman's face as she passed—a black face. Even as that realization was working its way into my consciousness, I swung my eyes back to the post office. The postmistress was standing in the big picture window, staring out at me with her arms folded across her chest, the corners of her mouth turned up ever so slightly.

I swore again, coaxed the Bronco's stick shift into first gear, and tore off after the Chevrolet.

CHAPTER 3

THE woman in the Caprice turned east onto the main highway. In the seconds it took me to read the situation and get the Bronco headed in the right direction, a hulking dump truck with a plowblade on the front and a load of sand in the bed had gotten between me and my quarry. I cozied up to the truck's rear and eased the Bronco to the left, out over the solid double dividing line, managing to catch a glimpse of the Caprice. All I could make out of the mud-splattered license plate were the first two letters—Y and I—before an oncoming pickup sent me careening back into my own lane.

The woman was up to cruising speed already, easily outdistancing the slowly accelerating dump truck. In another minute she'd be gone, and I'd've blown my best chance to track down Frank Wooley.

I urged the wheel fractionally to the left again and, with my head pressed against the side window, peered past the rumbling truck. We were cresting a rise. Up ahead I could see two vehicles; the Caprice, moving away, and a compact sedan, coming up the hill toward us. I waited for the small car to flash by, then I put the gusting snow and the slick road conditions out of mind and made my move. I angled out into the oncoming lane and downshifted into third gear, confident I had plenty of room and horsepower to pass. But the heavy truck was quickly gaining speed on the downslope and, as my hand guided the stick into high again, I saw the bearded driver glaring at me from his sideview mirror and I heard the rumble of his engine deepen as, his machismo challenged, he pushed the accelerator to the floorboards.

Everything was running fast but time. The seconds dragged by as we raced down the hill, the Bronco moving up on the dump truck inch by inch, coming even with the massive hood, slipping ahead by a nose, struggling to gain enough room to slip back into the other lane. Then, a hundred yards ahead, the Chevrolet's brake lights flashed and the left turn signal blinked. The trucker saw it too, the whine of his straining engine suddenly dying out, replaced by the urgent bleat of his horn. The woman in the Caprice, oblivious to the juggernaut bearing down on her from behind, started her turn onto a side road, putting herself directly in my path. It was too late to slam on the brakes; my only chance was to hold my speed and yank the wheel hard to the right, praying that the Bronco's rear bumper would clear the plow blade on the dump truck, and that my steelbelted radials would be able to keep their grip on the slippery grade.

At the last moment I veered to the right. The Bronco shot past the Caprice safely, but the back wheels began to slide away toward the embankment of plowed snow that paralleled the road. I kept the pedal to the floor to increase the distance between myself and the truck and tried to steer through the skid, but momentum and the slick macadam kept forcing the Bronco sideways. Then I felt the four-by-four's rightside tires drop onto the gravel shoulder and begin to grab. I straightened the wheel and pulled off the gas just as the dump truck whizzed past my left ear, horn blaring. The Bronco was completely onto the shoulder of the road now and quickly losing speed, but not quickly enough. My head banged against the roof and ricocheted off the door as the Bronco bucked and bounced over frozen ruts and slammed grille-first into the snowbank.

The first thing I did when the world stopped shaking was take a few deep breaths, just to make sure I still could. Then I took inventory. Both the truck driver and the woman in the Chevrolet were gone, he on over the next rise in the highway, and she down the dirt side road fifty yards to my rear. The Bronco was buried up to its wheelwells in snow, the front end angled down into the drainage ditch. My lower lip was bleeding—whether from banging it on the steering wheel or biting into it, I couldn't remember—and the strands of nerves along the back of my neck were throbbing like the strings on a viola.

All things considered, I figured I owed a rosary to whichever hallowed martyr is the patron saint of reckless fools.

"Fly casters, pah!" Ralph Cramer made like he was about to spit on the floor, then changed his mind when he caught his wife eyeballing him from the lunch counter.

"Got no use for the sons a bees m'self." He extended his left index finger—it looked about as old as the one Michelangelo had given God—and pointed toward the sporting-goods side of the building. "I don't even handle fly-fishing gear any more. Know why?"

I'd already heard Ralph's reasoning on this subject, and I wasn't in a mood to hear it again, but I knew how far that attitude would get me.

I sighed into my coffee cup. "Why don't you handle fly-fishing gear anymore?"

" 'Cause I got better things to do with my time than stand around all day while some city whelp agonizes over which waders go best with his L.L. Bean safari suit." Ralph stuck his jaw forward, working himself into a proper lather. "Years ago fly casters were maybe a little snootier than your normal angler, but you could deal with 'em. Now you got these 'dress for success' types comin' down and screwin' things up." He shook his head. "Why these yuppie punks don't stick to sail boats and leave me alone, I couldn't tell you."

We were sharing a booth in the eating half of Ralph and Kay's Diner and Outdoor Store, a one-story brick building set on Mohaca Springs's main street between a Rexall Drugs and the public parking lot. When not in the kitchen helping the short-order cook, or out on the lake trying a new plug the bass haven't seen yet, Ralph can most often be found chowing down in one of the diner's booths or assisting a customer in the adjacent sporting-goods shop. In either event, you can be sure his lips will be moving.

"They've been comin' outa the woodwork now the weather's turned decent again, stoppin' in here lookin' to buy flies and little wicker fish baskets and every other thing I don't handle,

21

just so they can go stand cheek to cheek down along the inlet. Jeez, I hate opening week of the trout season." He pushed the topic aside as easily as he pushed away the plate of french fries with vinegar he'd been nibbling at. "You look like you've had a pretty rough day yourself, Sheridan."

"A pretty rough day and a half," I admitted.

It was now two o'clock on Wednesday afternoon, nearly twenty-four hours since I'd ended up in the snowbank. It had taken me the rest of Tuesday's meager daylight to dislodge the Bronco. Even with four-wheel drive, I never would've gotten free without a tow if there hadn't been a collapsed barn down the road. I had to wedge several pieces of old barn planking under the wheels to provide traction, then rock the vehicle back and forth half a hundred times before it finally extricated itself. By the time I was back on the road, I was tired and wet and aching like an abscessed molar. All I had come up with for a day's discomfort was a pretty slim lead on the whereabouts of Frank Wooley—a black woman in a maroon Chevy Caprice with a license number beginning with Y.

I went home to a hot shower and an early bed. The next morning, still sore and a little stiff from Tuesday's debacle, I dug out a road map of the Finger Lakes region and studied it over coffee and a toasted bagel. In New York State, the first letter of a license plate usually indicates the registrant's county of residence. The system doesn't always hold true for the more populous counties, but we don't have many of those in our area, so it was reasonable to assume that the Y on the Caprice meant that the driver lived in Yates County, probably close enough to the little hamlet of Stewart to make it a convenient place to pick up the mail.

The area north of Stewart was crisscrossed with meandering secondary roads, many of them seasonal and no better than hard-packed dirt or gravel. I glanced out the window. The storm had played itself out overnight, leaving behind fifty-degree temperatures and plenty of sunshine and snowmelt—a combination guaranteed to turn any unpaved road into a muddy quagmire. Not that I had a choice. I put on jeans, a flannel shirt, and a pair of waterproof hiking boots, opened a can of goo for the cat, and, map and notepad in hand, headed back down to Stewart.

The side road the woman had turned onto the day before was

called Bath Road. I followed it northeast for about a mile, until a sign with a couple of deer slug holes blown through it announced that I was entering Yates County. I continued on another mile—driving carefully through huge muddy puddles, taking a long look at the small homes that popped up every so often in between the stands of pine and weed-infested fields—until I came to the first crossroad. I tossed a mental coin in the air, then turned left onto an even narrower dirt road, resigned to scouring the whole southern end of Yates County until I found a yard with a late-model maroon Caprice parked in it.

Three hours later I admitted to myself that my brilliant idea was another lost cause. The map didn't even show half of the twisting, rutted tracks I'd come across, and it had failed to warn me that many of the houses would be set back hundreds of feet from the road and further hidden behind trees and hills. Not to mention that the car I was looking for could as easily be tucked away in a garage or barn.

I gave up at noon and worked my way back to Stewart, stopping in at the Friendly Tavern to play my last hunch. The handful of faces I saw were mostly friendly, as advertised, and all white. I ordered a bottle of Labatt's and asked a few questions, but all that got me was a series of blank looks. You don't see many black people down this way, I was told by the rawboned youth behind the bar, and if there are any, they stick to their own.

Strike three. I drank down the beer, climbed behind the wheel of my Ford, and drove back to Mohaca Springs.

"So, Sheridan," Ralph was saying now. "You gonna tell me what's eatin' you? You look about as cheerful as a hound dog at a flea circus."

"Maybe it's just his ears are tired," Kay said, as she came out from behind the lunch counter with a glass of pop in hand. She used one of her substantial hips to shove her husband deeper into the booth and settled in beside him. "Although you do look a little under the weather, Sheridan," she said, turning her soft grandmotherly face toward the window overlooking the parking lot. "Your truck's half covered with mud—you been doing some off-roading or something?"

"I got hung up in a ditch down in Schuyler County yesterday," I said, dismissing it with a wave.

23

"Some bad roads down there when the snow's blowing," Ralph said. "What was so urgent that you were down runnin' around Schuyler County in the middle of a whiteout?"

"Ah, it's this story I'm supposed to be working on." I gave them a run through on the assignment and my so-far-useless efforts even to find the man I was supposed to be profiling. Kay had drawn a blank on Frank Wooley—her favorite national pastimes were flea markets and garage sales—but Ralph was enough of a fan to recognize the name.

"You remember him, Kay," he elbowed his wife. "He was in all those peace marches and protests back a few years. Colored guy, the papers used to call Black Sheep Wooley, 'cause of all the trouble he got himself into." He turned back to me. "Got thrown out of baseball for gambling or something, didn't he, Sheridan?"

"Something like that. Anyway, I told this editor, sure, I could locate Wooley, no problem. Famous last words."

"You say you ID'd the car, though, and you got a partial plate." Aside from largemouth bass and lake trout, Ralph's most consuming interest was private-eye novels. "You could maybe call your buddy the sheriff, have him run it through the state MVD computer."

"I may have to." Quincy County Sheriff J. D. Staub was a friend, and a willing resource to boot. But I didn't like using up his good will with something I should've been able to handle myself.

"You know who else might be able to help?" Kay said. I looked up at her expectantly, but she was squinting over at her husband. "This Wooley fellow is colored?"

"That's what I just said."

"And he's supposed to be living like a hermit down in Yates County someplace?"

"What's your point, girl?"

"Well, it seems to me if you're trying to locate a colored person in a ninety-nine percent white county, you'd do well to go ask another colored person for help. Like your euchre buddy Ruly. Birds of a feather flock together."

"Ruly Jackson," Ralph mumbled, trying out the idea, then looked at me. "You remember Ruly, Sheridan. Waits table up at the Pinewood's taproom?"

"I remember him well. In fact I talked to him when I was looking into my uncle's murder when I first moved here."

"That's right. Anyhow, I'll bet you old Ruly knows every black face between Geneva and the Pennsylvania line. And if he doesn't, his wife does." He winked at me as he added, "Y'see, every once in a while wives do come in handy for something."

CHAPTER 4

HAVING convinced myself that Ruly Jackson would keep for a day or so, I spent the remainder of the afternoon puttering around the cottage—fixing the hasp on the storage shed, raking wayward gravel back onto the drive, braving the soggy soil to pick up the twigs and branches that the storm had deposited around the small yard. There had been several acres to the place when I inherited it from my uncle, but I'd sold most of it to Allison Humbert, who needed additional vineyard acreage along the lake to plant vinifera grapes for the family winery. Now the cottage was flanked by ordered rows of young vines, each one carefully tied to a wire that ran between stakes set at regular intervals. In a few years, Allison had told me, with care and luck and any cooperation at all from the fickle elements, the vineyard would begin producing white grapes of a quality that would enhance the reputation of the Humbert label. In the meantime, the sale of the land had assured me a comfortable nest egg and neighbors that never threw loud parties or asked to borrow anything.

After the yard work I washed off the grime with a hot shower and had an early supper. That evening I called Kate to confirm our Friday dinner date at her place in Rochester. Then I eschewed the Mets game on cable for a couple of hours up in my writing nook in the loft, fleshing out an article on the state parole system I was doing for one of the Rochester dailies. I planned to drop off the copy at the newspaper building Friday afternoon on my way to Kate's.

Thursday morning I rolled out of bed at eight, had coffee and toast, and took a brisk walk along the lakeshore before washing up and digging out some slacks that weren't nearly as dirty as I'd thought when I'd thrown them in the hamper. By ten o'clock, I was on the road again.

Ruly Jackson lived in Harley Corners, a small crossroads settlement like Stewart that straddled the Quincy-Yates County Line Road about four miles west of Mohaca Springs. The Finger Lakes region includes eleven lakes spread between ten different counties, with each county's boundary lines laid out as illogically as a gerrymandered voting district. Officially the region is about a hundred miles square, running north-south from the shores of Lake Ontario to the Pennsylvania border and east-west from Otisco Lake near Syracuse to Letchworth Gorge, thirty-five miles south of Rochester. But the heart of the region—the part that perhaps best illustrates its combination of lakes and hills, gorges and valleys, wineries and dairy farms and villages—is a twenty-five-hundred-square-mile block that encompasses four of the larger lakes; Cayuga, Seneca, Keuka, and Canandaigua. Yates County had somehow managed to capture long shorelines on three of those lakes, missing only Cayuga.

Harley Corners was tucked away in the back hills, far enough removed from the nearest lake to be of no interest to vacationers and developers. It had a mom-and-pop grocery with a couple of gas pumps out front, an old cinderblock garage advertising small engine repair, and half a dozen modest houses sited too close to the road. The Jackson place was a neat bungalow with a deep veranda. The front yard was freshly mowed, no simple task considering the obstacle course of lawn ornaments that filled much of the space.

I had parked in a gravel turnaround and was walking toward the front door when a woman's voice hailed me from somewhere behind the house. I followed my ears to the back and a brick-in-sand patio, where I found Mrs. Jackson seated at a picnic table, perusing a seed catalog.

"All this miserable weather gonna mess up the planting schedule, but I don't let it keep me away from my gardening," she said through a welcoming smile. "I know you, don't I?"

"Sheridan," I said. "From Mohaca Springs. I'm a freelance writer."

"That's right. Ruly introduced us that time over at the vegetable stall. You bought some snap beans."

"And two jars of your homemade raspberry jam."

I took the seat she offered on the bench opposite her, and we spent a few minutes exchanging views on the major questions of the day: did it look like spring was finally here to stay; would the late snow hurt the grape production. Like her husband, Mrs. Jackson was slim and sinewy with dark coffee skin made brittle from years of working the little truck farm that took up every sunny inch of the deep back yard. When he wasn't working at the Pinewood's taproom or hiring out for seasonal work at local wineries, Ruly helped his wife tend the garden and haul crops to their stall at the farmer's market in Mohaca Springs on Saturdays. This morning, Mrs. Jackson told me, Ruly was up in Penn Yan trying to locate a set of replacement tines for their rototiller.

"I'm sorry I missed him, ma'am," I said. "But you may be able to help me. I'm trying to locate a man for a story I'm working on." I told her of my efforts to find Frank Wooley and described as best I could the black woman in the maroon Caprice. "I was hoping Ruly—or you—might know of such a woman living somewhere down in southern Yates County near the line with Schuyler County."

"Hmm." Concentration pushed her features into a frown. "I never pay attention to sports myself, but I remember Ruly used to think a lot of this fella Wooley, leastwise until all his personal problems come along. I remember him joining the ball team up in Geneva, too—our two youngest boys used to go to a lot of the games before we packed 'em off to college. I didn't realize Wooley stayed in the area after the Cubs let him go. Wonder what decided him to do that."

"That might be where the woman in the Caprice figures in."

Her eyebrows arched. "Y'know, come to think of it, there's this girl I know of—well, not a girl, except compared to me. She's probably your age, maybe a little older. Name's IdaRose Mack." She broke off, the frown returning. "I don't know if I should be telling you this, Mr. Sheridan. It isn't a Christian thing to do, spreading gossip about people."

"I'm only interested in writing Frank Wooley's story, Mrs.

Jackson. Anything you tell me—whether it helps me find him or not—will stay between the two of us."

She considered that for a few seconds. "Well, I couldn't say it's her you saw in that maroon car. But IdaRose does have a place down that way." She rested her elbows on the seed catalog and leaned forward. "Y'see, IdaRose lost her husband a few years ago in a trucking accident—he used to drive semis for Seneca Foods down to Dundee. Jackknifed on the thruway and broke his neck, God bless him. Anyway, we go to the same church up in Penn Yan. And for a time there after the accident, IdaRose was real active in church affairs and socials and all, which is how I come to know her so well. But in the last couple years, nobody hardly sees her except at Sunday services and . . . well, the rumor is she's got a man living with her."

It took a couple more minutes before she worked herself up to describing IdaRose Mack's place for me. Then we spent another five minutes scrutinizing the map I kept in the Bronco's glove compartment before she could decide which of the dirt tracks leading off from Bath Road were most likely to take me to the house. By the time I finished my thank yous and left Mrs. Jackson to her garden planning, it was approaching noon.

I drove west on Harley Corners Road, itself a grader-scraped dirt affair, and picked up Route 14A, a well-paved two lanes that connected Penn Yan and Dundee.

In addition to the usual roadside stands that sell sweet corn and raspberries and grape pies in season, Route 14A is notable for intermittent highway signs featuring a silhouette of a horse and carriage, a warning to watch for slow-moving buggies trundling along the wide shoulders. The area is home to several Mennonite farms, and possibly some Amish as well. Telling the difference between the two religious sects is beyond me, like trying to distinguish a Sunni Moslem from a Shiite, or a Southern Baptist from the regular kind. All I know is that both groups favor simple dress and shun modern conveniences, which, ironically, has made them unwilling tourist attractions in many parts of the country. Perhaps it was the notoriety and its attendant intrusions that had pushed them to settle in the land-rich, people-poor underbelly of Yates County. And perhaps a similar need had brought Frank Wooley to the area.

Following Mrs. Jackson's instructions, I drove south for seven miles, then reluctantly surrendered the smooth sailing of the main highway for another dirt track, this one called Porters Corners Road. I followed it to Bath Road and headed south again, picking my way around the now-familiar potholes and puddles until I turned on to what I hoped would be the last leg of my journey: Lookout Run.

As Mrs. Jackson described it, Lookout Run ran off to the west toward Keuka Lake, but dead-ended—the real estate pros would call it a cul-de-sac—somewhere in the hills this side of the lake. The Mack place was on a lane that forked to the north maybe a mile up on Lookout, as best she could remember from her single visit to the house.

I missed the turnoff the first time and had to drive another mile before I found a driveway to turn around in. The road itself was too narrow for turning and, even though most of the snow had been reduced to isolated patches along the north slopes of the hills, I had no desire to tangle with another of Yates County's bottomless drainage ditches.

When I finally made it back to the side lane, I noticed a pair of crude signboards nailed to a gnarled box elder. Each had a name printed on it in flaking white paint; the top one said simply STURDEVANT, the bottom one MACK. I followed the twisting lane into a valley hemmed in by steep hills. The first clearing I came to held an old house trailer with bales of straw tucked under it in lieu of skirting and tires on the roof to hold down a sheet of black polyethylene. The overgrown yard featured a new four-wheel-drive pickup truck and an enormous satellite dish, either of which was probably worth more than the trailer. The name painted onto a boulder near the driveway said Sturdevant.

I drove on another two hundred yards, down a tunnel of overhanging trees and sumac scrub, until the dirt lane abruptly became a long blacktopped driveway. It doglegged left, ending at a newer looking two-and-a-half car garage. Up a short rise from the garage sat a house similar in style to the Jackson's bungalow except this one was considerably larger, with a second story under a steep roof and a sizeable addition along one side. There was a satellite dish beside the garage, but that was the only thing it had in common with its neighbor. The house's cedar siding was stained a light gray, with white trim; the gently sloping front lawn was neatly clipped and edged, and the evergreen shrubs planted along the perimeter of the house had been fussed into perfect geometry by someone who knew how to handle a pair of hedge clippers.

I drove up the smooth ribbon of blacktop and parked in front of the garage. No maroon Chevy in sight, but this had to be the Mack place. I took the peastone path around to the porch and rang the doorbell. I could feel more than hear music with a heavy bass beat playing somewhere inside the house, but no one responded to my ringing.

I came off the porch and headed around to the back, following the path to a terrace that ran along the rear of the house. Sliding glass doors led onto the terrace from the new addition, but heavy drapes shut off any view inside. I continued on to a small entry porch and knocked on the solid door. Again no answer, and now I couldn't sense the music playing within.

Prowling around a strange house out in the middle of nowhere isn't the smartest thing you can do. People who live in such places obviously value their seclusion, sometimes guarding their privacy with xenophobic zeal and a loaded shotgun. But I was certain someone was inside and, with the travails of the last few days fresh in mind, I was feeling just frustrated enough to forget smart.

I tried the knob, and felt it turn in my hand, pushed the door inward, and stepped into a corridor that led into the kitchen. I started to call out my intentions, but before I could open my mouth, the door suddenly swung shut behind me and something heavy pounded into the small of my back, shooting a wave of pain up my spine and driving me to the floor.

"Uhhn—Jesus!" I rolled onto my side and held my hands up defensively and yelped out a cry of surrender to my attacker.

He stood over me, his feet planted wide apart, an angry glare fixed to his obsidian face, his hands nervously waggling a baseball bat as if he were about to drive a pitch into the left field alley.

It was exactly how I had always pictured the great Frank Wooley.

CHAPTER 5

"WHO sent you?"

"*Sporting Life* magazine." I propped myself onto one elbow, groaning at the effort. "Christ, you nearly broke my back with that damn thing."

"You stay right there." He jabbed my shoulder with the bat. "I didn't hit you with this, sunshine, I used my knee. Anyway, where d'you think you get off sneaking into a man's house like that? I oughta kick your ass just on principle." He lowered the bat to his side. "If you're from *The Sporting Life*, let's see some ID that proves it."

"I'm a freelancer. All I've got is an old press pass from my last newspaper job and a guild card that expired four years ago. My name's Sheridan." I pulled out my wallet and started to come up again, but so did the bat. "Look, who the hell else would I be? I've been trying to find you for three days to do a profile. I finally tracked you here. I knew somebody was inside, but you didn't come to the door. I also know you might be . . . reluctant to be in the public eye again, so when I saw the door was unlocked . . . "

"You decide to barge right on in and start shoving questions at me. I guess that makes you a reporter, all right. Burglars have better manners." He lowered the bat again and stepped past me, away from the shut door. "Now that's settled, you can haul your sorry butt outa here."

I returned the wallet to the hip pocket of my jeans and rose to my feet one aching joint at a time. Once I was eye to eye with him, my first reaction was surprise. I'd known all along that he was a small man by the standards of professional sports, but my mind's eye had never made the connection. To the kid who still lived inside me, guys like Frank Wooley were larger-than-life characters who filled up a TV screen, dominated a box score. They had to be bigger, stronger, faster, better in every way than us mere mortals. But standing in front of me was this stunningly ordinary man, an inch shorter than my five-nine, perhaps 160 pounds, seeming to swim inside a pair of baggy khaki slacks and an oversized navy sweatshirt. Only the eyes—defiant, determined, and piercing—lived up to the image I'd carried with me since boyhood.

"Look, Mr. Wooley," I said. "Like it or not, you're a public figure. People are going to write articles about you; in fact, they already are. Stories based on old newspaper accounts and anecdotes from former teammates. Stories that quote everybody but Frank Wooley." I turned my palms up. "Don't you want to set the record straight?"

He hesitated, a sudden, elusive softening working the edges of his hard-set mouth. But then the private man reemerged—the bitter recluse who'd been burned too many times to risk moving back into the spotlight.

He laid the bat across his right shoulder. "What I did on the diamond got me to Cooperstown. All anybody needs to know about that, they can look up in the stat books. 'Numbers don't lie.' Jackie Robinson said that."

" 'You can run, but you can't hide,' " I countered. "Joe Louis said that. Don't you think it'd be better if . . . "

In one smooth move he brought the bat off his shoulder and poked the barrel end against my chest. "You don't come in here and tell me how to think, not on your best day. You hear me, sunshine?"

I heard him all right, but three days of bad roads and blizzards and snowbanks hadn't left me in a mood to heed. "If I was out of line, I apologize, okay?" I said, my voice rising. "But you can take the 'sunshine' bit and the Louisville Slugger and shove 'em up your ass. And if you prod me with that bat one more time, I'll do it for you."

He smiled coldly. "A scribe with balls. Must be a mutant or something." Slow and deliberate, he propped the bat in a corner of the corridor and turned back to challenge me. "I'll say it again, boy; not on your best day."

He had once been a world-class athlete, with speed and power and agility, and it was clear that more than a remnant of those skills remained. But he was twenty years older than I, his close-cropped hair was spattered with gray, and the dark skin that once stretched tight across his sharp features had given in to time and gravity. It would be a fight I couldn't win, no matter which of us ended up on his feet.

I sighed. "This kind of crap belongs in a high school parking lot. You don't want to talk to me, that's your right. But *The Sporting Life* will still publish a profile on you—and there'll be even more people after your story as we get closer to the induction ceremonies. If I could find you, others can, too. You can do the Greta Garbo routine, sure, but all that'll get you is more media, tripping over each other to get an exclusive. Or you can let me do an interview now and hope the others will lose interest."

It sounded self-serving even as it came out of my mouth, and it appeared Wooley was about to tell me as much. But then his eyes drifted off me, his anger replaced by a look usually seen on small boys caught with their hands in cookie jars.

"He's got a point, Frank."

I turned toward the voice. A tall black woman stood on the entry porch beyond the now open door, hugging a grocery bag with each arm. She had high cheek bones and large, fluid eyes and full lips arranged in a wan smile. She was probably forty, give or take a couple of years. The maroon dress she was wearing was a shade darker than the Caprice I assumed was now parked out in the driveway.

"You must be Ms. Mack," I said, seizing the moment. "Can I help you with those bags?"

"Thank you, Mr. . . . ?"

"Sheridan," I said as I hefted the groceries.

"Well, welcome to our home, Mr. Sheridan. Won't you come in and have a cup of tea?" I followed her into the kitchen past Wooley, who looked like someone had just rung him up with a three-two curveball. "You want to bring in the rest of the bags, Frank," she trilled over her shoulder, "while I put the pot on?"

"Maybe you should turn the music off, Frank."

"Not on my account," I said as I fought to balance a mug on one knee and my notepad on the other. "That's the King Cole Trio, isn't it?"

Surprise replaced the scowl Wooley had been wearing since we'd settled in the den. "Most people don't even know Nat played piano," he said.

"Most people don't know what they're missing."

He grunted, then lapsed into a maddening silence. So far most of what I'd learned had come from IdaRose Mack. The two of us had hit it off immediately, gabbing across the kitchen counter like old friends while she steeped the tea and quick-thawed some little dessert squares in the microwave. She was open and gregarious, the complete opposite of her man. In the space of a five-minute chat, I learned that she and Wooley had met at a charity bazaar sponsored by the Ecumenical Society the week he first came to Geneva to take the coaching job with the Cubs. They started dating and after he, in her phrase, "left the ball club," they decided to move in together "to see where the relationship would lead us."

After nearly two years, it hadn't yet led to the altar, but it was plain that IdaRose was a patient woman. She'd have to be, living with a mercurial character like Frank Wooley. He had said little, occasionally grunting neutrally at one of IdaRose's comments, following docilely along while she walked me through the first floor of the house and pointed out the improvements Wooley had made: the living room, where he had stripped and refinished the oak trim, a little powder room he'd carved out of a former pantry. The pièce de résistance was the den, where we now sat sipping tea and nibbling crumpet substitutes. A contractor had been hired to build the shell, IdaRose told me, but Frank had done the rest himself.

It was obvious he knew the working end of a hammer. The den was roughly sixteen-by-fourteen feet, with French-style sliding doors leading to the rear patio, a vaulted ceiling, and built-in bookcases flanking a fireplace at the gable end of the room. The walls were painted Navajo white and decorated with framed art posters and a pair of photos, one of a smiling black man in his early thirties standing beside a fancy pickup truck, the other of a light-skinned young black woman wearing a graduation gown and a self-conscious grin. Conspicuously absent were any photos or mementos from Wooley's playing days.

"My late husband," IdaRose explained when I asked about the two pictures. "And Frank's daughter Martina, taken last May at her commencement at Brown. She's in her first year at Cornell law school now."

Wooley tried to remain aloof, but the proud papa in him couldn't bring it off. "She graduated Brown with honors," he said, looking at me for the first time with anything other than a glare. "Pretty good in a place like that."

"I'd say so." I gave up on the mug and set it on an end table. "Pretty expensive, too. A pair of Ivy Leeague schools, the tuition must be out of sight." It was meant as a casual remark. I wasn't consciously probing, but sometimes the working professional in me slips out at the wrong time. Rather than helping to break the ice, my off-hand comment brought the frozen stare back to Wooley's face.

"I pay my end, if that's what you're getting at," he snapped. "Tuition, board, books—we split up all Martina's expenses, me and my ex-wife's husband. I do my part."

"I didn't mean to suggest otherwise." The room went silent but for Cole's subdued piano solo. IdaRose was watching Wooley out of the corner of her eye, like a cook expecting a pot to boil over any second. Meanwhile, I was berating myself for mishandling the tiny opening Wooley had given me, and trying to think of a way to get the interview back on track. I'd have to ask a lot of prickly questions before I could do an honest profile of the enigmatic man seated before me. But I'd need Wooley's cooperation and at least a little of his trust to get anywhere, which meant I had to start out slow and easy.

I figured my best bet was to ignore my earlier gaffe and brazen forward with a non sequitur.

"You must've been excited when you were notified of your selection to the hall of fame," I said.

"You mean surprised, like everybody else," he said sourly. "Everybody figured the 'character' clause'd keep me out forever, thanks to the ex-commissioner."

"Still, it has to be gratifying, knowing you'll be enshrined with so many great names like Ruth and Cobb and Robinson...."

"Yeah. Me and all the dead heroes." He shifted forward in his chair. "Ty Cobb was a racist cracker. They say he used to bet on games, too—but that didn't keep his lily-white ass from going into the hall." He glanced at IdaRose. "Excuse my French."

She grabbed the opportunity to try and ease some of the tension that coursed between Wooley and me like a high-voltage wire. "I have a theory on the hall of fame balloting, if you're interested, Mr. Sheridan."

"I'm very interested," I said, picking up my notepad.

"Well, I think some of the younger baseball writers took a look at Joe Morgan's career statistics, then took a look at Frank's, and they realized how similar they were, if you allow for how many more years Morgan played. And since they were going to vote Morgan in, they recognized what an injustice it would be not to vote for Frank, too."

"I've got nothing but respect for Joe," Wooley interjected. "But, except for his power hitting, there wasn't anything he could do at the plate or out at second base that I couldn't do as good or better."

"I agree. With both of you." I looked at IdaRose. "You're knowledgeable about the game."

"Oh, I've been a fan since I was a kid. I'm only sorry I never had a chance to see Frank play—in person I mean. I've never been to a major-league game."

"I saw my first big-league game in 1966 at Yankee Stadium," I said.

"That was my last year with the Yanks," Wooley said.

"I know. It was a late-September afternoon doubleheader against the Senators. My junior high class was visiting the city on a two-day field trip. We were allowed to choose between the game or a matinee performance of *The Impossible Years.*"

IdaRose smiled. "Not a difficult choice for a boy."

"No. Both teams were already out of the pennant chase, but it was a magic afternoon for me anyway. In the first game, Maris and Mantle hit back-to-back homers."

"I remember that day now," Wooley murmured. "Gray and gloomy, nobody in the stands. I made a pretty good play in the second game."

"It was a great play," I said. "Hawk Harrelson lined a shot right over the second base bag. Somehow you managed to dive and pick it off, then get to your knees and throw to third, doubling up the runner and saving the win."

For the first time, I saw Frank Wooley smile.

CHAPTER 6

ELSTON Howard was a quiet guy. Soft spoken, even tempered. What Gus Oldham used to call 'a credit to his race.' " Frank set his coffee mug on the kitchen table and paused to look out the window. The sun was streaming into the breakfast nook bright enough to give me a blue-eyed squint, but Wooley, staring into the rays, didn't even blink. After a few seconds, he turned back. "As you can guess, Oldham never used that line on me— I'd've laughed in the old bastard's face. Ellie didn't mind, though. He was perfect to be the first black player on the Yankees when you think about it. A great catcher, no politics to speak of."

It was nearing eleven o'clock on Friday morning. The previous afternoon's session, after a perilous start, had ended in a fragile truce. Wooley—at IdaRose's gentle cajoling—had grudgingly consented to continue the interview the following day. We agreed to meet for breakfast and conclude by noon so that Wooley could get back to the woodworking project he had going in the garage, and I could get an early start on my trip up to Rochester.

"Ellie made the team in '55; I came along three years later as the team's second black." He nudged the mug aside and rested his elbows on the table. "They wouldn't ever admit to it, but the ballclubs had a policy in those days we called stacking. You know the term?"

I shook my head negatively.

"The owners were afraid too many blacks on the roster would hurt the gate—they didn't believe your average white fan would stand for it. So they had this unwritten rule where they'd only use blacks at certain power positions, like first base or the outfield. I was one of the first black middle infielders to come along since Jackie Robinson."

I scribbled a few lines in my pad, then I glanced at the digital counter on the tiny recorder I'd placed between us and made a notation of the number so that later I could readily compare my handwritten notes to the information on the tape.

The morning session had gone reasonably well, establishing a sort of dentist-patient relationship between us. My role was to try to extract a lifetime of experiences from a man who squirmed in his chair and balked at my every probing, but stayed put because he didn't see how he could put off the inevitable any longer. IdaRose had provisioned us with coffee, fruit cups, and a plate of toasted English muffins before leaving for her job in Penn Yan. Her departure seemed to relax Wooley a bit, as if he could better handle the discomfort if his woman wasn't there to see it.

I flipped back to the prep notes I'd taken while studying the clips on Wooley. "What about the spring training incident in '64," I asked. "Where you first got in hot water for speaking out on discrimination. I didn't find any quotes from Howard in any of the stories."

"You mean when I blasted the club for putting up the white players in the Hotel Soreno in St. Pete, while me and Ellie had to stay with local black families." He shook his head, bemused. "Ellie was in Clearwater that day playing in a split-squad game. Next day he told a couple writers that he supported the voting rights legislation, too, but I don't think it ever made the papers." He sipped at the tepid coffee. "Ellie was okay. In fact, I loved the guy—and you can quote me on that. Hell, my wife and I bought a house in Teaneck, New Jersey, just because Ellie and Arlene Howard lived there."

In two days of interviews, I'd learned a lot about the young Frank Wooley. How he'd been born in Mobile, Alabama, in 1936, but was raised in Gary, Indiana, where his father found a good-paying job in a steel mill during the war. How he'd learned to throw and hit on a hard-packed dirt field in the shadow of a smoke-belching coking plant. The joy he'd felt when, as an eleven-year-old in 1947, he heard on the radio that Jackie Robinson had made the Brooklyn Dodgers, breaking for good professional baseball's color barrier. And how lucky he'd felt after being discovered in 1953 by a Yankee scout, who there and then signed the future hall of famer for a five-hundred-dollar bonus.

"Branch Rickey used to say, 'Scout with a broom,' " Wooley said. "Sweep up as many young prospects as you can for as little money as you can, then let the cream rise up through the farm system. It took five years—and plenty of all-night bus rides—but that's exactly what I did."

He was animated when he talked of the good times with the powerhouse Yankees of the late fifties and early sixties, wistful but candid when he detailed the team's eventual fall from grace as the stars grew older and infirm and, one by one, faded into retirement or moved on to other teams.

"By the time they traded me to Philly after the '66 season," he had told me, "I didn't give a damn. Half the team was already gone or went in trades the same year—Berra, Kubek, Maris, Boyer. They sent Ellie to Boston in '67, and within a year both Whitey Ford and Mantle hung it up. Hell, I was glad to be going to Philadelphia."

At that point, early on in our breakfast interview, I had brought up his marriage to Evie March. Was it true, I asked, that the interracial marriage had as much to do with Wooley getting traded as did his continuing activism in the civil rights and antiwar movements?

"That was just a good excuse," he said dismissively. "Oldham was trying to move me for two years, because I was outspoken—wouldn't be his house nigger."

Wooley had then successfully deflected the conversation toward the Vietnam War and his reasons for opposing it, citing the disproportionate numbers of young blacks who were being sent off to fight and die. I let him lead me away from his marital problems because the Vietnam stuff was important to the profile, too, and because I was still wary of antagonizing the man, triggering the angry defenses that would cause him to retreat back into his shell.

But now, as he fondly reminisced about the little Cape Cod

house he and Evie had bought in an integrated neighborhood near the Howards, I saw a chance to ease the interview back to his controversial marriage to the young nightclub performer.

"You kept the Teaneck house after you were traded to Philadelphia?"

"Yeah. My wife liked the place, and we were sorta established in the community. That meant a lot, us being, you know, a mixed couple." He flashed a frown at me across the table, then abruptly pushed his chair back and stood. "It was too far to commute every day, but a ballplayer spends half the season on the road anyway. I took a room at a hotel in Philly during the season and drove up to Teaneck whenever we had an off-day scheduled. It wasn't so bad."

I pivoted on my chair, watching him as he walked to the kitchen sink and began rinsing dishes, making busy work.

"Do you think the separation—you in Philadelphia or on the road, and Evie up in Teaneck—contributed to the problems you had later on?"

He shrugged, his back to me as he bent over the sink. "Our breakup you mean? Sure it did. Check the record on ballplayers and you'll find plenty of broken marriages. It's tough on a woman, staying home alone for most of the season. You get so you start to lose touch with each other."

"Tough on the man, too, I'd guess. I mean, living away from his wife and his home for so much of the time. Finding himself sitting in a hotel room night after night, plenty of money in his pocket and time on his hands before the next game." I waited for Wooley to respond, but he didn't. He just kept running tap water over plates that didn't need it.

"There must be plenty of temptations out there for a star ballplayer," I went on. "The women, the high life, the hustlers, and the hangers-on."

"You mean hustlers like Harry Lundquist," he said, turning, finally. "Like maybe I was the same as a lot of other ballplayers? Too much money too soon, and not enough . . . what? . . . sophistication or education to handle it. Except instead of bedding down with the baseball groupies who hung around the hotel lobbies, or pickling myself with a bottle of Jim Beam, I killed time betting the ponies and maybe playing a little poker. That's what you mean, isn't it?" The dark eyes bore into me like x-rays, daring me to deny what lay hidden beneath the surface.

I nodded. "That's what I meant. It was the gambling ties that eventually got you banned from the game. I'm just trying to understand how you got into all that. Particularly why you continued your association with Harry Lundquist after the commissioner. . . . "

He pointed his index finger at me with the same menace with which he'd wielded the ball bat the day before. "The gambling and all the rest, that was a lot of overblown crap." He dropped his arm and began pacing the kitchen's short galley. "Lundquist was just . . . a guy I knew. We hung out together once in a while in Philly, sure, but I never bet a nickel on a baseball game in my life, no matter what that damned commissioner thought." He strode past me, muttering, "End of discussion. It's getting late."

I got up and followed him into the den. You learn to take a lot of things when you're a reporter, but taking a hint isn't one of them. Wooley was standing at one of the bookcases he'd built in beside the fireplace, running his eyes over the books.

"You did a nice job on those shelves," I said. "In fact the whole room looks like a pro did the work. How'd you get so handy anyway?"

"I worked in construction down in Jersey after I left baseball, to make ends meet until I could collect my pension. Got so I liked working with my hands, making something . . . lasting." He continued to scan the spines of the books as he talked. There were dozens of titles on the shelves, the authors ranging from Ralph Waldo Emerson to Ralph Waldo Ellison, and the books showed the wear of heavy use. He found the one he was looking for and pulled it. It was the autobiography of George Washington Carver.

"My father named me after this guy. Franklin George Wooley. The Franklin was for Roosevelt." He studied the book for a moment, then said quietly, "We're gonna have to call it a day, Sheridan. I got things to do."

"Sure," I said. "I'd like to come back Monday, though, if that's good for you. There's a lot we haven't covered."

He seemed about to protest, then shrugged it away. "Come back or don't, it's up to you. But I'm not going to talk about

Harry Lundquist or gambling or my ex-wife. That stuff's all behind me, and I'd just as soon leave it there."

" 'Packy Penguin says pick up a party pack today.' " Kate peered at me across the dining room table. "So?"

"Very alliterative."

"That's key. Bram says a campaign slogan has to have a rhythm to it, so it's easy for people to remember." Bram Goddard was Kate's boss and self-appointed mentor at the agency, a man I hadn't met but already disliked.

"Like 'Peter Piper picked a pack of pickled peppers.' "

Mandy stared at me wide-eyed, then tittered, but her mother didn't see the humor.

"Exactly." Kate nodded, her auburn hair springing off her shoulders. "Memorable and cute enough so even kids won't be able to forget it."

"I didn't realize the *Sesame Street* set was a target group for wine coolers."

She rolled her eyes and put on an exaggerated grimace for her daughter. "Men are impossible. Remember that."

Little Mandy nodded solemnly. "You told me that before, Mommy."

"Mmm. Let's move on to a new topic." Kate turned back to me. "Your eyes look tired, Sheridan. Are you sure you want to drive all the way back down to Mohaca Springs tonight? We could fix up the couch later. . . . "

"No, I'll be fine." We had already agreed that there'd be no sleep-overs while her daughter was home. "I always get a little blurry after a few hours of staring at a VDT."

"Rough afternoon at the paragraph factory?"

She meant the newspaper building downtown. After leaving Wooley's, I had gone home to shower and change into clothes that hadn't recently been liberated from the hamper. Then I drove the seventy miles to Rochester to file my parole-board story, with an eager young assistant metro editor looking over my shoulder and critiquing every line as I typed. By the time we finished it was nearly six, and I had to fight the last of the rush hour traffic to make it to Kate's northside home in time for dinner.

"It went okay considering the editor I was assigned seems to have a bias against freelancers." I took a sip of the Wagner Chardonnay, a Finger Lakes vintage I'd brought along, and sighed contentedly, then patted my middle. "I think the only thing wrong with my eyes is that they're bigger than my stomach."

The dinner—orange-pineapple chicken and seasoned wild rice—had been delicious, and the conversation around the table enjoyable. Six-year-old Mandy, when she wasn't quizzing me about my cat or my boat, had eaten sparingly, insisting that none of the individual items on her plate should mingle with any of the others because that would be too yucky. Kate, meanwhile, took double portions of everything and ate with a gusto common only to professional football players and svelte young women with the metabolism of a gibbon.

Mandy glanced down at my waistline, then up at my face. "Your eyes aren't that big, Sheridan," she said innocently.

When her mother and I stopped laughing, we cleared the dishes and brewed coffee. Mandy was excused so that she could go up to Kate's room to watch television.

"You know, you really could take the couch," Kate said as we settled in the living room.

"Rules are rules," I said. "And this one happens to be a good one."

It was the right thing to say. The tiny stress lines along Kate's forehead disappeared as she sank back into the plump couch. She smiled and sipped her coffee. "So, tell me about the rest of your week. You decided to take the assignment on that retired baseball player—what's his name?"

"Frank Wooley." I frowned. "Yeah, I took the assignment, but I almost wish I hadn't. The guy's an old hero of mine—I'm not sure I need any more disillusionment at my age."

"Disillusionment sells, according to Bram," she said. "He claims people love to read about their 'fallen idols' for some perverse reason. Hence the tabloids."

"Mmm."

She reached out and poked my arm. "This is no time to go all strong and silent on me. You know I'm a journalism junkie—tell me why the Wooley assignment is a problem."

I set my cup on the end table and stretched out my legs. "Well, to begin with, he's so—I don't know. Reticent isn't strong enough." I turned so I was facing her. "Usually I deal with your average career criminals and sociopaths—guys who love to brag about themselves and what they've done, always finding ways to put their own spin on it. They rationalize, like everything they ever did was someone else's fault. But Wooley, he makes no attempt to alibi. He just clams up or changes the subject whenever I get too personal." I shrugged. "I feel like I'm sparring with a hemophiliac, y'know? Like if I hit too hard with my questions, I'll cut him and he'll just bleed to death."

"This guy was that important to you as a kid?"

"It seems silly now, I know. But, for me, coming of age in the late sixties, Frank Wooley touched all the bases, pun intended. Baseball, civil rights, the antiwar movement. He had a handle on everything—but then it all fell apart."

"What happened?"

"Everything. You remember, I told you about his left-wing politics and the controversy over his marriage. But it was the gambling rumors and his decision to take on baseball's status quo that really started him down a slippery slope—that and some well-publicized domestic problems."

"Domestic problems?"

"Yeah, it was right after Wooley lost his case against baseball's reserve clause. He was arrested for allegedly beating up on his wife and daughter. Apparently he'd been drinking, and he was undoubtedly depressed about . . . "

"Wait a minute, Sheridan." Kate sat up suddenly. "This so-called hero of yours abused his wife and daughter?"

"That was the charge. . . . "

"And you're willing to excuse it because the bastard had a bad day?"

"I'm not trying to excuse anything, Kate," I protested. "It's just, I'm having a hard time accepting Frank Wooley as the sort of man who'd do something like that."

"Look who's rationalizing now." Her face was stiff, the rich brown eyes glassy. "The world is full of men like Frank Wooley. Why anyone would want to glorify him in a magazine story, I don't know—and I don't give a good goddamn how many home runs he had!"

She rose abruptly, leaving me staring up at her, mouth agape. I had wounded her somehow, that much was obvious. She had never said much about her ex-husband, and I hadn't asked—probably because I was too busy avoiding talk of my own failed marriage. But it didn't take an investigative reporter to divine a connection between Frank Wooley's checkered family history and Kate's sudden, impassioned outburst.

"Look, I'm sorry if I—" I began, but she cut me off.

"No, no, it's nothing. I'm fine." She tried to plaster over her embarrassment with a brittle, apologetic little smile. "It's just that . . . I'm a little tired, Sheridan. Tough week on penguin duty. I think we'd better call it a night, all right?"

CHAPTER 7

THE scene with Kate was still with me when I drove back down to see Frank Wooley midday Monday.

I had stayed at her house another hour Friday night—the second time in a day I had refused to take a hint. Unlike the earlier episode with Wooley, however, I managed to get Kate to open up a little. It wasn't easy for her; she seemed embarrassed, as if being the victim was somehow worse than being the aggressor.

In a quiet, tempered voice, she told me that her ex-husband Michael had started physically abusing her soon after they married—only her, never their daughter, she hastened to add. At first it had been slaps across the face—shocking and hurtful, but something she thought she could deal with—but as time went on the open palm became a fist, and Kate was finally convinced that it was time to get out of the marriage. Michael had moved to Buffalo after the divorce and hadn't bothered her in two years. He had been granted supervised visitation rights with Mandy, but gradually stopped exercising them. That left Kate stuck in the middle: sorry for the hurt his abandonment caused their daughter, but relieved that she herself no longer had to spend every other Sunday in the presence of a man who had caused her so much misery during five years of marriage.

That was as much as she had been willing to tell me, and I hadn't pushed. But when I left her that night, I had a new appreciation for Kate Sumner, and, perhaps, a different perspective on Frank Wooley.

Now, as I drove up the muddy lane that led to IdaRose Mack's place, I replayed Kate's angry accusation. Had I been rationalizing Wooley's failures? Making up excuses for him, giving him the benefit of the doubt because of who he was? Letting him slip all the tough questions, not because I was worried about losing his cooperation, but because I was trying to prop up a fallen idol?

He was standing in the open door of the garage when I pulled up the drive, this time holding a block plane instead of a baseball bat. A late-model Chevy Blazer was parked in the turnaround, but the Caprice was gone.

"So you decided to come back anyway," he greeted me. He was wearing jeans speckled with sawdust and an old cotton work shirt. His expression was neutral but calm. "If we're gonna do this, we'll have to do it in my shop in back here. I told IdaRose I'd have her closet doors rehung by the time she gets home from work."

The workshop took up the rear of the extra-deep garage. I pulled a folding lawn chair from a hook along the side wall and sat down, resting my notepad on my knee and the pocketsized tape recorder on a stack of tires. Wooley concentrated on planing the edges of a pair of sturdy chestnut doors while we talked. The going was easy at first, a few throw-away lines about the spring weather, some asides about the best method for refinishing old crackled wood, a story or two about the good old days on the diamond. I let him ramble until the small talk ran its course, then I let my instincts take me, asking the first question that came to mind.

"When I showed up here unannounced last week, the first words out of your mouth were 'Who sent you?' " I said. "Not 'Who are you?', but 'Who sent you?' What'd you mean by that, Frank?"

He had told me to call him Frank at the outset of our second session, but I hadn't been able to do it. It had seemed somehow inappropriate, like meeting up with your third-grade teacher twenty years later and calling her Edna. But my experience with Kate made me change my approach.

"I didn't say that," he said without looking up from his work. "I asked you what you were doing in my house."

"That's not how I remember it."

"Yeah, well, too bad we don't have instant replay. You'd see you remember it wrong."

"Who did you think I might be?" I persisted.

"How the hell did I know who you might be?" He took a couple of aggressive strokes with the plane, thin curlicues of wood shavings rolling out the back like party favors. "A burglar, ringing the bell first just to make sure nobody was home. Or a snoopy reporter."

"Is there somebody else looking for you, Frank? Not reporters, but somebody you think means you harm? Is that why you've hidden yourself away out here. . . . "

He flung the block plane onto the work bench, scattering a tray of wood screws. "I'm not hiding from anybody or anything. I live with my lady and she lives here. Maybe that suits me right now." He took a deep breath. "I had the limelight for a lotta years, Sheridan. It got old, some things went wrong. So I found a place where I could get some peace, and an honest woman who doesn't harp on things neither one of us can do anything about. Maybe I just decided to take the easy road for once, all right?"

I let it go, pausing a moment before moving on. "Tell me about the decision to challenge the reserve clause."

He relaxed a little, his hunched shoulders seeming to shrink under the blue cotton shirt. "Seemed like a good idea at the time," he said, a small rueful grin playing at the corners of his mouth. Then he got serious. "You know that professional baseball was given a special antitrust exemption by the Supreme Court back in 1922?"

I nodded. "I read about it when I was preparing for this story. But I'd like to hear your views on it."

He leaned back against the work bench and folded his arms casually across his chest. "That exemption firmed up what the owners claimed was their right all along—to treat a ballplayer's services as a personal asset owned by the club. They claimed this right under what's called the reserve clause, which went into every contract. From the first time you signed on as a green seventeen-year-old kid, you became the property of whichever team had your contract. And you were bound to that team for your whole professional life, unless they decided to trade you. See, the owners claimed the reserve clause gave them a perpetual option on your services. What I did, I went to court after the Phillies tried to trade me to Kansas City and I argued that I should be a free agent—free to choose where I worked just like anybody else. You follow me?" he asked as I jotted a few notes.

"I'm with you."

"All right. It was my argument that I'd fulfilled the contract with the Phillies and, since the contract had expired, I should be free to peddle my services elsewhere." He shrugged. "The court ruled against me. They said the Phillies had a preexisting right to trade me under the contract I'd signed. But they also told the owners that this idea about a perpetual option was trouble, and that at some point the owners were going to have to revise it, or the court would do it for them. A few years later, when a couple pitchers challenged the reserve clause again, that's pretty much what happened. They were declared free agents and the baseball owners had to scramble to negotiate a new deal with the players' union. Too late to do me any good, though."

"It was a courageous thing to do."

He laughed joylessly. "Courage didn't figure in, Sheridan. We, my wife and me, didn't want to move to Kansas City, that's all. I had two choices; retire or go to court."

"Four years earlier you were traded to Philadelphia from the Yankees and you didn't protest. In fact, you told me you were happy to make the move. What was different the second time around? Why is it you decided to risk your career rather than accept a trade to Kansas City?"

"I told you before, we had a nice place in Teaneck, an integrated neighborhood where we were pretty much accepted. Only about a hundred miles from Philly, so I could get home a lot during the season. Plus we had a baby by then." His dark face softened. "Martina came along in '68. I named her after Reverend King. Evie wasn't crazy about it, but . . . "

It was the first time I'd heard him use his ex-wife's name. It had slipped out in an unguarded moment, when his thoughts were on his daughter and the comfortable house in Teaneck. He seemed surprised and mortified to hear the name escape his lips, like a monk who'd inadvertently broken a vow of silence.

"Anyway, I was a thirteen-year veteran. I should've had some say in where I played. Today's players do, but you go ask 'em how many remember that I had something to do with their getting it." He shook his head solemnly. "I was a hot ticket for a while there. The head of the players' union was drooling, he wanted so bad to stick it to the owners. Everybody was on my side, the big Washington lawyer they hired for me, the union, Richie Hirshberg, my wife. . . . "

"Richie Hirshberg?" I asked. "The political activist Richie Hirshberg?"

"He was, in the sixties," Wooley said, nodding. "You probably remember him from one of the antiwar rallies. Had hair halfway down to his ass, always giving speeches about some 'new economic order' we were all gonna help create. But like a lotta those guys, he got unradical real fast after the draft was abolished. Now he's an agent for professional athletes, living in northern Jersey near where . . . my wife and her new husband live."

"Hirshberg was your agent?"

"Financial adviser. We didn't actually have agents in those days. I got to know him at an antiwar rally, found out he was a big fan and a financial whiz to boot, with a degree from Columbia. Anyway, we got friendly, and I started using him to help me with my contract negotiations and investments and things. He did a pretty good job, too, but I ended up having to cash in half of what we'd built up after I left baseball. My ex got the rest when we divorced in '74."

"You say Hirshberg lives near your ex-wife in Teaneck?" I asked, grabbing the opportunity to bring Evie March back into the discussion.

"Not in Teaneck. Further out toward Saddle River. My ex sold the place in Teaneck after she remarried."

"You have an address for her?"

He studied me for a moment before answering. "It wouldn't do you any good if I did. Much as she likes to gab, she won't talk to you about the bad old days with me. Her new sugar daddy wouldn't like it and, besides, we signed a paper when we got divorced. Neither one of us is supposed to talk about—certain things."

"You mean like Harry Lundquist," I suggested. "Or the assault charges leveled at you for . . . "

"The charges that were dismissed two days later," he said heatedly. "Only that time it didn't make banner headlines like the arrest did. My usual luck; the day the charges were dropped the goddamn newspapers broke a big Watergate story. That's all anybody remembers.''

"You know what I don't understand, Frank? What you were doing with Lundquist when you tried slipping away from the courthouse that day. After the agreement you made with the commissioner. . . . ''

Wooley pushed himself away from the work bench. "He just showed up with the lawyer, that's all. I didn't plan it that way. I tried to tell the commissioner, but that arrogant son of a bitch wouldn't listen.''

"It does seem hard to believe, Frank," I pressed. "If you really had severed your relationship with Lundquist, why would he show up with your lawyer?''

The dead stare came into his eyes and his lips compressed into a tight frown. He turned away and began gathering up the scattered wood screws from the bench, putting them back in their tray.

"That's it, Sheridan. I already told you I wasn't going into this stuff. I told you, Evie—my ex-wife and me both signed an agreement not to talk about all that.''

"Whose idea was that?''

It was an accusation more than a question. I'd promised myself there'd be no more soft-toss; the big boys always play hardball. If I was going to do the assignment right, I had to open Wooley up and see what was on the inside. But there was a big difference between a surgeon and a butcher, and as I sat there on the lawn chair my pen suddenly felt as heavy as a meat cleaver. A moment later, I found myself wishing it was.

Wooley stiffened, his back to me as he faced the work bench. Then he whirled, his hands balled at his sides, and came at me across the dusty concrete floor. "Get the fuck outta here," he said in a low growl.

I stood clear of the chair and raised my arms, holding the pen and notepad in either hand, my fingers splayed.

"Take it easy, Frank. I was only. . . . ''

His arms exploded upward, the heels of his fists pounding into my chest and driving me backward against the sidewall of the garage.

"Don't be an asshole," I said angrily. "If you . . . ''

He caught me on the mouth with a hard left, knocking me into the wall again. A rake came off its hook and landed on me as I went down on one knee. I dropped my pad and pen and scrambled up just as Wooley threw a right. My elbow deflected the punch, and I countered with a right of my own, connecting solidly with Wooley's jaw. He staggered into the work bench, the impact rattling the tools suspended along the back wall's Peg-Board. Then he recovered and came at me again, arms swinging wildly.

It went on like that for what seemed an hour, but it couldn't've have been more than a minute. Wooley, a silent, seething battering ram, kept launching himself at me and I kept fending him off. But it was like pounding on a speed bag: The harder you hit it the faster it comes back at you. Finally, just as I thought my own lungs would burst, I sank my fist deep into Wooley's stomach and heard the air rush out of him and felt his body slacken. His legs buckled and he dropped, first to his knees, then to all fours. His head hanging, his arms quaking with fatigue, his breath coming in tortured gulps, he still managed to spew a string of obscenities at me.

I stood over him for a moment, my chest heaving. Then, with a muttered curse of my own, I gathered up the tools of my trade and stormed out of the garage, vowing that I'd never again waste a minute of my time on Franklin George Wooley.

CHAPTER 8

BUT it wasn't quite that simple.

By the time a couple of days had passed and the bruises on my face had almost disappeared, I knew I had to think about Frank Wooley again, if only to call Pete Calvett at *The Sporting Life* and explain why I was bowing out of the assignment. But Pete wouldn't hear of it. He figured my three sessions with Wooley had provided me with enough personal information and quotes to put together a good profile. And he loved the part where Wooley and I knocked each other around in the garage, claiming it made for the perfect gonzo journalism ending for the piece.

I wasn't enthusiastic. As far as I was concerned, I only had a snapshot of Wooley; a flat two-dimensional image. In the end, though, I agreed to write the piece, not as a profile per se, but as a personal account of one reporter's encounter with one of baseball's most enigmatic figures. It was a business decision more than anything. I had time and effort invested in Frank Wooley and a professional commitment to Pete Calvett. I wanted to get paid and I wanted to maintain my relationship with *The Sporting Life.*

I let things simmer for a few more days, then settled in at the word processor, my notes and tape recorder spread across my desk. The piece took two days to write and came in at around twenty-two hundred words. I sent it off to Pete the next day, dissatisfied with the result, but knowing it was the best I had in me. I felt hollow when I put the last period on the article, but also relieved. For better or worse, I was finally through with the Wooley story.

Or so I thought at the time. Several weeks later, I found out I'd just gotten started.

May brought generous doses of sunshine, gentle evening rain showers, and swaths of yellow and red along the driveway where the daffodils and tulips bloomed. On the weekends, West Lake Road saw more and more boats on trailers and minivans packed with household gear and children as families from the cities came down to open up their cottages for the season ahead. Kate and I smoothed things over—although glossed them over might be a better term. On the occasional nights out we were able to arrange when she was in town on business, we talked about everything and anything, so long as it didn't include her ex-husband Michael. Spring fever kept me away from my desk as often as not but, in between a couple of chilly early morning fishing excursions with Ralph Cramer, I managed to complete a few assignments.

By the third week in May, my work schedule had hit a momentary lull, and I was able to catch up on a few social obligations without feeling guilty. Lead item on the agenda was dinner at the Pinewood with Kate, along with Karen DeClair and her husband. An old friend of mine from our days together on a Rochester newspaper, Karen was now the managing editor of the *Finger Lakes Daily News*, headquartered in Geneva, and the six-month-new bride of the paper's owner, publisher, and editor-in-chief, Bob Kaufman.

"She's really . . . " Karen turned to her better half with a saccharine smile. "Adorable. Is that the word I want, Bob?"

"The word you want is young, dear," he said, his eyes amused behind the wire-rimmed glasses.

"Kate is twenty-nine," I said defensively.

"She looks twenty," Karen said. "I'm surprised the waiter didn't card her when she ordered the gin and tonic."

"Sorry, Sheridan," Bob said. "I just don't know what to do about this woman of mine."

"Have you thought about having her de-clawed?"

Karen let go a laugh that froze the rest of the diners for an instant. One didn't parade one's emotions in the sedate surroundings of the Pinewood Lodge.

"Touché, Sheridan," she said. "Kate's really beautiful and she seems very nice. I'm just jealous of her disgusting perkiness. Make that youthful exuberance."

Bob gave me his best deadpan look. "I've always been drawn to cantankerous old broads myself, as you can see." Karen shot him the evil eye, then barked out another laugh.

She was only thirty-seven and, if you disregard the incongruously throaty voice, she could pass for thirty. She was short and small boned, with a round face and an explosion of frizzy hair. Her life revolved around her work and her husband, order of importance yet to be determined, according to Bob. He was a year or two past forty, of middle height and also small boned, with a mild paunch and receding sandy hair. The two were as natural together as Burns and Allen, or perhaps burritos and Alka Seltzer.

"I knew I was in trouble the minute you suggested this dinner," I told Karen. She'd been bugging me about meeting Kate ever since the jungle drums had first informed her that there was, in Karen's words, "a steady girl" in my life. At first I tried the old dodge about Kate and I merely being good friends and when that didn't scan, I used conflicting work schedules as a way to beg off. But Kate and I had been seeing each other off and on for two months now, and the inevitable always has a way of catching up.

"Oh, c'mon, Sheridan," Karen said. "I'm only teasing. I'm glad you've got someone to share your life with. I didn't know how important that was until I got hitched," she added, with an affectionate glance at her husband.

"We're not 'sharing our lives,' Karen, we're just dating. We see each other maybe once every couple of weeks if we're lucky and we've managed to spend two weekends together, including this one." I poked a fork at the last of my brandied cheesecake, then nudged the plate away. "Neither one of us has even mentioned the infamous *m* word."

Bob looked at Karen. "He can't even bring himself to say it."

"He's gun-shy," Karen agreed. " 'Fool me once, shame on you. Fool me twice, shame on me.' "

"Linda has nothing to do with it," I lied. My wife and I had been apart for almost three years, divorced for two. It was inevitable, our splitting up, and we were both probably better for it. But I was raised an Irish Catholic boy, for whom the phrase "till death do us part" was a commandment, not an aspiration. Karen's jibe had hit closer to home than I liked to admit—which I had no intention of doing anyway. "I don't believe in whirlwind romances."

Just then Kate crossed in front of the huge stone fireplace centered on the far wall and began a serpentine return to our table in the center of the Pinewood's main dining room. It had been the living room back in the early days, when the place was a private summer residence for a wealthy downstate businessman. The east wall had triple French doors leading to a stone terrace with a sweeping view of Seneca Lake. The score of tables were all filled, as they usually were on a Saturday night, both in and out of season. The Pinewood Lodge, located a few miles south of Geneva, was the top local dining spot for those who preferred traditional over trendy. The service was good, the food excellent, and the tab not too exorbitant if you were careful with the wine list.

"I hope I didn't miss anything interesting," Kate said as she settled into her chair. She had passed on the dessert cart in favor of a trip to the ladies' room to powder a nose that didn't need it.

"Only about a thousand empty calories," Karen quipped.

"I'll bet you were exchanging wild stories about your experiences," Kate said, then sighed wistfully. "God, it must be exciting, being a real working journalist, tracking down stories, facing that deadline pressure every day. . . . "

"Editing the farm report," Karen interjected.

"Negotiating a new contract with the typesetter's union," Bob threw in.

"All deadline pressure ever gets you," I said, "is stomach ulcers and prematurely gray hair."

"Now that you mention it, Sheridan." Karen squinted at the side of my head. "There do seem to be a few silver strands amongst the gold."

"Thank you for noticing, Lady Clairol."

Conversation lagged for a moment as the waiter came around to refill our coffee cups. Had it been earlier in the evening, he might've been lax on the refills in hopes we'd clear out and free up the table. But it was almost ten, and there were no more patrons cooling their heels in the lobby.

"Anyway," Kate continued after the waiter faded away, "it's a lot more exciting than setting up an appearance schedule for a guy in a penguin suit. I mean, I'm not complaining—I love my job and all—but it just doesn't have the urgency of journalism."

"You give us more credit than we deserve, Kate," Bob said. "Believe me, the mundane far outnumbers those few instances of high drama. Of course, it's only the dramatic events, like the Gulf War, let's say, or the Berlin Wall coming down, that people remember."

"I suppose so." Kate nodded. "But I don't just mean the big, earthshaking stories like that. It just has to be such a rush knowing that every day there's something new. That even a simple assignment could turn out to be exciting or important, or even dangerous. Like that awful baseball player you had that brawl with a few weeks ago, Sheridan."

"It wasn't a brawl, really. . . . "

"Whoa!" Karen leaned over the table and peered at me like an owl focusing on a field mouse. "I see your interviewing technique is still a little rough around the edges, but never mind that. Who's this famous baseball player you completely forgot to tell me about?"

I suppressed a groan. I hadn't mentioned Wooley because I knew the minute I did, Karen would try to wheedle his whereabouts out of me so she could send one of her reporters down there to do an article for the *Daily News.* If the piece was any good at all, it would be picked up by one of the wire services and fed to hundreds of papers all over the country. Which meant my piece for *The Sporting Life* would lose what little import it had.

I tried to brazen it out with an inscrutable silence, but Bob, who was a baseball fan, figured it out on his own.

"You dug up Frank Wooley. That's it, isn't it, Sheridan." He grinned at me, then turned to his wife. "You remember, Karen, the retired ballplayer who was a star second baseman for the Yanks in the sixties? The guy who was elected to Cooperstown over the winter?"

"The one with the bad attitude who worked for the Cubbies for a while, until he got fired for fighting," Karen said, nodding slowly. "Sure. We had Johncox do a story on the guy when he joined the team three years ago, but it was a piece of fluff. Johncox, that son of a . . . I told him to get ahold of the Cubs' management in January to find out what happened to Wooley, figuring we might do another story if he was still around. But Johncox said Wooley had left town."

"He did," I said. "But he only went about forty miles."

"Sportswriters," Karen muttered. "Hand 'em a shovel, and they still wouldn't know how to dig." An eyebrow arched. "So where's this hotshot Wooley hanging his hat these days, Sheridan?"

I smiled at her over the rim of my cup. "Go fish."

A little over an hour later, Kate and I were back at the cottage, nestled together on the old leather sofa, half listening to a Marcus Roberts CD, when the phone cut the mood like a chain saw.

"Damn."

"Let the machine get it," Kate murmured.

"Yeah."

I tried to filter out the distraction, but the music was very low and the buzzing of the phone was insistent. On the fourth ring, the answering machine on my desk in the loft picked up. There was a click, a few seconds of quiet anticipation followed by a familiar beep, and then an equally familiar voice echoing down off the great room's vaulted ceiling. I had left the machine's volume control on high.

"Sheridan? Karen. I know you must be back home by now so let go of Kate and pick up the phone."

"She never gives up," Kate said, sighing.

"That's why she's such a good newspaperwoman." We both assumed Karen wanted to take one more shot at cajoling, threatening, or begging me to tell her where to find Frank Wooley. As it was, she'd harangued me all the way from the Pinewood's dining room, out into the lobby, and across the parking lot to our cars. "We'll just let her use up her minute and hope she doesn't keep calling back," I said.

"I only wanted you to know I'm not mad at you anymore for stiffing me on the Wooley story," Karen was saying. "I stopped at the newsroom on the way home to see that everything was in order, and Brian MacKay was there doing the final police call around before deadline, right?"

I said to Kate, "You watch. Whatever this is about, she'll time it right down to the last second before the tape shuts her off."

" . . . so the watch commander at the sheriff's office in Penn Yan tells Brian they caught a real bloody one tonight. Down in southern Yates County . . . "

I slowly pushed myself upright on the sofa.

" . . . gives Brian the tentative identification on one of the bodies . . . "

I stood up and began looking around for the cordless phone.

" . . . preliminary indications point to a murder-suicide," Karen said, pausing before adding, "Frank Wooley is dead, Sheridan."

Click.

CHAPTER 9

IT wasn't IdaRose Mack.

That had been my initial fear; that Wooley, in an uncontrollable rage, had struck out at IdaRose, killing her and then taking his own life.

But it wasn't IdaRose. The murder victim turned out to be a man named Mike Delfay. As best the sheriff's people had been able to determine, Delfay had arrived at the house earlier in the day driving a rental car he'd picked up at the airport in Rochester. The materials in the briefcase he had with him suggested that Delfay was a writer. Apparently he had flown up from New York City on Saturday morning and had found his way to the house, looking for an interview with the new hall of fame inductee, just as I had a few weeks earlier. Only Delfay hadn't gotten off with just a sore jaw and a badly bruised ego. He and Wooley had been found by IdaRose when she got home from work and shopping around seven that evening. Both bodies were on the floor of the den, Delfay with a bullet hole in his chest, Wooley with a single entry wound in the neck just under his chin, his fingers still wrapped around a .22 caliber handgun.

That's as much as I was able to learn Saturday night. After receiving Karen DeClair's message, I had immediately called her back at the *Daily News* office. Her initial bantering gave way to hard facts as soon as she read the tone in my voice. She put me on with her police reporter, Brian MacKay, who gave me what he had on the story and then hung up abruptly so that he and Karen could get back to the frantic task of rearranging the paper's front page. I then put in a call to the Yates County Sheriff's Office in Penn Yan. The night duty officer I spoke to read me the standard release on the investigation, but couldn't or wouldn't elaborate.

Sunday morning's edition of the *Finger Lakes Daily News* didn't tell me much more. The headline took up almost as much room as the story itself. The article listed the murder victim's age as thirty-five and said that Delfay had been a resident of Brooklyn. There was no information beyond that provided by the sheriff's official release.

The rest of the weekend with Kate was a washout. We went through the motions with a big breakfast Sunday morning at Ralph and Kay's, followed by a visit to a flea market and antiques show down in Watkins Glen. The weather was perfect for strolling around the open-air exhibit stalls—sunny and near seventy—but it was wasted on me. By mid-afternoon, Kate gave voice to what we'd both realized since Saturday night: that I was too preoccupied with the Wooley tragedy to concentrate on homefries or English pine cupboards or even the attentions of a beautiful brunette. She left for home a few hours earlier than we'd planned, giving me a warm goodbye kiss, but clearly irritated by how things had turned out.

I spent the remainder of the afternoon and early evening sitting out on the deck, cocooned in a heavy cable-knit sweater, watching a strong northern breeze whip up the lake surface and trying to understand how so much talent and intelligence and guts can go so far wrong. It was almost eight o'clock when the buzz of the phone through the patio door's sliding screen brought me in out of the growing chill.

"Mr. Sheridan?" The voice, muted but steady, belonged to IdaRose Mack.

I started into the standard speech. How shocked and sorry I was to hear about Wooley's death; how I wished I'd gotten to know the man in better times, under different circumstances. That's when IdaRose cut me off with a burst of pent-up anguish.

"That's just it, Mr. Sheridan, these were better times for Frank. And for me. What you saw . . . the trouble you had, that was because of who you were, not because of who Frank was."

I shook my head wearily in the gloom of the cottage's great

room and sighed through the phone line. "Look, IdaRose, I know how upset you must be, but . . . "

"I'm not blaming you for anything, don't get me wrong," she said. "You're a journalist. It's your job to ask questions, dig up the past. But that's the one thing Frank can't—couldn't stand to do. Pressure him about his old life, and he became a changed man; he'd tighten up and get all defensive. That's why a man in your work couldn't get close to the real Franklin Wooley, Mr. Sheridan. It's taken me two years of loving and trust and patience, and still there was so much he kept locked inside."

"Well, I'm sure you're right about that," I said. "All I know is he was one of the angriest men I've ever met. If I somehow brought that out of him, triggered something that—made him do what he did, then I'm very sorry. I don't know what else I can say."

"You can say you'll finish what you started."

"Excuse me?"

"That day you first came out to the house, you said you wanted to write about the real Frank Wooley. I was hoping you'd succeed, so the rest of the world would get to know the sweet, gentle man. . . . " She broke off for a moment. "The gentle man I knew. I still want you to find and write about the real Frank Wooley."

It was the same thought that tugged at me as I brooded out on the deck. Who was the real Franklin Wooley? I realized I still wanted to know the answer to that question. But I also knew that IdaRose Mack didn't. The 'truth' she wanted told was her truth; an absolution for a man she could only see through the tunnel vision of love.

I moved over to the chair by the fireplace and settled into the comfortably battered seat cushion. In the beginning, I had been ready to sympathize with Wooley, to give him the benefit of the doubt, if only he gave me something in return. A reasonable defense of his actions. An explanation for a life gone sour. But things had changed; Wooley was no longer the principal victim of his failings. Now there was a dead man named Delfay to factor in.

"I don't think you understand what you're opening yourself up for, IdaRose," I said. "If it's a eulogy you're after. . . . "

"I said I wanted the truth, Mr. Sheridan," she cut in. "Starting with what really happened out at my house yesterday afternoon."

"The police say they know what happened."

"They're wrong. Frank supposedly killed this man for who knows what reason, then turned the gun on himself? Does that sound like the Frank Wooley you met?"

"I've been asking myself that question all day, IdaRose. Did he seem capable of killing someone over some real or imagined slight? I'm afraid I'd have to answer yes. As to whether he would turn the gun on himself . . . "

"There's another question you should be asking," she said. "The gun. Where did Frank get the gun?"

"Well, I assumed he had it around the house someplace."

"Not in my house, Mr. Sheridan. I can't abide guns and Frank knew that."

"He may've kept it stashed away someplace."

"He didn't," she stated flatly, then hurried on over my objections. "What about that first day you came out to the house, Mr. Sheridan. The day I got home just in time to find you two staring each other down in my back hallway. Frank caught you sneaking around, thought you might be a burglar or something, remember?"

"I surely do. He could've taken my head off with—" I hesitated as her meaning sank in. "—with that baseball bat."

"That's exactly right. So ask yourself another question. If a man had a gun in the house, why would he try to stand off a burglar with a Louisville Slugger?"

I didn't have a ready answer for her that time, but then she wasn't waiting for one.

"I don't know what happened between Frank and that other man," she went on. "But I know the police got it wrong. They won't listen to me, Mr. Sheridan. Their minds are already made up. What about yours?"

I stared into the fire for a moment and listened to the mild static of the cordless phone and the tense but controlled breathing of the woman at the other end of the line. Then I said, "I still don't write eulogies, IdaRose. But if you're really prepared to help me find answers, no matter what those answers turn out to be, then I think we should talk. Face to face."

I heard her sigh, as if an oppressive weight had been lifted away. "I'm staying with friends near Penn Yan. We could meet here tomorrow morning around ten o'clock."

I told her that was fine and wrote down the address she gave me. After we hung up, I thought about digging into my files for the notes and tapes of my interviews with Wooley, but I couldn't work up the ambition. Tomorrow would be soon enough, I told myself, after my talk with IdaRose. Instead, I put a disc on the CD player and stretched out on the couch and studied the great room's vaulted ceiling while I listened to Van Morrison.

Enlightenment—he sang—don't know what it is.

Next morning at eight I was back in the morris chair, savoring a second cup of coffee, when Pete Calvett called.

"You must've gotten to the office bright and early today," I said. "Very industrious. Did the Japanese buy up *The Sporting Life*, or are you just turning over a new leaf?"

"Bite your tongue, Sheridan. I'm not at the office yet, as a matter of fact. I'm in my car, stuck in traffic on the GW bridge with about a thousand other suburbanites. We high-powered executive types all have cellular phones, y'know. It comes with the package, along with an ulcer and a wife who lives to shop."

"The man in the gray-flannel Saab."

"It's an Audi, but close enough. Anyway, I'm sitting here listening to WCBS. The happy-news guy who sounds like Gary Owens, right?"

"I'll take your word for it."

"And what do I hear, but that your favorite ex-ballplayer and mine has shuffled off this mortal coil."

"Frank Wooley is dead, if that's what you're trying to say, Pete. Sometime Saturday afternoon. You're just hearing about it?"

"I spent the weekend on my publisher's boat out on the Sound," Calvett said. "No phones, no papers, no fun—no shit. Anyhow, I'm sitting here waiting for New York's finest to scrape another bike messenger off the tarmac, and this happy-news clown comes on and tells me that not only did Wooley off himself with a .22 handgun, but first he took out another guy. And the other guy is none other than Mike 'As Told To' Delfay. Is this for real, Sheridan?"

"It's for real." I filled him in on the official police version of the incident, leaving aside my conversation with IdaRose Mack the night before. "You knew this Mike Delfay, Pete?"

"Sure. Everybody in town who works in sports publishing knows Delfay. He writes—make that wrote—celebrity bios on big-name jocks. We had serial rights for his last book, that so-called autobiography by Trenton Towner, the Knicks' forward? All Towner did was tell a few war stories, if he ever did that much. Delfay actually wrote the thing."

"Which means he worked under contract with his subjects?" I asked, frowning into the handset.

"Sometimes yes, sometimes no," Calvett said. "Delfay would do some preliminary research on a person he thought had 'saleability,' if you will, then he'd approach the jock or the jock's agent with a book proposal. If they went for it, Delfay would write an authorized 'as told to' biography, usually with plenty of dirt on everybody but the subject himself. The Towner book, for example, blamed Towner's coke habit on a college coach who he claims introduced him to steroids. Trenton Towner comes out looking like a misguided choir boy. That's how Delfay plays it when his subjects sign on the dotted line."

"And if they don't?"

Calvett chuckled. "Then it gets nasty, if Mike the Knife decides he's put in too much research time to dump the project. He goes ahead and does an unauthorized biography, no holds barred. Play ball and you get the sympathetic touch, say no thanks and you get filleted. Most of his subjects decide to cooperate, if only to save the aggravation. You must've seen the unauthorized hatchet job he did on Pete Rose, didn't you? It was a best seller for about an hour and a half last year."

"I guess I missed that one." I paused for a moment. "Apparently Delfay tracked down Wooley and tried to talk him—or threaten him—into cooperating on an autobiography."

"Looks like it. Only he picked the wrong guy to intimidate this time. Which brings me to the reason I called, Sheridan. The profile you wrote for me? And the other seven-fifty I owe you on publication?"

"Yeah?" I frowned into the phone, knowing what was coming. My piece, scheduled to run in the July 15 issue of *The Sporting Life*, was obsolete now. Which meant that the article would be scratched and I wouldn't be seeing the second half of my fee. I had expected as much, but that didn't mean I had to like it, particularly now that IdaRose had convinced me to give the subject a second look. I'd been hoping to get Calvett to give me another shot.

"Well," he said in that blustery voice of his, "how'd you like to see that seven-fifty turn into five thousand?"

The question so caught me off guard that I didn't say anything for a second, a void Pete rushed to fill.

"I know you said you didn't want anything more to do with Wooley," he said. "And I can understand. You're disillusioned because your old boyhood idol turned out to be a major-league jerk. But, listen, Sheridan, you're a pro, right?"

"Well—sure."

"And a pro doesn't let personal crap get in the way when there's a job to do. Am I right?"

"Yeah, you're right."

"So here's the deal, Sheridan. You take the research you already did and you start digging again. I mean really dig this time, because I want to know everything there is to know about the tragic life and death of Frank 'Black Sheep' Wooley. Everything." Calvett paused to take a breath—I could hear car horns blaring in the background—then plunged ahead. "You get me the whole story before the hall of fame ceremonies in July, and I'll give you five grand and maybe even the cover of *The Sporting Life*. And this time I'm not gonna hang up until you say yes."

"Well, since you put it that way, Pete—yes."

CHAPTER 10

SHE wasn't the same woman I'd met just a few weeks before. The dark eyes had glowed then, and her long, graceful body had been at ease with itself. Today her movements were quick and small, her glance tentative and questioning and somehow apologetic. Her somber charcoal dress hung homely as sackcloth from her slumped shoulders.

"I'll be all right," she said again. "I've been through this before, when my husband died. You get so—your mind loses its place every so often, y'know?"

I smiled reassuringly and leaned back against the fat sofa's antimacassar. IdaRose Mack sat across from me on a brocaded antique chair, the fingers of her left hand worrying at the doily draped over the chair's arm. We were in the overfurnished living room of a couple named Birney, who owned the gift shop where IdaRose worked. After learning of Wooley's death, they had offered her their guest room and as much time off as she needed. Both husband and wife were away, working at the shop, when I arrived.

I had spent the first hour coaching a reluctant IdaRose through a painful, meandering recounting of the scene she had come home to Saturday night. Her memory, stunted by shock and grief, came in disjointed fragments. She recalled the unfamiliar car, a small white sedan, parked in the driveway; the unsettling stillness she sensed when she entered the house through the back door. Then the horror she nearly tripped over in the den. Frank lying on his side, his throat and the carpet beneath him stained brick red, his fingers frozen around the textured grip of a small automatic. The other man—a stranger—lying on his back, eyes and mouth open, suitcoat flung wide to reveal a crimson splotch the size of a half dollar on his white shirt. It didn't seem fair, she remembered thinking, that the other man had bled so little while Frank had bled so much.

"They wouldn't really do that, would they?" she asked me now. "I mean, the hall of fame, that's all Frank has left. They won't take that away?"

"I don't know, IdaRose. I think it's just speculation right now by someone who needs to fill up a column every day." There had been an article in the morning paper, a syndicated sportswriter calling for Wooley's July induction in Cooperstown to be canceled. There were sure to be more such articles, and it was anyone's guess whether anything would come of it. "Right now, the best thing we can do is try to prove your theory of what happened on Saturday," I said, nudging the conversation back on course. "If Frank was just trying to defend himself—and if we can demonstrate that somehow—then the hall controversy will go away."

IdaRose stiffened. "There's no 'if' about it! That other man must've threatened Frank with the gun, and Frank fought him for it, and they both ended up shot. That had to be it. The other man had to've brought the gun into my house, you know that."

"No. I'm sorry, but I don't know that." I held up my hand to ward off her protest. "I know that Frank used a ball bat, not a gun, the day he waylaid me in your back hall. And I know that you knew nothing about a gun, wouldn't allow one in the house. That's enough to convince me that the police may've gotten it wrong. But it doesn't prove anything yet—not to me or anyone else."

She accepted that more readily than I'd expected. "At least you're keeping an open mind, Timothy," she said, shaking her head. "That's more than the police will do."

I had been trying to get her to call me Sheridan since the day we met, but that hadn't jibed with IdaRose's sense of decorum. So it had been "Mr. Sheridan" until this morning, when I finally broke down and invited her to use the name that only my parents and other assorted relatives still used.

"You were telling me about Frank's frame of mind on Saturday," I prompted her. "You said he seemed fine, not on edge. And he never said anything about this Delfay coming to interview him?"

"Not a word. That's why I say he didn't know the man was coming. He would've told me if he was expecting a guest and, anyway, Frank was relaxed when I left for work. Upbeat even. If he knew a journalist was coming, well, I don't need to tell you how tense that would make him."

"No," I said, reflexively rubbing a finger across my lower lip where Wooley had connected with one of his roundhouse rights. Delfay's showing up out at the Mack place had bothered me since the beginning. I'd assumed at first that the man had been invited—that Delfay had tracked Wooley down by letter or phone and convinced him to give the book proposal a fair hearing. But after I'd seen Frank and IdaRose together, the respect and caring they showed for one another, it seemed unlikely to me that Frank would have kept her in the dark about meeting with Delfay.

But if Frank hadn't been cooperating, then how had Delfay managed to turn up on the Mack doorstep on Saturday afternoon? Maybe it was just ego talking, but after the time I had tracking Wooley down, I just couldn't see a New York City sportswriter hopping a flight to Rochester, signing out a rental car, and, a couple of hours and eighty miles later, showing up at the right house on a dirt road dead end in southern Yates County. Not without a detailed map, at least, and maybe not even then.

"Did Frank keep an appointment book of any kind?" I asked. "A calendar with important dates marked on it, anything like that?"

IdaRose allowed herself a small laugh, and for a moment the woman I'd first met came through. "The only appointments Frank ever had were to get the cars serviced or pick up some material at the lumber yard," she said. "It's a lucky thing I'm such a homebody myself. Oh, we'd go out for a Sunday drive now and then, maybe catch a late dinner up in Penn Yan or down to Hammondsport. But only in the off-season, when there wouldn't be much chance of some downstate tourist figuring out who he was. He couldn't abide people gawking at him." She sighed. "As far as important dates, he didn't need a calendar to keep track of those. There was Martina's birthday and my birthday and Christmas—and the first and the third Tuesday of every month, of course." She read the question on my face and explained, "His checks from the players' pension fund."

I nodded, then frowned. "The first and third Tuesday, you said?"

"Usually. I mean, they didn't always show up on a Tuesday, the postal service being what it is. But they're supposed to be mailed on a Monday, so on Tuesday one of us would always—"

"But you're saying he got two pension checks a month?"

This time IdaRose nodded. "He'd use the first one for household expenses, bills, spending money. Most of the second one he sent off to his daughter to cover his share of her college expenses."

"Odd," I said. "I spoke with a guy at the pension fund office when I was trying to locate Frank. He told me the checks came out once a month."

"You must've misunderstood, Timothy, because Frank's checks came two a month. He'd sit down around the middle of every month and write a nice letter to Martina and then, when the second check arrived, he'd go do his banking and put a money order in with the letter and send it off. It was his favorite ritual, I think."

"Hmm." I studied IdaRose for a moment before asking, "Did you actually see these checks? The mid-month checks?"

"Well," she said, her brow wrinkling, "I saw the envelopes they came in but—I guess, now that I think about it, I never actually saw the checks. Like I told you, Frank would have a letter ready for Martina the middle of the month and, when the pension money came, he'd take the letter and the pension check, stop at the bank, then mail everything off to Martina at school."

Today was the third Monday in May. "You should be picking up a check tomorrow then?" I asked.

"I suppose so. I forgot all about it until just now. I'm not even sure where I stand regarding Frank's pension money—legally, I mean. I know I'm listed as co-beneficiary on the life insurance the pension fund provides, along with Martina. Not that it mattered to me," she said, shaking her head emphatically from side to side. "I came into an insurance annuity when my husband passed away and, between that and my job at the gift shop, I don't need anything else."

I told her to let me know if and when the second check arrived, then I asked, "D'you know how much he sent Martina?"

"Yes. A thousand dollars."

"Every month?"

"Cornell law school isn't cheap, Timothy," IdaRose reminded me. "And neither was Frank. The way he explained it to me, Martina's stepfather paid her tuition, and Frank saw to it that she had a monthly allowance to cover her living expenses—food, rent, books, car insurance, whatever. It was important to Frank that he 'pay his end,' as he liked to say. More than important, when you come down to it."

"How do you mean?"

There was a large picture window spanning the long wall of the living room behind IdaRose's chair. She got up and stared out at the sloping front lawn and the gray two-lane road beyond, her arms crossed loosely across her chest. Wondering how much to tell me, how much Frank would want me to know? Perhaps reminding herself that Frank was gone and that all his secrets hadn't managed to keep him out of harm's way. I watched her shoulder blades rise and fall inside the dour dress as she thought things through. Then she turned.

"Martina's coming up today, did I tell you that?"

"No."

"Frank hasn't . . . Frank's body hasn't been released by the police, but when it is we'll have him cremated. That's how Frank wanted things done. No service or public viewing." She looked down at the Oriental carpet, then back up at me. "Anyway, Martina's coming up to help me straighten out his affairs. And just to spend some time with me. She's a good girl, Martina." She took a deep breath. "She's due in any time, and I don't know whether she knows about this, but I figure it's something you need to know if you're ever going to understand what sort of man Frank really was. So this is just for your information—off the record, okay?"

"Okay."

She prefaced it with another long sigh. "Did Frank ever mention his own father to you, Timothy?"

I searched my memory for a few seconds. "I remember him saying his dad named him Franklin after FDR. And that the family moved from Alabama up to Gary, Indiana, so his father could get work in a steel mill."

"That's not exactly how it was," IdaRose said. "Frank's father went up to Indiana on his own. He sent money back and, eventually, Frank's mother took the kids—there was Frank and his brother Louis—and came up to Indiana herself. Uninvited. The fact is, Frank's parents were never married. Frank was illegitimate."

It was a term that didn't carry much weight today, judging by the latest figures on teen pregnancy. But when IdaRose and I were kids—and even more so for Frank Wooley, growing up in the forties—having a child out of wedlock was at best a family embarrassment and at worst a public disgrace. I wasn't sure how to react, but it was clear that IdaRose expected some sort of response, so I chose the neutral path and said, "I had the impression that Frank was close to his father."

She shrugged. "I guess he was for a while, but it didn't last. When Frank was a teenager, his father got laid off at the mill. After a couple months of waiting for a callback that didn't come, he just took off. Frank told me he never heard from his father again until years later, when he was a famous ballplayer." She frowned. "The old man was looking for a handout. Frank's mother and brother were gone by then—Louis was killed in a car wreck when he was seventeen, and Frank's mother died a few years later. So Frank sent his father some money every month and exchanged letters with him until he passed away, too."

"Anyway, I'm just trying to tell you how Frank felt about family obligations," she said. "He didn't have to send money to his father all those years, but he did it. And he certainly doesn't have to send any to Martina at Cornell—his ex-wife married a rich man. But he insisted on doing his part." The light from the window sparkled in her damp eyes. "He told me once how, when he was a boy, he'd fight any kid in the neighborhood who called him a bastard—and there were plenty who did. I think that helps explain why he turned out the way he did. So prideful, I mean, and protective of his privacy and his family. . . ."

She broke off at the sound of a car coming up the drive. I joined her at the window and watched a slender young woman dressed in a forest-green skirt suit ease out from behind the wheel of a newish Toyota Corolla. Even at that distance I could tell that the photo I'd seen of her on the wall in IdaRose's den, the one showing her in cap and gown, hadn't done her justice.

"Why don't you wait here, Timothy, while I get Martina." She hesitated before adding, "I haven't had a chance to tell her about you yet."

I nodded and returned to the sofa while IdaRose went out to the driveway. I was making a few notes when, five minutes later, the two women came into the front hallway. I got to my feet while IdaRose made the introductions. She was wearing a game smile, but it was underlayed with trepidation, as if she were Martina's tax accountant and I was the local IRS agent.

"Martina, this is the journalist I was telling you about, T.S.W. Sheridan. At least that's how he's known professionally. Once you get to know him better, he may let you call him Timothy."

Until that moment I'd had trouble seeing anything of the father in the daughter. She was both tall enough—perhaps five-eight in the flat tan pumps she was wearing—and beautiful enough to be a fashion model rather than a first-year law student. Her complexion was tawny, her copper-colored hair was medium long and wavy. She had full lips and a narrow, graceful nose and bright hazel eyes that, at present, were doing their best to look straight through me. Which is where the resemblance to her father began and ended; the Wooley glare.

"I don't really care what he likes to be called," she told IdaRose. "And I don't plan on getting to know him at all."

CHAPTER 11

Is it just me, Ms. Wooley, or are you rude to everyone?" I said.

She pursed her lips, no doubt preparing a rebuttal worthy of the law review, but IdaRose wasn't having any.

"Timothy is here because I asked him to come, Martina," she said, quiet but firm. "He's going to get your father's story out for us. The honest story this time, not some . . . "

"Is that what you think reporters are after, IdaRose?" Martina forced a laugh. "The honest story? More like any story at all, so long as it sells papers. What's the 'angle,' what sort of 'spin' can we give it?" She turned the glare back on me. "Aren't those the terms you people use?"

"Yes, those are some of the terms we people use." I tucked my notepad and pen away in my jacket pocket, using the time to count to ten and to remind myself that the angry young woman before me had just lost her father. I should've counted to twenty. "We also use terms like accuracy and attribution and cross-checking. But you apparently took a journalism course in your undergraduate days, so I guess you know everything there is to know about the news business."

"Enough to know that's all it is; a business. Or do you do this for free, Mr. Sheridan?"

IdaRose began to speak, but I held her off with a wave. "It's okay. Comes with the territory. I saw a poll a while back that said a majority of the public lists journalism as one of the least admired professions. But we came in about two notches higher than lawyers."

I'll admit that baiting her wasn't the best way to finagle her into cooperating, but I figured I'd taken my limit of verbal abuse from Wooleys for this lifetime. At least this one hadn't tried to reorient my nose. Not yet, anyway. Martina was still busy trying to think up a cutting rejoinder when IdaRose piped up.

"Listen to you two!" she said, pressing her hands to her hips. "My Lord, you sound like those two teenaged brats on *Married . . . With Children*. And I can't stand that show."

For some reason, her scolding did the trick. Martina's lips quivered for an instant, then gave way to a tiny grin.

"I never cared much for it, either," she said.

"The theme song's good," I said. "Sinatra."

It got a little better after that. Not great, but better. We both offered up tacit apologies; Martina mumbled something about being moody and irritable over her father's death, and I confessed that anyone but a natural-born wiseass would've been sensitive enough to keep his mouth shut. IdaRose beamed at us like June Cleaver used to right after Wally and the Beav had patched things up.

She gave Martina a sisterly hug and asked, "Does this mean you're not mad at me for encouraging Timothy to do an article on Frank?"

"I could never be mad at you for long, IdaRose."

"Does it also mean you might cooperate?" I asked. "Let me interview you for the piece?"

She considered it. "I don't know how I feel about that, to be honest. I'm just not sure what's to be gained by it." She snuck a glance at IdaRose. "Dad was—a very complicated man. Part of me thinks that maybe in the long run it would be better to let people write whatever they want and just ignore it all. Let it run its course. I don't know," she said, ending with a shrug.

IdaRose patted her shoulder. "Well, you think about it, see how you feel in a few days. Right now let me show you our room so you can get settled."

I waited in the foyer, ready to take my leave when IdaRose came back downstairs. It had been a rough few days for her, too, and I didn't want to wear out my welcome. When she returned,

I asked her for the name of the investigating officer from the sheriff's department. I also asked if she had a phone number or an address for Evie March. She said she thought she had the number at home, if I didn't mind waiting a few days until the police decided to let her back into her house. I could've suggested she ask Martina, but I wasn't sure how that would go over so I agreed to get back to her later in the week.

Just before I went out the door, she said, "I think Martina will come around when she's had time to think about it. It's just, she grew up with her mother and stepfather. She loved her father, but Frank wasn't always able to be there for her and it's made her sort of—confused about him, if you know what I mean."

I told her I knew just what she meant.

Keuka Lake is shaped like a child's first attempt to draw a Y. Penn Yan is sited at the top of the Y's east fork. As with most Finger Lakes towns, tourism, wineries, and farming figure strongly into the local economy, but Penn Yan also has Birkett Mills, which bills itself as the world's largest manufacturer of buckwheat products. A few years back, at the annual Buckwheat Festival, the local citizenry earned its way into the pages of the *Guinness Book* by cooking up the world's largest pancake—a record since eclipsed by a hungry crew of Dutchmen. Proving, I suppose, that pancakes and whimsy are international in appeal.

Main Street is flanked by brick-and-stone buildings bunched in close to one another and the sidewalk. Most of them were built before or just after the turn of the century, and all of them look a little shopworn but still able, and a lot more appealing to the eye than the fast-food joints and strip plazas that squatted out on the town's fringes. The sheriff's office—or, more precisely, the Yates County Public Safety Building—is an exception. It's a modern, single-story affair of no particular distinction located on the north end of Main across from the public library.

I parked next to a red-and-white county cruiser and made my way across the parking lot, through a set of glass doors, and into a reception area that would've been right at home in a medical office building. A portly, middle-aged deputy who could've played a nonspeaking role in a Burt Reynolds movie interrogated me with a crooked eyebrow. I asked him where I could find Detective Sergeant Leek. An amused grin hyphenated the deputy's jowls, and he wordlessly jerked his thumb toward a corridor that ran off to the left.

I passed by a small squad room, empty at the moment, and stopped at the first private office I came to. The door was open and inside, seated behind one of two beige metal desks, was a blond, moonfaced young man wearing a short-sleeved white shirt and a bow tie, blue with little red dots. He was frowning at a set of eight-by-ten glossies that were spread across the desk, but he quickly shuffled them together and tucked them away in a folder when he noticed me standing in the doorway.

"Yes, sir?"

"I'm looking for Sergeant Leek."

"Come in, please." He stood up behind the desk and extended his arm. "I'm Arthur Leek." He was one of those people who look round, but not fat. The face was less boyish up close, but I still pegged him as no more than thirty. His manner was open and his smile friendly—not what I've come to expect from a homicide detective. The bow tie bobbed up and down on his Adam's apple as he spoke. The only people I could recall who still wore them were the conservative columnist George Will and kiddie comic Pee-wee Herman. I wasn't sure which of the two the sergeant was trying to emulate.

"My name's Sheridan," I said as we shook hands. "I'm a freelance reporter."

"T.S.W. Sheridan?"

"Yes."

"I've seen your byline." He motioned me into a seat opposite the desk and sat back down himself. "You did a bang-up job with that series last fall on the terrorist group in the Thousand Islands."

Another surprise. I wasn't used to having policemen compliment me on my work. Most of them consider journalists an unnecessary nuisance, along with judges and juries. I mumbled a thank you and got down to business, telling him about the assignment for *The Sporting Life* and my previous contacts with Frank Wooley and IdaRose Mack. Then I told him about my first encounter with Wooley—the episode with the Louisville Slugger.

"Put that together with IdaRose's insistence that Frank didn't keep a gun out at her place," I concluded, "and it makes me question if it really was a homicide-suicide out there. If maybe IdaRose has it right when she says Delfay must've pulled the gun, Wooley fought him for it, and both men ended up dead."

Throughout my whole spiel, Leek had listened politely, attentively, never once interrupting or breaking off eye contact to gaze out the window or fiddle with the stack of papers piled in his in basket. It was almost eerie, how damned pleasant this guy was, and I was starting to wonder if there was an ulterior motive lurking somewhere in the vicinity—or if Doris Day had a son who went into law enforcement.

"Well, that's an interesting piece of speculation, Mr. Sheridan," he said when it was clear I had finished. "In fact, I was intrigued by it when Mrs. Mack first presented it to me. She seems like a fine lady, and I don't question her sincerity for a moment. I also understand why she clings so desperately to this idea that it was Delfay's gun. It's hard to accept it when a loved one commits suicide. It's only natural to look for other explanations. But there are at least three reasons why her theory doesn't work." He propped his elbows on the desk. "First, I've already contacted the airline that flew Delfay up to Rochester. He had only a carry-on valise with him when he checked in, and both Delfay and valise passed through security without a problem. No gun."

"He might've picked it up in Rochester after. . . . "

"Extremely doubtful. The time frame doesn't allow for it. But, as I said, there were at least three reasons."

"The other two?"

"The preliminary lab report says that with the weapon used and the type of load it was carrying, there should've been some degree of powder burn if the gun was fired anywhere within three feet of the victim. But there was no powder residue on Delfay's shirt, which means the two men couldn't have been wrestling for the gun when it fired."

I didn't need to hear reason number three, but Leek told me anyway.

"Lastly, Delfay's fingerprints were not found on the gun; Frank Wooley's were." He shook his head. "There's just no two ways about it, Mr. Sheridan. Mike Delfay didn't bring that gun into the house."

"No," I admitted. "It doesn't sound likely."

The tiny office lapsed into silence while I sat there picking at the wire binder on my notepad, trying to come to terms with what now seemed conclusive; Frank Wooley, provoked or not, had killed Delfay and then turned the gun on himself.

I looked up to find Sergeant Leek gazing serenely at me across the desk. I felt as if I'd been checkmated in six moves by some well-adjusted child prodigy.

"You know what I'd really like to know, Sergeant?" I said. "How did Delfay find the place so easily? You mentioned the time frame; the information given the press says Delfay arrived at the airport in Rochester at about ten thirty Saturday morning and that you speculate he arrived at the Wooley place no later than one o'clock. Is that right?"

He bobbed his head. "The medical examiner says loss of body temperature indicates both men died sometime between around noon to one thirty or so. Allowing for a little time to get in the door and get settled. . . . "

"So Delfay picks up a rental car about, what, ten forty-five?"

Leek nodded again.

"Which gave him about two hours to make an unfamiliar eighty-mile drive, more than half of which is on a series of two-lane secondary roads. Quite an accomplishment."

"What is it you're suggesting, Mr. Sheridan?"

"I don't know what I'm suggesting, Sergeant. Reaching for straws, I guess." I tried a wry grin. Leek's expression remained placid and studious; the perfect professional laying on his best game face for the overwrought civilian. This much nice was starting to annoy me.

"Look," I said. "I know you must think this is a waste of time. . . . "

"Not at all. I'm enjoying the interplay."

I shook that one off and went on. "Did you turn up a map or anything on Delfay, or in his car? Maybe a detailed set of directions to the Mack place?"

"Nothing of that nature. His valise contained a couple of stenopads, a tape recorder, a fresh shirt. What you might expect a writer to pack for a day trip." He anticipated my next question. "Delfay was booked on a flight back to New York at eight thirty that evening, so this was obviously intended as a short get-together. As for directions to the house, Wooley may've described the route to him over the phone."

"That's the thing," I said. "IdaRose doesn't think Frank knew Delfay was even coming."

He held up his hand like the traffic cop he probably once was. "Mrs. Mack already explained her theory on that score as well. What it amounts to is more emotional projection on her part. The fact that Wooley was in a good mood and that he failed to mention that a visitor was coming doesn't add up to much—not when weighed against the physical evidence."

"In other words, Sergeant, the case is closed?"

"Not officially, until all the lab work is in," he said. "But practically speaking, yes. As things stand, our preliminary call—a homicide-suicide, with Frank Wooley as the perpetrator—is the one the department is prepared to stand behind."

"Uh huh. Well . . . " I was about to tip over my king and make a graceful exit, but Leek wasn't through yet.

"Of course," he said, drawing out the words, "if you should find something concrete—some anomaly that truly contradicts the official version of events—I'd be obligated to give you a fair hearing."

I perked up a bit. "Are you saying that you have some doubt about what really happened out there?"

"No. I'm merely telling you that we're always open to, umm, informed suggestions, even if we don't always have the time or resources to pursue them the way we might like to. In police work, there are certain methodologies, procedures we stick to religiously. We always start with the physical evidence, for example, and work toward the direction that evidence suggests. Appearances rarely deceive. If a crime seems on the surface to have gone down a certain way, it almost certainly did happen that way." He shrugged. "That's the premise we operate under, anyway. Of course, you and I have different objectives, Mr. Sheridan, so we may differ on how we approach our jobs."

"Different objectives?"

"As a policeman, my interest in Frank Wooley begins and ends with the events out at the Mack house last Saturday afternoon," he explained. "Once we've arrived at a plausible explanation—motive or lack thereof notwithstanding—we rapidly lose interest in delving any deeper. On the other hand, you're interested in writing about a man's life; not how he ended up, perhaps, but why he ended up as he did. Is that a fair characterization, would you say?"

"Yeah, I'd say you were right on the money."

"So, regardless of the department's findings, you'll continue to dig around, see if you can make any sense of things. To put the 'why' into your story."

"That's right."

"And I expect you'll be doing the usual; visiting the crime scene once we've cleared it—which should be by the end of this week—canvassing the neighborhood for comments and quotes, that sort of thing."

"You have a problem with that, Sergeant?"

"No, not at all. You have your job to do, too. All I'm suggesting is that, in the unlikely event you uncover something germane to the Wooley-Delfay case, you bring it to my attention." He smiled enigmatically. "As I said, I kind of enjoy the interplay."

CHAPTER 12

I left Penn Yan and drove over to Geneva, my conversation with Sergeant Leek reverberating through my mind with each passing mile. On the one hand, he was telling me the Wooley case was closed; on the other, he seemed to be inviting me to investigate further, draw my own conclusions. Curious.

I stopped in at the Quincy County Sheriff's Department on the off-chance I'd find J. D. Staub with his feet up on his desk and a little free time to kill. I wanted to get a line on a couple of people—Arthur Leek, for one—and I figured J.D. was a good place to start. As it happened, he was in his office, but up to his epaulets in cost analyses, flow charts, and graphs, each designed to support his argument that the department needed a ten-percent funding increase from the county legislature for the upcoming fiscal year.

"Gotta have all this crap ready for a preliminary budgeting meeting Wednesday," J.D. informed me, a dead El Producto clamped between his teeth. "I can give you a listen over lunch Friday, Sheridan, high noon. You know Pinky's? Kitty-corner from city hall on Castle Street?"

I told him I'd find it, then I backed out of the office and left him to his statistics. Out on the street again, I thought about heading straight back to the cottage to begin working the telephone. But since one of the places I needed to call was the ballpark there in Geneva—and because it was a brilliant spring afternoon—I decided to drive over instead, hoping someone with the club management would be on hand to answer a question or two.

McDonough Park sits on the city's west side, just an open field separating it from the mostly residential blocks that flank it to the south and east. The field serves as extra parking on those few occasions when the crowds, drawn in by bat day or ten-cent beer night, can't be accommodated by the small gravel parking area near the grandstand. Geneva, a farm team of the Chicago Cubs, plays in the New York-Penn League, a short-season Class A league that features a mix of fresh-faced teenagers who've managed to survive a year of rookie ball and college prospects, many of them making their professional debuts after standout careers at places like Oklahoma State and Stanford and Seton Hall.

The ballpark is a cinderblock, plywood, and corrugated metal hybrid painted a shade of blue two tones lighter than the navy trim found on the home team's uniforms. I parked under a handpainted sign that read McDONOUGH PARK, HOME OF THE GENEVA CUBS. Taking my cue from a simple white arrow that was also painted on the wall, I went through an unlatched chain-link gate and around a corner and ended up standing in front of a door marked GENERAL MANAGER. Before I could knock, the door swung in and a tall, craggy-faced man in his sixties, his eyes glued to a clipboard, almost ran over me.

"Oh, jeez! 'Scuse me." He backed up a step. "Didn't know anybody was out there."

"No harm done," I said. "Are you with the ball club?"

"Sure am." He thrust out a big, knobby hand. "Al Hargis, GM of this crazy circus for the last thirty years," he said. "Part time, anyway. Mainly I run a furniture-and-appliance store over on Exchange, but it's hard to kick the baseball bug once you been bit. See, I used to be a catcher in the Cardinals' organization just after the war."

"You've got the hands," I said, wincing at the strength in the man's gnarled fingers. "My name's Sheridan. I'm a freelance writer, working on a story for *The Sporting Life*."

"*The Sporting Life?* Hey, that's great." He pulled me into the office and guided me into a green Naugahyde chair. Then he tossed the clipboard onto an old oak desk that had seen its share of extra innings and sat down on one of its corners. "We could sure use some pub. Our season opens in a few weeks, and our advance ticket sales have been, well, not up to projections, let's say. What're you doing, a thing on life in the minors or something?"

"No, I'm trying to get in touch with your ex-manager, Hub Jefferson, for a piece I'm doing on Frank Wooley."

"Oh." Wooley's name took most of the wind out of him. "Well, you're a week early. Hub's the organization's director of player development now. He makes regular rounds to all the Cubs' minor league teams—he's due in town next Tuesday." He moved behind the desk and slumped into his chair. He had thick eyebrows that looked like they'd been knitted by someone's grandmother and doleful brown eyes. "Frank Wooley—now there's a bad penny I knew would come back to haunt me."

"How so, Mr. Hargis?"

He slowly combed one hand through his thinning gray hair, composing his answer. "Don't get me wrong, Frank never gave me any grief. Our relationship was maybe a little cool, but professional. It's just . . . I had this intuition, I guess, from the minute Hub told me he wanted to bring Wooley back into baseball. I just knew Frank would find a way to screw it up."

"Did you know Wooley personally, I mean from before he signed on to coach here in '88?"

"No, all I knew about him was what I read in the papers, like everybody else. But that was enough. See, as general manager, I'm held responsible for the players and coaches by the Cubs' organization. And as a businessman, I've got my own reputation to worry about. If the ballclub makes me look bad, I don't sell as many TVs and sofas. That's just a sad fact." He stared down at the notepad I'd taken out moments before. "Lookit, can I tell you something off the record here?"

"Sure." I closed the pad and tucked the pen away.

"I kept pretty close tabs on Frank when he first came here, okay? I don't mean I tailed him around, nothing like that. Let's just say I know a lot of people—bartenders, Off-Track Betting officials, some guys up at Finger Lakes Racetrack. I'd touch base with people, just to make sure Frank wasn't maybe getting into something he shouldn't. And he didn't, not for the entire three months he was up here, as far as I ever heard. He'd do his work with the team, maybe go out for beers with Hub. Usually he spent his free time with his lady friend, Mrs. Mack." Hargis sighed. "No trouble at all until that last weekend, the one that ended up with him going into the stands after a fan during a Sunday doubleheader. I didn't see the brawl; I was in here going over the gate receipts. But I already knew I had a potential problem because of what I saw on Saturday during the card show."

"A baseball card show?"

"Yeah. Well, a memorabilia show really. There were signed balls and bats, uniforms, pennants, posters—lots of stuff being bought and sold besides baseball cards. They had the convention floor in the basement over at the Stanton Motor Inn out on five and twenty. You know the place?"

I nodded. I had stopped at the bar there once with a date. It was a typical budget-level motor lodge, geared toward traveling businessmen and families whose idea of a vacation was to lie around an Olympic-size swimming pool while four lanes of traffic whizzed by fifty feet away.

"The big draw for the card show was the autograph sessions," Hargis continued. "The promoters brought in a bunch of retired big leaguers to sign baseballs or whatever. You pay two bucks just to get in, then anywhere from ten to twenty bucks for the actual autograph, depending on how popular the player was." He frowned. "It's a damn racket, but that's how it is these days. You have more adults than kids, but even the kids act like they're futures traders on the floor of the New York Stock Exchange."

I was itching to pull my pen back out, but I didn't; I was losing some great quotes, but it was better than losing Hargis's cooperation.

"Wooley attended the card show?" I asked.

"Yeah, he was one of ex-stars they lined up for the autograph session. He didn't want to do it at first, but I asked him to—I figured it was good pub for the ball club and, anyway, he was getting a nice chunk of change from the promoters, twenty-five hundred I think it was. I was on hand because we were sort of cosponsoring the thing. We had the ex-big leaguers out to the park for an old timers game that afternoon before our regular game, then I went over to the show later to press a little flesh, do a little PR. But, anyway, it wasn't the autograph session that bothered me, it was after."

I waited Hargis out while he teetered back and forth in his swivel chair. After a few seconds, he leaned forward and locked onto me with those sorrowful eyes.

"Okay," he said. "Here's the thing; if people like to play some cards and they've got a few bucks to toss around, that's none of my business. Unless I see one of my coaches—a guy with a reputation like Frank Wooley—getting involved."

"You saw Wooley in a card game at the Stanton?"

"As good as," he said, nodding grimly. "After the show there were some parties going on upstairs in the rooms. I went up to one of them with one of the promoters. On the way to the room where our party was, we passed by this other suite. Lotta people coming and going, the door half open. Anyway, I saw a table set up for cards and a few faces I recognized from the memorabilia show sitting around it. Well, I didn't think much about it. They're grown men, they can do what they want, right? But about a half hour later, I'm leaving the party in the room down the hall and I almost bump right into Frank and this other guy going into this same suite."

"Nothing wrong with a friendly game of cards," I said. "Even if your name is Frank Wooley."

"Course not, but it was the guy who was with Wooley that bothered me. Seeing the two of them standing there like that, it rang a bell, but I couldn't figure out why. But then, just before Wooley saw me coming up to him in the corridor, I heard him call this other guy by name. Harry, he called him. And that's when I remembered that famous picture of Wooley and the lawyer and the gambler sneaking out of the police station. Harry Lundquist, that's who he was with."

CHAPTER 13

MY infatuation with the news business began when I was a little boy sitting around the breakfast table with my family, each of us grabbing off our favorite part of the morning paper almost as soon as it hit the front stoop. My father went straight to the op-ed page, reading it with a furrowed brow and every so often looking up over the brim of his coffee mug to grumble a carefully edited curse at the Republicans. My mother would browse through the features—the women's page, as it was called then—while my older brother studied the box scores in the sports section. For me it was the funnies, where I would check out the latest foibles of *Beetle Bailey* and the triumphs of *Steve Canyon* and wonder yet again if anyone actually read *Rex Morgan, M.D.*

But it's my grandmother I remember best, sipping her cup of tea each morning as she calmly perused the death notices on the obituary page. I asked her about it once, why she made it her first priority.

"It's a bit like your brother with his sports, Timothy," she explained to me in the gentle brogue of west Ireland. "I like to see who's winnin', God or the divil."

I was starting to believe that, in Frank Wooley's case, the divil was piling up an insurmountable lead. Apart from Sergeant Leek's impeccable detailing of events out at the Mack place and Al Hargis's bombshell about the gambler Lundquist, I had my own personal history with Wooley to deal with. The more I learned, the more it seemed that the private and the public man were one and the same. That wouldn't come as a surprise to Pete Calvett or the rest of the sporting press; all they were interested in were the gritty details. But IdaRose Mack had half-convinced me that the world was wrong about Frank Wooley and, despite the objectivity that was supposed to be the cornerstone of my business, I had wanted her to be right.

Tuesday morning I called Campbell, my contact at the players' pension fund office in New York. As I expected, he verified that the retired players received only one monthly check, which was mailed the first Monday. He had no idea why Wooley would've been receiving a second mailing mid-month, but he was certain it wasn't a pension check.

Later I called IdaRose at her employers' house in Penn Yan and related what I'd been told. She insisted that Frank had been getting two checks—or two envelopes, anyway. I asked if she'd had a chance to visit the post office in Stewart and she told me she'd driven down there that afternoon, but that no second check had come.

"You don't really think this pension business is important, do you, Timothy?" she asked me. "It's probably some procedural thing your man doesn't know about."

"Maybe," I said. "I've asked the guy to look into it a little deeper, let me know what he turns up. Not to change the subject, but have you had any luck with Martina?"

"Hard to say. Right now she's trying to concentrate on her law finals next week and she doesn't really want any more distractions than she already has. In fact, she's driving back to Ithaca tomorrow to hit the books. Maybe if you could wait until the end of the month, after her exams?"

"I guess I can hold off another week," I said.

"She did give me her mother's phone number and address in New Jersey. Hold on." She came back on the line half a minute later and read me the information on the former Evie Wooley, who was now Mrs. Lou Garci. "I take it they have quite a spread down in Saddle River," IdaRose said. "Mr. Garci owns a laundry business, I gather. It's funny, but I think I've learned more about that part of Martina's life in the last few days than Frank told me in over two years."

That came as no surprise to me. I asked IdaRose if she'd heard anything from Sergeant Leek and she told me he'd given her permission to move back into her house on Friday afternoon. She was eager to hear how my research was going, but I put her off. She was sounding much more like her old self, and I didn't want to destroy her mood any sooner than necessary—at least, that's how I rationalized it.

Wednesday and Thursday, I divided my time between the Wooley piece and a couple of mundane magazine assignments that, nevertheless, had deadlines of their own. I wrapped up an article on home security systems for a regional magazine and sent it off and, in between, made some personal calls—one to my brother and a couple to Kate, both of whom I was planning to visit in Rochester over the upcoming Memorial Day weekend. The few calls I made on the Wooley assignment didn't gain me anything. The ex-baseball commissioner, through a spokeswoman at his law office, declined to be interviewed about his run-ins with Frank Wooley—"He's writing an autobiography of his own, you know," the woman told me—and each time I called the number IdaRose had given me for Wooley's ex-wife, I got an answering machine.

By late Thursday afternoon, while staring out the window at the glorious weather, I almost managed to convince myself that I could think better out on the lake with a fishing line draped over the side of the boat. But I reluctantly decided to return to my desk to continue transcribing my notes from the Wooley assignment onto the computer's hard disk. As that Irish grandma of mine liked to say, you can't plow a field by turning it over in your mind.

Friday noon, I parked at a meter on Castle Street just across from Geneva's turn-of-the-century city hall and walked half a block south to Pinky's. It turned out to be a narrow, dim place that despite its prominent location on the main drag had the ambience of a working-class neighborhood tavern. I let my eyes adjust, then moved down past the bar to the back dining area, where I found Quincy County's sheriff holding down a Formica-topped table with both elbows and a bottle of Genesee Twelve Horse Ale.

"Never seek elected office," he said by way of a greeting.

He normally looked about a decade younger than his fifty-six years, but not today. His long, lanky body seemed ready to curl in on itself, and the deep-set eyes were dull with fatigue. The beer bottle he was cradling with both hands had lost most of its label to his fidgeting fingers.

"Don't tell me," I said as I sat down. "The county legislature told you to read its lips."

He snorted. "Kiss its ass is more like it. They got this war on drugs thing backwards. Everytime I request more manpower to deal with the problem, they just say no. The early line says I'll be lucky to come out of next Tuesday's budget vote with only a five-percent cut."

We trashed politicians for a few minutes more, pausing long enough to order sandwiches and a round of Twelve Horse from one of the guys who came out from behind the bar. By the time the food had come and gone, J.D. had finished his rant about the legislature and was finally ready to hear what was on my mind.

"I'm doing a big magazine piece on Frank Wooley."

"The murder-suicide down in Yates," he said, nodding. J.D. was a cop, not a baseball fan. "From what I hear on the grapevine, it's an open-and-shut case."

"It's looking that way, but that's not my concern at the moment." I gave him a rundown on Wooley's past troubles, particularly his association with Harry Lundquist back in the early seventies and his resulting ban from baseball. "And then I find out from the Cubs' G.M. that Lundquist and Wooley were seen palling around together here in Geneva in 1988, the same weekend Wooley ended up getting booted out of his coaching job. Hargis—the general manager—saw the two of them after a big baseball memorabilia show over at the Stanton. He claims they were heading into a poker game going on in one of the suites upstairs."

"Your man Wooley must've been a slow learner." He frowned thoughtfully. "I vaguely remember something about that memorabilia show—some request we got from another department, I think." He shook his head. "Can't recall just what it was. It didn't have anything to do with Frank Wooley, though."

I poured my glass full with beer, then decided to stop stalling. "The thing is, J.D., I really need to locate this guy Lundquist."

"Ahh. And so you figured we should get together for this

wonderful repast—which you're paying for, by the way—on the off chance that I could turn this guy for you."

"I was thinking you might contact the NCIC, ask 'em to run Lundquist's name through their computers. I know he did time on gambling-related charges back in the sixties." The National Crime Information Center is a sort of clearinghouse used by police organizations from all over the country. It attempts to keep tabs on known felons—anyone with a criminal record of note.

J.D. stared down at the remains of his sandwich, then squeezed his eyes shut for a moment before looking up at me. "We both know you had a lot to do with my getting this job."

I started to protest, but he waved me off.

"It was you that broke your uncle's murder case, and me that got most of the credit." He pointed his right index finger at me. "But here's the thing: Official police channels are for official police business. I can't put a request through the NCIC without a good reason, and the fact that I owe a young journalist friend of mine a favor isn't a good reason."

"Understood," I said. "Forget I mentioned it, J.D., I was just being lazy. I've got some newspaper contacts. . . . "

"Hold on. I said I can't use official channels." He sipped from his bottle of ale, then grinned. "I didn't say anything about the unofficial ones. Give me everything you know about this Harry Lundquist, and I'll see if I can't track him down."

"You're sure?"

"For chrissake, kid, I was just putting you on. I haven't had many laughs the last few days. Give."

So I gave—all I had on Harry Lundquist, culled from the newspaper clippings Pete Calvett had sent me, and the rest of the information I'd picked up while putting together my original piece for *The Sporting Life*.

"I'll see what we can come up with," J.D. said as he wrote down the information on a piece of notepaper I'd given him. "Now, unless you've got something else on your mind, Sheridan, I've gotta head back over to the county campus to twist a few arms."

"Well, there was one other thing."

"There always is with you."

"Sergeant Arthur Leek, the guy in charge of the Wooley case for the Yates County Sheriff's Department. Know him?"

"Don't recognize the name. Tony might. He liases a lot with the neighboring departments." Tony Areno was J.D.'s undersheriff and former chief of detectives.

"Could you check with Tony?" I asked. "See if he knows anything about Leek?"

"Sure. What's the matter, the guy giving you a hard time with your story?"

"Just the opposite. He was so damn accommodating, it threw me. But it wasn't just his manner—it's like he was toying with me for some reason. First he lays out the case one, two, three, neatly shooting down my theory of events in favor of the official finding of murder-suicide. But then, after he's got me convinced I'm off base, he all but invites me to snoop around on my own and get back to him if I come up with any 'new evidence.' "

"You have a problem with the murder-suicide scenario?"

"I just thought there were a few inconsistencies, that's all." I told him about IdaRose Mack and her edict against guns in the house, about my first encounter with Wooley and the baseball bat, and how Wooley's behavior on the morning before Delfay's visit suggested that Wooley wasn't expecting a sportswriter to show up on his doorstep. "I also don't understand how Delfay found the place without a map—it's really out in the boonies—but, like I said, Leek had an answer for everything."

"You amaze me sometimes," J.D. said with a chuckle. "You're always taking a bunch of unrelated oddities and trying to mold them into a mystery. Cops, on the other hand, don't like mysteries. We like closed cases. And from what I've heard on this Wooley thing, the weight of evidence is all on Leek's side."

"I've already admitted that," I said. "So why would he encourage me to keep digging?"

"That probably wasn't his intention. I'd guess he's just an ambitious young detective—he is young, right?—who wants to climb higher in the department, maybe even go for sheriff someday, bless his foolish heart. And the last thing an ambitious young man wants to do is antagonize a member of the local press."

I teetered back in my chair and studied J.D. across the littered tabletop. "You think that's all there is to it?"

"That would be my best estimate." He got to his feet and lazily stretched out his long arms. Then he picked up the check, gave it the once over, and tossed it in my direction. "Not that I expect you to pay the slightest bit of attention—to me or Leek."

CHAPTER 14

LOOKOUT Run wasn't any smoother than it had been during my last visit nearly six weeks earlier, but it was a good deal drier. The snow was long gone, but the heavy spring rains had left their mark in deep tire tracks and erosion channels that the warmer weather had begun to bake into scar tissue. By July, when the heat and humidity in the region would rival the Carolina Piedmont, the narrow dirt road would be a dusty, lung-choking ordeal for anyone foolish enough to drive it with the windows down.

But by July, I assured myself, the Wooley story would be on the newsstands, I would be chasing down a new assignment, and Lookout Run would be merely a fading signpost in my memory's rearview mirror.

After lunch with J.D., I had walked around the corner to the *Daily News* building and pestered Karen DeClair into letting me comb the paper's clips library for old items on Wooley's short coaching stint in Geneva. I found one reference to the abusive fan that Wooley had attacked—a local man named Eberling—and a feature on the memorabilia show at the Stanton, including a listing of the ex-big leaguers who had attended the autograph session. I wrote the names in my pad and made a mental note to check with each of them later.

Back at the cottage, I made more phone calls. The first went to Pete Calvett at *The Sporting Life.* I needed background on

Delfay, including the name of his publisher and either his literary agent or a family member—anyone who might be able to tell me more about Delfay's professional interest in Wooley. After securing Pete's promise to get back to me in a few days, I called Wooley's old high school in Gary, Indiana. I was hoping to find someone who could give me something useful on the young Frank Wooley, but it had been nearly forty years. His old baseball coach was dead, I was told, and none of the current faculty were old enough to have been around in the early fifties.

It was after three when I gave it up and drove into town. I'd be away in Rochester for the long weekend and I had a formidable do-list; leave the cat with Allison Humbert, pick up and drop off at the dry cleaners, buy food and drink at the Big M, do my banking. My last errand completed, I drove out of Mohaca Springs and headed southwest.

There were seven houses strung out along Lookout Run proper, plus two more on the little side lane: IdaRose Mack's place and Sturdevant, her neighbor in the rusty trailer. Four of the houses were located well beyond the Mack turnoff, but I planned to canvass them anyway. I tried the trailer first—nobody home—then backtracked to the three houses I had passed on my way in. One had a FOR SALE sign in the unkempt yard and a deserted feel about it. No one answered my knock there, either. At the next place, I spoke with an elderly couple who could barely hear or see me, never mind remember if any strange vehicles had come by the previous Saturday. Only at the last house, the one nearest the highway, did I turn up anything.

"I was hanging out my wash just after lunch on Saturday?" Her name was Karnes. She was a reedy, nervous woman who ended every statement as if it were a question. While we talked out on her front stoop, two tiny boys, their mouths rimmed with grape stains, held onto the legs of her jeans and stared up at me as if I'd just stepped out of a space ship. "And I saw this little white foreign car go by real slow, like he was looking for an address?"

"The driver was alone in the car?"

"Uh huh." She squinted at me curiously. "You sure you're not a policeman? Because you sound just like that sergeant, the one who talked to me the day after the shooting? He asked was there anybody else in the car, too."

"I'm just a reporter, ma'am." I wrote Leek's name in the margin next to her response and circled it. "This may be a little tricky, but did the sergeant press you on that point? I mean, did you get the impression that he thought there was more than one person in the car?"

"Nothing like that. He just asked did I see anyone else besides the driver. He was real polite, y'know?"

"He's a very polite guy," I agreed. "The driver—he was heavyset, with dark hair, a beard, and glasses?" I was using the description of Delfay that had been released by the sheriff's office.

"I think so. I saw the glasses and stuff, but I'm not sure about the beard because of the thingie he was holding."

"A thingie, ma'am?" I asked, feeling like Joe Friday.

"Like an address book? That's how it seemed anyway, 'cause he was holding it up to look at, you know, like it was directions or something?"

I asked if she had told Leek about the address book. When she said yes, I scribbled an asterisk next to the circle.

I checked out the remaining four houses with a new sense of optimism, but it faded quickly. No one answered my knock at any of them. The last two, located at the crest of the hill that had given Lookout Run its name, were seasonal rental properties. Attached to a pole near the driveway entrances for each cottage were metal lockboxes for keys and small signboards listing a number to call for rental information. From what I could tell, they had fine views of Keuka Lake a mile or so to the west, but no direct access down to the lakeshore, an inconvenience that doubtless kept the weekly rates low.

I turned the Bronco around in one of the gravel driveway aprons and drove back to IdaRose's house. She had just come home and was busy cleaning up the mud the sheriff's investigation team had tracked through the place. The only room they had been careful with was the den, which was just as well, IdaRose said, because she didn't have the heart to spend any time in there yet.

I assured her I wouldn't be staying long; I had only stopped to see that she was getting on all right and, reluctantly, to tell what I'd learned so far. She was disturbed when I told her Wooley had been seen with his old pal, Harry Lundquist, back around the time of his firing from the Cubs, but she insisted there had to be a reasonable explanation. She was even more upset after hearing about my discussion with Sergeant Leek; no matter what he—or I—believed, she told me, she'd never be convinced that the murder weapon had belonged to her man.

"Frank wasn't a murderer, Timothy," she said, her somber eyes boring into me. "I can't be wrong about that."

I decided not to pass along what the woman up the road had told me, mostly because I wasn't sure what to make of it myself. Did Leek have reason to believe there may have been a third party involved in the Delfay-Wooley deaths? Or was he merely being thorough, eliminating possibilities no matter how unlikely? If so, that didn't explain why he hadn't mentioned Mrs. Karnes's contention that Delfay had been checking an address book when he drove by her house—or why his investigation hadn't turned up the book in Delfay's belongings or the rental car. But that was a can of worms I didn't feel like dipping into just then—not until I'd had a chance to brace Leek again.. Instead I asked IdaRose to make a careful search of the house when she had a chance, and to let me know if she found anything of interest; check stubs from the players' pension fund, correspondence, an appointment book or diary. I didn't expect she'd find much, but at least it would give her something to keep busy.

After leaving IdaRose, I drove back up the rutted lane a few hundred yards and stopped in front of the neighboring property. A gleaming Dodge 4X4 pickup was now parked beside the decrepit house trailer. I thought about driving on; it was getting late, I had a full weekend planned, and I wanted to get an early start in the morning—all the usual Friday excuses for cutting out on the job before the whistle. But the reasons for stopping outweighed the excuses—I was there, the occupant was also apparently there, and I had to check him out sooner or later—so I switched off the Bronco's engine and trooped on up past the giant satellite dish in the yard and rapped once again on the trailer's dented metal door. This time my knock was greeted by simultaneous, frantic barking and the unmistakable click-and-scratch of a dog's nails as it tried to find purchase on a linoleum floor.

"Shut up, Queenie, you goddamn mutt!"

I heard a thud and a yelp, then the barking ceased—canine and otherwise—and the door swung inward.

"What?"

He was a thickset man with black, heavy-lidded eyes that made him appear half asleep. He was bald on top, with a bushy beard to compensate, and he wore an oversized flannel shirt untucked above a pair of crusty jeans. There was an unnatural bulge under his shirt riding on one hip, and I didn't think it was because he was glad to see me.

"Mr. Sturdevant?"

"That's right." When he spoke, the corner of his lip rose, as if he were doing Elvis.

"My name's Sheridan," I said. "I'm writing a magazine piece on your neighbor. . . . "

He put his hands on his hips, deliberately pulling back enough of the shirt to reveal the butt of the handgun he had tucked into his belt. Under different circumstances, I might've laughed at his comic macho. "That jig wasn't no neighbor I'd claim. Shackin' up with that other one—couple a damn monkeys fell out of a tree, you ask me."

I resisted the urge to do a slow take on the mess that surrounded us; the weedy yard, the battered trailer, the man himself. Only the shiny pickup truck and the expensive satellite dish appeared to be well maintained. I reminded myself that the world was full of people who need a dog to kick or someone with different skin to hate to keep from giving themselves a good look. Then I took a deep breath and got on with it.

"I'm wondering if you saw anything last Saturday, the day of the shootings," I said. "I imagine the police have already spoken to you."

"Yeah. Some priss in a bow tie." The left side of his upper lip arced a little higher. I expected him to break into "Hound Dog," but he just chuckled. "Sweetie-boy name of Leek. Some kinda name, huh?"

"Could you tell me what you told Sergeant Leek?"

Sturdevant shrugged. "I was just comin' home, up the road there. I make the bend and I come up nose to ass on a little Toyota movin' like a damn snail. Almost ran over the damn thing with my truck. That's all."

"Uh huh. And I imagine the sergeant asked you how many people you saw in the car?"

"Yeah. I told him I didn't see nobody. I was right on that Toyota's ass, sittin' high up in the cab of my pickup—I got heavy-duty suspension on my rig. I couldn't see nothin' but the driver's elbow pokin' out the window."

"That was all you could tell him, then?"

He blinked his lizard eyes slowly. "That's all I did tell him," he said. "Maybe not all I coulda told him."

"You saw something else?"

His right hand caressed the gun butt, a Freudian move if ever there was one. "Let me ask you a question, buddy," he said. "You get paid for writin' this stuff?"

"Yeah."

"Well, I figure my time's valuable, too."

I sighed and shook my head. "I'm a reporter, Mr. Sturdevant, not a TV gumshoe. I don't pay for information."

"Then you ain't any more use to me than that fuckin' cop." The lip curl turned into a full blown snarl as he slowly eased the gun out of his belt—a big, shiny .357 that was also probably worth more than the trailer. He kept the gun at his side, tapping the long barrel against the leg of his ratty jeans, hoping I'd swoon.

"I'll tell you this much, buddy boy. I hear that coon used a candy-ass twenty-two. Those things ain't good for nothin' besides plinkin' cans and puttin' down stray cats." He grinned through the bush. "Now, this here's one of the most powerful handguns in the world. It'll blow a man's head clean off."

"Go ahead—make my day," I said, returning the fool's grin. "Clint Eastwood as Dirty Harry Callahan. I take it you get HBO with that satellite dish of yours?"

He immediately dropped Clint and went back to the Elvis sneer. "You're wastin' my time. Get offa my property. Now." Then he took a step backward into the gloom of the trailer and slammed the door. I heard the dog whimper and scurry away for a new hiding place. On the way back to the Bronco, I tried to decide who I should call first, the sheriff's department or the SPCA.

CHAPTER 15

BEFORE my Tuesday meeting with former Cubs manager Hub Jefferson at McDonough Park, I stopped in at the Geneva public library and looked up some background on the one-time major leaguer. He was born Hubert Lawson Jefferson in 1947, I learned, raised in a coal town in western Pennsylvania. He signed with the Phillies in 1966 after a year of junior college ball. His quick feet and swift hands served him well at second base, and he moved up rapidly in the Philadelphia farm system, landing a spot on the big club's roster in 1969.

I returned the baseball materials to the sports reference shelves and looked at my watch. Still forty minutes before I was due at the ballpark. I thought back to my weekend in Rochester with Kate—our discussion about Frank Wooley and the infamous "domestic incident" involving his wife and daughter, and Kate's anxiety as she talked around the edges of her own tragic marriage.

I glanced at the time again, then I went over to the checkout area and asked the librarian if she could recommend an informative book on family violence.

"It's all in the wrist, sweetheart. See, like this."

The lime-green disk left my hand on a low, flat trajectory before suddenly catching the air and sailing high over little Mandy's head, landing with a splat in Great Aunt Dorothy's potato salad.

"Oops."

"Nice toss, Sheridan," Kate called out as her daughter retrieved the Frisbee from amidst a group of flabbergasted old folks. "Thank God they've outlawed lawn darts."

I threw up my hands. "It must've caught a thermal."

"Pilot error, if you ask me."

"Can't fly on one wing. I think I need another beer."

We took different routes to the picnic pavilion, Kate and I, while Mandy ran off to the playground with a gaggle of her cousins—much to my relief. It was unseasonably warm for Memorial Day, and my weary body could think of nothing better than a shady seat and a cold draught. Kate and I converged at the keg, where one of her many uncles drew us each a cup of beer. Then, as Kate schmoozed for a moment, I grabbed a lawn chair and propped my feet on an ice chest and watched the Sumner family reunion swirl around me while I tried to recover from too much weekend.

I'd done my sleeping—what there was of it—at my older brother's suburban split-level. When I wasn't busy visiting with my brother and his wife or playing Nintendo with my niece and nephew, I was out with Kate, our itinerary taking in local museums, movie theaters, restaurants, and, on Sunday afternoon, a long, fast walk on the pedestrian trail that runs along the Genesee River and the Erie Canal.

"You look like you could use a pillow," Kate said as she pulled a lawn chair up next to mine and stretched out her bare legs. She was wearing running shoes, shorts, and a pink polo shirt. Her hair was pulled back into a short pony tail.

"A coffin might be more appropriate," I said. "I can't wait to get back to work tomorrow so I can get some rest."

"Poor baby," she teased. She reached over and stroked my arms languidly and smiled, the corners of her eyes crinkling mischievously. "I don't remember you complaining about the late hours last night, Sheridan. On that lumpy couch at your brother's house."

"Well—it wasn't that late. Or that lumpy," I said. "Besides, I would've done anything just to lie down for a few minutes. Ouch!" I pulled my arm back and rubbed the red mark where Kate had pinched me.

She laughed. "Serves you right for being such a liar. If it had only been a few minutes, I'd be the one with a complaint."

We sat quietly awhile, sipping at our cups of beer. Then Kate asked matter-of-factly, "Speaking of work, how's the Wooley thing coming along?"

I held my hand out flat and waggled it. "So-so. I need to do a lot more digging, but I've got another month, so I should be all right."

"Are you still having trouble reconciling the hero jock with the man who beat up on his wife and child?"

A warning bell went off in my head—we'd gone down this road before—but Kate remained calm.

"I suppose I am," I said after a moment. "I want to hear what Evie—Wooley's ex-wife—has to say on the subject, but I haven't been able to reach her. I just hope that when I do, she'll be willing to talk about it."

"Mmm." Kate stared straight ahead. "It can be difficult to—forget the shame. To stop feeling like your life's on hold. She might not want to reexamine any of it."

I followed her gaze out toward the park playground, where Mandy was happily negotiating the jungle gym. "I did meet Wooley's daughter Martina—she would've been about four when the incident happened. She wasn't ready to open up about her father, but she didn't seem . . . angry or bitter, really. More like protective, and maybe a little sad."

"Children are resilient, Sheridan. Much more so than their parents." She frowned. "A father can cause a little girl a lot of hurt—psychologically if not physically—and she'll still be willing to forgive him."

I spoke carefully, quietly. "That's not altogether a bad outlook, is it, Kate?"

She turned back to me and, for an instant, there was ice in the warm brown eyes.

"How do you forgive someone who never shows remorse? Whose only concern is his own—" She broke off, looked away again. "Sometimes I think it's better not to let yourself care in the first place. Then you never have to worry about forgiving. Or forgetting."

* * *

"I was basically Frank's caddy for my first two years in Philly," Hub Jefferson said as he fired up a cigarette.

We were sitting in a pair of box seats behind home plate. Out beyond the shade of the grandstand, the carefully manicured diamond sparkled in the midday sun.

"There was no way I was gonna unseat Frank Wooley from second base, he was just too good. But I was being groomed to take over if he went down with an injury or retired or whatever. Nobody expected that to happen so soon. It was the gambling and the suspension that screwed him up. He ended up having a bad season and the club traded him to K.C." He smiled ruefully. "Course a bad year for Frank was still better than me or ninety percent of the other second basemen in the league could do. I had the glove, but I couldn't touch Wooley with the bat or on the bases."

I said, "You had a solid career."

He shrugged it off and exhaled a plume of smoke. "If you're going to quote me on anything in your story, quote me on this. Whatever Frank Wooley did or didn't do, I'll always remember him best for how great he treated me those two years we played together in Philadelphia. He spent hour after hour working with me, showing me how to get a lead off first base, how to make the double-play pivot. And that was unusual in those days, believe me. Most veterans, they see some kid come along looking to take their job, they'd sooner shit on you than say hello."

"Your own teammates?"

"You gotta remember, Sheridan, this was before we got free agency—another area where Frank was ahead of his time. Guys who played in the sixties, the established players, they did okay. Maybe made what a dentist or an accountant would earn, but nowhere near what even a journeyman major leaguer pulls down today. You were lucky if your career lasted ten years, and after that it was back to the real world. You had to hang on as long as you could and put away as much as you could and hope you didn't end up back at your old man's gas station when it was all over."

I scribbled a few notes in my pad. "So he was a generous man, in your experience."

"That's a good word for it. He was generous with his time and even with his money, particularly with the younger guys. When

I first came up, he loaned me a few hundred bucks to help me get by until our first paychecks came. We didn't get paid during spring training in those days." Jefferson looked out at the diamond. "Maybe he saw a little of himself in me. A young black kid from a poor family trying to catch on in the big show. Anyway, he was always there for me in my first year. The second year he wasn't quite as accessible, but that's understandable."

"You mean because of the trouble he was having with the commissioner?"

He nodded. "The suspension only lasted for a month in the early part of the season, but it seemed to drag Frank down for the whole year. When he started playing again, he was, I don't know, a little listless. Like he'd lost the fun, y'know? He was having a tough time on the field and he wasn't his old self in the clubhouse, either."

"Still, you were friendly." When he acknowledged that with a nod, I asked, "Did you know before the suspension about the gambling in general or Wooley's relationship to Harry Lundquist?"

Jefferson stared at me warily and, for a moment, I could see the imprint of his former mentor flashing in his dark eyes.

"Look, Sheridan, I'm not a betting man, never was. Make sure you get that down, too." It was the sort of statement that always has a but attached to the end of it. I scribbled a note in the pad just to make him feel better, then looked up expectantly.

"But you're right," he continued. "Frank and me were friendly. One spring down in Florida, I tagged along with him to the dog track—he played, I didn't. I think he lost maybe fifty bucks all day. Other than the card games that the guys get up in the clubhouse and on planes, that's the only time I actually saw Frank do any gambling with my own eyes. But, sure, I knew he liked to go to the track once in a while, play a little poker. So did a lot of players and nobody ever said anything about it."

"Unless they started associating with pros like Harry Lundquist," I said pointedly.

Jefferson grunted. "Shit, other guys got away with stuff all the time, but Frank couldn't because he was too outspoken. There was definitely a double standard. Club owners can own race horses and even race tracks, and the commissioner doesn't say a thing. But let Willie Mays or Mickey Mantle take a lollipop job at an Atlantic City casino, playing golf with the highrollers and shaking a few hands, and they get banned.''

''You're saying Frank Wooley's relationship with Lundquist was blown out of proportion?''

''Hey, I don't know Harry Lundquist from the man in the moon. All I know is what I read in the papers, okay? And twenty years ago, when the commissioner's office was on Frank's case, all you newspaper guys ever could find out was that Frank was spending some of his free time at the track with this guy Lundquist, and that Lundquist had a minor record for gambling and stuff. Sounds like a case of guilt by association, you ask me.''

I stopped writing and leaned into the stiff wooden back of the box seat. The atmosphere of the ballpark was starting to get to me; my throat craved a paper cup filled with beer and my cramped legs longed for the seventh-inning stretch.

''You're a loyal friend.''

''I owe him. He was there when I needed him.'' Jefferson squirmed self-consciously, the cigarette bobbing in the corner of his mouth. ''Truth is, I was pretty impressed to be sharing a locker room with Frank Wooley. He was sort of a hero of mine when I was a kid.''

''You went out on a limb when you decided to hire him as your coach here.''

''I figured he belonged in baseball. I knew from my own experience that Frank had a great head for the game and that he could teach young players. The front office in Chicago wasn't happy about it, but they'd already guaranteed me the right to do my own thing—I wouldn't't've agreed to take the managing job otherwise.''

''You've moved up the organizational ladder in a hurry,'' I said. ''From an A-ball manager to director of player development. Apparently no one held you responsible for what happened— Wooley going into the stands after that fan, I mean. Getting himself fired after only three months.''

''To be accurate, he wasn't fired. He quit. Gave me his walking papers and cleaned out his locker that same afternoon.'' Jefferson took a long, last drag on the cigarette and pitched the butt out into the aisle. ''I was relieved, you wanna know the truth. We both knew I would've had to fire him. That was part of our agreement when he signed on—any disruptive behavior or bad press and he was gone. I still don't know what the hell got into him, although, as I remember it, he was in a pretty lousy mood all that day, even before the game started."

"That heckler must've really been on his case."

"Yeah, some drunk bastard. Happens all the time, usually on the road. I couldn't hear the guy—I was in the third base coach's box. I guess every time Frank went out to coach at first in the bottom of the inning, this clown would start in with some shit about Frank being a no-good gambler."

"And that was enough to set him off?"

"Obviously it was. Luckily a couple of the kids got ahold of Frank before he could do anymore than rip the guy's shirt, or we could've had a major lawsuit on our hands."

"Considering all he had to lose, it has to make you wonder if there was something else bothering Wooley—something more than a heckler in the stands." I waited for a response, but none was offered. "Did you know about what went on the day before, after the memorabilia show at the Stanton?" I asked.

Jefferson frowned. "You mean that Frank was seen with Lundquist? Al Hargis told me about it after the fan incident. By then it didn't matter—Frank was already out of the picture as far as the Geneva Cubs were concerned."

"Didn't you wonder what he was doing with Lundquist? Why Wooley would be foolish enough to get mixed up with the guy again?"

"I wondered about it," he conceded. "I figured maybe Lundquist was trying to wheedle his way back in with the old crowd from the Philly days: Frank, Alfie Klem, Gimp Smith."

"Hold it a second," I said as I flipped back through my pad. I found the page from my visit to the *Daily News* clips library the previous Friday, where I had noted the names of the retired ballplayers who had appeared at the autograph session with Wooley. Alfie Klem and Gimp Smith were on the list. Anyone who followed baseball knew that Klem had been a star pitcher for the Phillies and several other teams during a career that ran from the fifties to around 1980. Smith, as I recalled, had been a so-so relief pitcher back in the sixties. What was news, at least to me, was that Frank Wooley and the other two had been close during Wooley's stint in Philadelphia—and that Harry Lundquist apparently had known all three in the good old days.

I looked up at Jefferson and caught him sneaking a peek at his watch. "I won't keep you much longer. Just a few more questions. You're saying that Lundquist, Wooley, Klem, and Smith used to buddy around together?" I asked.

Jefferson hesitated. It was funny how often that happened—a person would hear his own words restated by a reporter and suddenly begin to hedge.

"Maybe I went a little too far," he said. "I mean, I don't want to bad-mouth somebody—especially not in print."

"But you did imply that Wooley, Klem, and Smith were friends off the field," I pressed. "And that Lundquist figured in somehow."

"Shit," he muttered. Then, "Off the record?"

"If that's how you want it."

He accepted that with a curt nod. "Klem was a star for a while and he liked the star treatment, including an entourage. Gimp Smith, who blew out his arm when he was with the Mets, was trying to catch on with Philadelphia as a coach, batting practice pitcher—any kind of job that would keep him in the major leagues. Anyway, Gimp and Klem knew each other from when they were both with the Mets. When Gimp was hanging around in Philly, he started running with Klem again, being his gofer basically. Klem liked to party a lot and sometimes he had Gimp drive for him." He shook his head. "All the black players thought Gimp was a Tom, a Steppin Fetchit. Klem used to boss him around in that Arkansas good-old-boy twang of his. All in good fun, supposedly, but it was pretty pathetic."

"Where do Wooley and Lundquist figure in?"

"Like I said, Klem was into the night life, including the horses and stud poker. Frank was, too, so they started hanging out sometimes. As for how Lundquist figured in, I told you before I never even met the man. But if he was running with Frank in the old days, I guarantee you he hung with the others, too."

Jefferson uncoiled himself from the seat. "All I'm saying is maybe Lundquist was in Geneva that weekend to try and get in with the old gang. All I really know is that Frank was stupid to get anywhere near him again. Now, if that's it. . . . "

"Just one more thing," I said. "You know how I could get hold of either Smith or Klem?"

"Well, I'm sure you could reach Klem through his agent.

Klem's real popular on the nostalgia circuit, rakes in a lot of money doing autograph sessions and card shows."

"You know the agent's name?"

"Richie Hirshberg, Hirshberg Management Group—he handles quite a few jocks, retired and active. He's in the Manhattan book," Jefferson said. "Matter of fact, Hirshberg was another old buddy of Frank's way back when."

And another name I knew I had filed away somewhere in my earlier notes. I wrote it down again and circled it.

"And Gimp Smith. Any idea how to reach him?"

He turned it over for a second. "Mmm, he could be handled by Hirshberg, too, I'm not sure. Gimp wasn't a star, but if he does card shows, he's got at least some earning potential, so he could be agented. The easiest way to go, though, would be to check with the players' pension fund office, also in the Manhattan book. Last I knew, Smith was working there as a player liaison."

CHAPTER 16

I drove back across town with a carful of names to keep me company: Harry Lundquist, Gimp Smith, Alfie Klem, and Richie Hirshberg. Four old friends of Frank Wooley, three of whom attended the memorabilia show at the Stanton and a fourth—Hirshberg—who was an agent for Klem and had once been financial adviser to Wooley.

Could the weekend at the Stanton have gone down the way Hub Jefferson had characterized it—Harry Lundquist showing up uninvited, trying to worm his way back in with the old crowd? Or was it something else? Maybe I was focusing too much on those two days in 1988, but my instincts kept telling me there was something there—that somehow the presence of Lundquist and the others had contributed directly to Wooley's frame of mind when he charged that fan in the stands. Now factor in Gimp Smith's job with the players' pension fund office, and the fact that Wooley seemed to have been receiving an extra check—or at least an extra envelope—from that office every month. If Smith was behind the extra check, then who was behind him? And why?

The Quincy County Sheriff's offices are located just off Main in a modern smoked glass-and-steel ribbed building that would've been just fine if it hadn't been tacked on as an appendage to the old county jail. The jail itself was a looming Gothic monster heavy with cut stone and gargoyles. The two were butted together shoulder to shoulder, an incongruity akin to seeing Christopher Wren with his arm around I. M. Pei.

I parked down the block and backtracked to the main entrance, giving a wave to the desk sergeant on duty as I passed on into the squad room. It was not unlike a small newsroom, with its orderly rows of desks and adjoining computer terminals, banks of file cabinets, and the ubiquitous overhead fluorescent lighting. I nodded to a few familiar faces and worked my way to the back, where a uniformed receptionist guarded the corridor that led to the private offices.

"Afternoon, Alice," I said. "Is J.D. available?"

"Nuh-uh. He's not only not available, he's not even here." Alice was a plain, serious woman of about thirty-five. She had a long, flat face and mouse brown hair lacquered into a permanent knot on the back of her head.

"Okay, how about Tony?"

"I'd have to buzz him to see if he was free."

I waited for her to do just that, but she didn't. She continued to squint up at me expectantly, like a trained beagle anticipating its next command. Finally I said, "Could you buzz him, please, Alice?"

"Sure thing."

I was staring up at the acoustical tile ceiling, imploring the heavens to give me patience, when Tony Areno came down the corridor behind Alice's station.

"Hey, Sheridan, what's shakin'?"

"My faith in the criminal justice system."

"Join the crowd. You're looking for the info you asked J.D. to get, am I right?" Without waiting for a reply, he backtracked up the hallway, waving the folder he was carrying like a semaphore to let me know I should follow him. I caught up to him at his office door.

"C'mon in, have a seat." He moved over behind a heap of papers and files I assumed were camouflaging a desk. Areno, the county undersheriff, was a stocky, blunt, shambling man who had gotten where he was by hard work and perseverance and loyalty to the man who had last held the job, J. D. Staub. He was somewhere in his forties, with thick jet-black hair and a broad, fleshy face that most often held a look of mild bewilderment.

I sat down in the offered chair and waited for him to find whatever it was he was looking for.

"Where the hell—ah, here we go. Jesus, I gotta clean off this desk someday." He grabbed a piece of green computer paper from the pile and sat down. "Okay, you wanted some background on . . . " he scanned the printout, "Harold Thomas Lundquist, aka Harry Lundquist, Harry Lundy, Hank Lester, and so on."

"Mostly I need to know where I can find the guy."

"That's easy." He tossed the sheet over to me. "He's locked up in Auburn, doing a nickel for check fraud."

"Five years for bouncing a check?" I asked, as I looked over the printout. "That's a little stiff, isn't it?"

"Look at the guy's rap sheet, Sheridan. He's a three-time loser—four if you count the stretch in Leavenworth the army gave him in 1958. Besides, Lundquist wasn't just bouncing a few bad checks, he was papering half the Eastern Seaboard from a dozen different phony accounts." Areno frowned. "Anyway, the asshole'll be out in two if he does good time."

"Mmm. I see he served time in New Jersey in the sixties on the same offense," I said. "Fifteen months."

"And in between, in the late seventies, eighteen months in Pennsylvania—one of those federal minimum-security country clubs. His name came up in a gambling probe, and they ended up tagging him for tax evasion. Same old dog, same old tricks, huh?"

"Looks that way." I glanced at the information at the top of the sheet. Lundquist was now fifty-seven years old, born in Omaha, Nebraska. In addition to the three prison terms and his army record—a dishonorable discharge following the stretch in Leavenworth for desertion—he'd been arrested five other times on fraud or gambling-related charges, with two dismissals, two failures to convict, and one conviction that involved probation only. Over the years, I'd seen similar resumes on a number of small-time grifters. The only thing that set Harry Lundquist apart was his friendship with Frank Wooley.

"Auburn Correctional Facility," I read. "Started his sentence last October. Well, his bad luck, my good luck." Auburn was only about twenty-five miles east of Geneva. Of all the people I needed to contact for my story, Lundquist was the one I figured

I'd have the most trouble locating. Petty crooks don't usually stay in one place very long, unless it's a prison.

Now that I knew where to look, I was reasonably sure he'd talk to me, even if much of what he said turned out to be a fantasy. Outside of a few old-time mob guys who still stuck by the Sicilian code, most of the career criminals I've dealt with love to brag about their exploits; how clever they've been and how dumb the cops and "the squares" are. The fact that they're usually talking from behind a set of bars doesn't seem to register with them. Getting caught is always bad luck, never bad judgment.

I held up the printout. "Can I keep this?"

"Yeah, sure," Tony said. "Just don't tell anybody where you got it. J.D.'s up to the county campus right now tryin' to save our budget. If the legislature hears we're runnin' computer checks for reporters, they're liable to cut us another five percent."

"I'll keep it close to the vest. Thanks for doing it, Tony. This is gonna save me some legwork."

He waved it off. "So, J.D. says you're doin' a thing on Frank Wooley for *The Sporting Life*, huh? I never could get too excited about the guy's politics, but, man, could he play ball. It's a damn shame he screwed up the way he did. How do you figure a guy like that, Sheridan?"

"That's what I'm hoping to find out. Why he did the things he did."

Areno shook his head. "I guess sometimes there isn't any 'why.' It's like these two brothers I knew growin' up, a couple of goombahs like me. Same parents, same house, same chances in life, right? Only Victor ends up a doctor downstate, and Paulie ends up dead in a Boston flophouse with a spike hangin' out of his arm, OD'd on smack. Go figure," he said, turning palms up. "Hey, J.D. says you had some problem with Artie Leek over in Yates?"

"I'm just having trouble getting a read on the guy," I said. "Sounds like you know him."

"Yeah, we crossed paths a couple times when I was running the detective squad—we team up with Yates once in a while when a case crosses county lines. He's a piece of work, isn't he? I'll bet he was wearing one of his bow ties. I'll tell you somethin' about Artie Leek, though. He's no dummy. Got a degree in criminal justice from up at Rochester Institute of Technology and a masters in sociology, I think it is. That's one of the reasons he's a detective sergeant over there, even though he fits in about as good as a salmon in a sardine can. He keeps aceing the civil service exams, getting himself on the top of the promotions lists.''

I shrugged. "So he tests well. But what kind of a cop is he?''

"Solid. That's the other reason he made it up the ladder so quick.'' He rested his elbows on one of the shorter stacks of files. "We liaised with Yates on a homicide a while back, right? A Geneva woman who'd just broken up with a guy from Penn Yan. She turned up missing and there was circumstantial evidence of foul play, only we had no body. Well, Leek sat on the boyfriend for weeks, just keeping tabs on his movements, until finally he catches the bastard trying to sell some of the girl's jewelry in a bar.'' He smiled with grim approval. "The son of a bitch folded like a pair of deuces. Led us to the body and everything. The collar went to us, but it was Artie's police work that made the case.''

"I'm surprised his superiors let him put in so much time on somebody's else's case.''

"Well, we get along pretty good with the sheriff over there. He's okay. Anyway, I got the feeling Artie did a lot of the surveillance on his own.'' Areno pushed back in his chair. "You know how detectives operate. A guy's got a caseload of maybe half a dozen active cases, he works 'em as he sees fit. You check out a couple leads on this one, make a few calls on that one—you got nobody hanging over you every minute to see what you're up to, see what I mean?''

I nodded. It was a lot like freelance work. You juggle as many stories as you can handle, giving priority where it's required on any given day.

Tony continued, "When Artie Leek gets his horns up about a case, he stays with it until he's satisfied. And if his bosses don't like it,'' he shrugged elaborately. "Like I always say, what they don't know won't hurt 'em.''

That afternoon I wrote a letter to the warden of the prison in Auburn, requesting permission to interview Harry Lundquist. It would take a week or so for the request to work its way through channels, but I had dealt with the department of corrections before and I was pretty sure that permission would be granted, provided Lundquist agreed to talk to me.

Correspondence completed, I made a few calls to the New Jersey state offices in Trenton to check out Frank Wooley's work history between 1972 and 1985, the years he'd been banned from baseball. Wooley had told me he'd worked in construction in New Jersey and I needed to verify. Labor and tax records showed that he had indeed worked as a drywaller and, eventually, a finish carpenter. Satisfied, I called Pete Calvett to find out what he'd been able to come up with on Mike Delfay.

"Hey, Sheridan, good timing," Calvett said, his voice cannonading through the line. "I got that stuff you wanted on Delfay."

"And you were just about to call me."

"You bet. Got a pen handy?"

"Better. I'm at my computer keyboard."

While Pete dictated, I pinched the phone against my ear and watched the computer screen's blinking cursor magically spill out the words.

Delfay had been busy in his short life. Before going freelance, he had worked as a sports reporter for *Newsday* and then as a contributing editor at *Inside Sports*. In addition to the unauthorized Pete Rose biography that Calvett had mentioned before, Delfay had cowritten six other biographies on well-known basketball, baseball, and football players, and was rumored to have ghosted half a dozen others. From Calvett's own impressions and those he'd collected from others, Delfay had been respected and even feared for his reporting skills, but was widely disliked for his ruthlessness and abrasive style.

"The guy was a bachelor, and his parents don't know from squat," Pete concluded. "But I got the name of his agent. He can probably tell you more about how Delfay operated, and what kind of a deal he had going with Wooley."

I fed the agent's name and number into the computer and thanked Pete.

"No problem. Let me know if you need anything else. I've got an eager intern in from Columbia for the summer, and she's itching to do something besides bring me coffee."

After hanging up, I dialed the Manhattan number for Delfay's literary agent, a man named Hugh Decker. He told me that he'd been representing Delfay for about five years and he confirmed that Delfay had undertaken the Wooley project strictly on speculation.

"Mike was intrigued with the whole Frank Wooley persona," Decker said in an accent that bespoke a Brooklyn upbringing filtered through a Connecticut education. "I know he did some background on him preparatory to actually contacting him about a collaboration. Of course, Mike would've done the book with or without Wooley's cooperation."

"Do you know how far he'd gotten before he died?"

"Mmm, not too far, I wouldn't think. Mike liked to know which way the project was going—authorized or unauthorized—before he invested too much time." Decker laughed, an unpleasant little trill. "He liked to know which side he was going to be on."

"So Delfay didn't have a contract with Wooley?"

"No. That's what the trip to the hinterlands was all about. He hoped to sign Wooley on, although frankly I told Mike he might have a bigger book if he went the unauthorized route."

"Two things you might clear up for me, Mr. Decker. How did Delfay locate Wooley, and was Wooley expecting him to show up at the house that day?"

"I'm not sure if Wooley was expecting him. Mike didn't say. As to how he got Wooley's address, he was having trouble with that early on, so I referred him to a sports agent I know who I thought might be able to help."

"Richie Hirshberg, by any chance?"

"As a matter of fact, yes."

CHAPTER 17

WEDNESDAY arrived cold and gray, an ethereal mist drifting over the lake surface and reducing visibility to spitting distance from the end of my dock. Almost June, I reminded myself while I hauled in an armload of wood for the fireplace. The cottage was well equipped with a baseboard heating system, but electric rates were out of sight and, besides, there's nothing like a roaring fire to chase away a morning chill.

The fire lit, I filled a mug with coffee, adding a splash of half-and-half and pouring the rest into a bowl for the cat. He was a stray tom I had named William of Orange, partly for his coloring and partly for his royal disdain for the Irishman whose home he'd usurped.

"Cool it, you greedy bugger," I growled as I carried the bowl to a favored spot near the glass sliders, the cat mewing and slaloming between my legs with every step. "If I spill this, you're out of luck until suppertime."

He craned his neck up at me and blinked slowly, dismissing my idle threat with a swish of his tail. I set the bowl on the floor and watched for a moment as William lapped at the milk. I've been living alone too long, I decided, as I grabbed my coffee mug and retreated to the writing nook in the loft.

I spent the morning alternately scribbling questions on a legal pad and placing a number of calls that, like the questions, went largely unanswered. The one thing I nailed down was that Gimp

Smith did indeed work for the players' pension fund. Campbell, my contact there, said that Smith was what he termed "a benefits counselor" for retired players. I called the number he gave me, and a switchboard operator put me through to Smith's office.

"Who you say you workin' for?" Smith asked warily after I gave him my name and my reason for calling.

The Sporting Life," I repeated. "As I said, I understand you were an old friend of Frank Wooley's and . . . "

"Who tole you that? I didn't know the man all that well." His slow, heavy voice was pure Mississippi Delta.

"The word I have is that you and Frank and Alfie Klem used to run around together back when Frank was with the Phillies," I said.

Pause. "Alfie and me used to do that, awright, but a lotta the boys would come along now and again. Wooley, too, I guess. That don't mean we was connected at the hip. Lord, I don't think I even seen Frank in twenty years or so, so I don't expect I can help you much with your article."

"Excuse me, Mr. Smith, but I'm a little confused. I understood that you and Klem and Wooley appeared together at an autograph session up here in Geneva less than three years ago."

Another pause. "That could be. I can't remember every— I do a lotta those things. What'd you say your name was?"

"T.S.W. Sheridan."

"Um, I'm sorry there, Mr. Sheridan, but I'm runnin' late for a meeting. Sorry I couldn't be more help."

The line went dead. I called back, only to be informed by the switchboard operator that Mr. Smith was not available.

I called IdaRose next, hoping she could tell me if any of Wooley's old crowd had kept in touch since he'd left his job with the Geneva Cubs, but she wasn't at home. Then I tried the Ithaca number IdaRose had given me for Martina Wooley, but there was no answer there either. I also called her mother, Evie, in New Jersey three separate times, twice getting a busy signal and, the last time, the answering machine.

By that point I was so frustrated I decided to call up an old friend from my New York City days, in part because I wanted to hear a voice—any voice—on the other end of the line, and in part because there was a slim chance he could be of help. Lev Ascher and I had shared a Greenwich Village apartment for a year, back when I was licking the fresh wounds of a failed marriage and simultaneously trying to pursue a freelance career in the big city. Since then, Lev and his girlfriend, Rachel, had traded in the Village and moved further south to a loft apartment above a former dairy plant in TriBeCa—the Triangle Below Canal Street. Lev was a successful copywriter for a Madison Avenue advertising firm who longed to be a successful playwright someday. As such, he and Rachel—an actress when she wasn't behind the cosmetics counter at Bloomingdale's—spent most of their free time working with off-Broadway theater groups.

"So what's the real reason you called?" Lev had asked after we finished catching up on the small talk.

I told him about my assignment and the problem I was having reaching Wooley's ex-wife, the former Evie March.

"It's a long shot," I admitted, "but I thought you might ask some of your showbiz friends if any of them knew her way back when. I know she was a dancer in some of the clubs back in the sixties—I'm not sure if she did any stage work."

"I can ask around, anyway. Actually, sounds like fun. But what is it I'm supposed to be finding out?"

"Anything about her life before Wooley, how they met, what either or both of them were like in the old days. I didn't have any luck trying to get any personal stuff from Wooley and I'm beginning to suspect that Evie won't be any more forthcoming. I could really use a few good quotes from someone who knew her."

Lev and I schmoozed for a couple more minutes, until his call-waiting cut us short. I decided to try one last call before driving into the village for lunch at Ralph and Kay's. Sergeant Arthur Leek sounded glad to hear from me, but then he was the sort who'd listen politely to a computerized phone solicitation. I asked if I could drop by his office for a little chat. He told me he was about to go out, then he asked if I was familiar with the parking overlook on Route 54, a few miles south of Penn Yan. I was instinctively wary at first—why did he want to talk out along a quiet stretch of highway instead of in his office? But I figured I already knew the answer. So I assured him I could find the place and we agreed to meet at two o'clock.

* * *

The sun made an appearance in the early afternoon, slipping out from behind an ominous bank of thunderheads that had spent the morning threatening a major storm, but had delivered only a mild rainshower. The damp air suddenly seemed ten degrees warmer, and I rolled down the Ford's window, then reflexively turned up the volume on the radio. A Rochester oldies station was playing a Beach Boys' tune, "Heroes and Villains,"—particularly apt for the mood I was in.

I was five minutes early, but Leek was already there. The roadside rest area provided a panoramic view of Keuka Lake's east fork. A mile in the distance, the high, wooded bluff that divided the upper portions of the lake seemed to shimmer in the sunny haze. I parked beside the only other vehicle in sight, a white late-model Plymouth sedan, and joined Leek at one of the overlook's half-dozen picnic tables. He was wearing a light blue cotton-blend suit with a white shirt and one of his signature bow ties, this one solid red. All he needed was a straw skimmer and a cane and he'd be ready for a road production of *The Music Man.* In front of him on the table were a paper bag held down with an apple, half a peanut butter sandwich on a square of wax paper, and a carton of milk.

He dabbed at the corners of his mouth with a napkin before speaking. "I hope you don't mind, Mr. Sheridan. Lunch hour is catch as catch can sometimes."

"Enjoy," I said. "I've already caught mine."

"Beautiful spot for it anyway," he said between bites. "I like to get out of the office and take in the fresh air whenever I can."

"Is that the reason we're out here?"

He frowned quizzically. "Excuse me?"

"I thought maybe you wanted to see me in a more private setting."

He chewed for a few seconds. "Why would I want to do that?"

"Oh, I don't know, Sergeant. Maybe you wanted to hear what I had to say without your superiors listening in and noting your continued interest in a supposedly closed case."

A sip of milk. "You're the one who's interested in a closed case, Mr. Sheridan. I'm just here as a responsive public servant— on my own time. But I would like to hear what you have to say."

"Fair enough." I put my hands flat on the rough surface of the picnic table. "To start, I went out to Lookout Run and interviewed some of the neighbors. One of them—a woman named Karnes—told me about seeing Delfay drive by her house the day of the shooting. She said he was consulting what appeared to be an address book, as if he were checking directions. She also said she told you about the address book."

Leek nodded, unperturbed. "But we didn't find an address book on the deceased or in his belongings."

"Probably because it was removed by a third party."

"Which third party would that be, Mr. Sheridan?"

"The one you were so concerned about when you asked Mrs. Karnes if she saw anyone in the car with Delfay."

I thought I had him for a moment, but he shook his head slowly, about to rook my king again. "I asked Mrs. Karnes a routine question; how many people were in the car? She said only one, the driver, who seemed to be scanning something in a book. 'Like an address book or a steno pad' is what she said. We found two such pads with Delfay's belongings; one was unused, the other had a few pages of notes and questions that he was presumably planning to put to Mr. Wooley. I suggest that, when Mrs. Karnes saw Delfay drive by, he was reviewing the list of questions."

I've done the same sort of thing myself before an interview, but I wasn't about to admit that to Leek.

"What about Sturdevant, the guy in the old trailer?"

"What about him?"

"You asked him if Delfay was alone, too."

The sergeant sighed, nearly a temper tantrum by his standards. "You're forcing me to repeat myself, Mr. Sheridan. My questions to Mr. Sturdevant were routine. He did see the Toyota come through, but from his vantage point at the time, he couldn't see into the car. The fact is, neither he nor Mrs. Karnes saw anyone but Delfay in the car."

"Maybe your questioning was a little too routine."

"Meaning what?"

I described my encounter with Sturdevant at his trailer, right down to the abused dog, the intimidation with the handgun, and the bald attempt to sell me information he claimed to have held back from the police. "The implication was that Sturdevant saw something out there a week ago Saturday," I summed up. "Something or someone who didn't belong."

Leek was slowly turning the apple in his hands, like a pitcher rubbing the shine off a new ball. "I think you may be reading a lot into what Sturdevant said. He probably only wanted to con you out of a few dollars. Still," he added, cutting off my protest, "I don't like being played for a fool. You say he brandished a gun—and mistreated his dog in your presence?"

"I didn't actually see him do anything," I admitted. "But I heard a thud, like a kick, and then the dog yelped. What does that sound like to you?"

"Like a good enough pretext to get me in the door at least," Leek said, turning it over. "Maybe I'll round up someone from animal control and pay Mr. Sturdevant a visit." He stopped fussing with the apple and looked me in the eye. "We'll treat this as an informal complaint at this time, but if it becomes necessary, will you verify that you requested the department to investigate Sturdevant for cruelty?"

"Necessary in order to prosecute Sturdevant, d'you mean, or necessary in case your superiors want to know why you're out messing around with Frank Wooley's neighbor?"

"The former, of course. Will you do it?"

I returned his stare for a moment longer, then exhaled. "Yeah, I'll back you up. I only wish you'd come clean with me, Sergeant. You know, or at least suspect, that something wasn't kosher out at the Mack place, don't you?"

"I only know what the evidence dictates, Mr. Sheridan." He pushed himself up from the table. "Right now I really have to get back to the office." He stuffed the wax paper and the empty milk carton into the paper bag, then tucked the apple into the pocket of his suit coat.

"Good luck with your story," Leek said. "And, please, feel free to call if you happen across anything you think might interest me. Not that I expect anything to come of it, you understand, but I . . . "

"I know," I said. "You kind of enjoy the interplay."

CHAPTER 18

IT was almost nine o'clock when IdaRose called. I was watching a Yankees-Angels game on cable, but the interruption came as a relief. The Yanks were making the Angels look good—which wasn't easy—and, like any die-hard fan, I was taking it personally.

"Am I disturbing you, Timothy?" she asked. "You sound a little upset."

I laughed. "Can you blame me? I just saw a shortstop with a seven-figure salary and a .233 lifetime batting average pop up a bunt to the pitcher."

"They don't stress fundamentals anymore," IdaRose said. "Frank used to complain about that whenever we sat down to watch a game together." Her voice caught on "together."

I gave her a moment before saying, "I'm glad you called, IdaRose. I tried reaching you several times today."

"I started back to work this week and I've been putting in some overtime. Our busy tourist season is just getting under way and—actually, I suppose the real reason I've been working late is so I don't have to spend as much time here at the house." She sighed. "I've decided to put it up for sale and move to a smaller place in town. I didn't mind the isolation when I had someone to share it with, but now I think I'd just as soon be with people."

"Sounds like a good idea."

"Listen to me, prattling on and not even giving you a chance to tell me why you were trying to reach me earlier."

"Well, to begin with, I was curious whether any of Frank's friends or teammates from the old days kept in touch after he left the coaching job in Geneva."

"No, unfortunately not. To be honest, Frank didn't encourage that sort of thing—it's like he wanted to completely divorce himself from the old life. That's why I find it so hard to believe he would've been associating with that man Lundquist after the card show," she added. I didn't debate the point. She continued, "The only time I met one of Frank's old friends was shortly after he moved in with me, right after he lost his coaching job. Let's see, he said he had to drive up to Geneva to meet with his old financial adviser to get some of his business affairs in order."

"That would be Richie Hirshberg?"

"Yes, the one who was a civil-rights activist back in the sixties. He's a sports agent now. Anyway, I convinced Frank to take me along so that I could do some clothes shopping while he met with Mr. Hirshberg. They talked business over lunch at that little Chinese restaurant on Exchange while I hit a few stores."

"That was the only time he saw Hirshberg, then? I mean, he never came down to the house?"

"No, he did drive down that evening for dinner." IdaRose made a clucking noise. "The poor man was staying over night at a hotel, then planning to leave for Syracuse the next morning to visit a minor-league ballplayer—a young outfield prospect he was hoping to sign on as a client. I told Frank the least we could offer was a home-cooked meal."

"Hirshberg's name seems to keep cropping up," I said. "What sort of a guy is he, anyway?"

"He seemed very nice. We chatted quite a bit about the civil rights and antiwar days, when he and Frank became friends. He told a few funny stories about some of the famous players and actors he knows. That was about it, as I recall. He left early to head back to Geneva; he was a little worried about losing his way after dark. He'd already messed up coming down—missed the turnoff and ended up all the way down to the dead end."

"Do you know what sort of business arrangement he and Frank had going?"

"Something to do with investments Mr. Hirshberg had apparently managed for him since his playing days. I had the impression it wasn't a whole lot—something along the lines of the life-insurance annuity I came into when my husband died, I think."

"Have you run into anything like that in settling Frank's estate?"

"Now that you mention it, I haven't." I could sense her frowning at the other end of the line. "Well, I was only guessing about the annuity thing anyway. Maybe he received a cash payment for the investment or something. The estate he left was mainly personal items, plus a few thousand dollars in bonds and the life insurance from the pension fund."

"While we're on the players' pension fund," I said, "did Frank ever mention Gimp Smith? He works for the fund."

"No, I don't think he ever did. Timothy, does all this have something to do with that extra check Frank was getting every month?"

"I think so—just don't ask me how it connects, or what it means." I could hear her breathing quietly on the other end while I stared into the middle ground and tried to think of something I hadn't already asked her. Most of the questions that were hectoring me dealt with Wooley's life before IdaRose—the genesis of his relationship with Harry Lundquist, for example. But IdaRose had already admitted that she had lived with Wooley for more than two years without ever getting him to open the door to his past life.

"The investigation by the sheriff's office," I said finally. "When Sergeant Leek questioned you about what happened that Saturday—what you came home to find, that is—were there any specific details he seemed to concentrate on? Did he seem overly curious about things you thought were insignificant?"

My wording was deliberately obtuse. I knew that if I mentioned my suspicions about a third person being on hand at the time of the shootings IdaRose would seize upon it as gospel, and I didn't want that. She was already clinging to too many thin straws in her blind desire to see Frank Wooley's reputation rehabilitated, and I wasn't about to hand her another—not unless I had something more than conjecture to offer.

"Well, you have to remember I was all broken up," she said. "At the time, everything he asked me seemed either stupid or pointless. Let me think. . . . There were several questions about whether I touched anything in the den. I told him I didn't even step into the room. I couldn't.''

I waited her out again, regretting that I had to push her to relive the horror of it.

"One thing I found odd,'' she said, sniffling. ''The sergeant asked me about vacuuming.''

"Vacuuming?''

"If I had done the room that morning. Well, it was obvious I had; you could still see the wheel and brush marks the cleaner leaves in that thick carpet. But he asked about it again the next day, during our second interview.''

"Interesting,'' I mumbled. ''Anything else?''

"Yes, he wanted to know if the patio doors were usually kept closed and locked. I told him they were. And he asked about the fireplace. Was there a fire in it when I left that morning. There wasn't, but Frank usually made one up when he sat down with his morning coffee. He liked to sit in front of the fire and sip his coffee and read.'' She exhaled. ''That's about all I can remember, Timothy.''

"That's plenty. I'll let you go now. I imagine you're tired after putting in such a long day.''

"I am . . . oh, don't hang up yet. I almost forgot why I called you in the first place. I spoke to Martina on the phone right after I got in. Her final exam is Friday and she's leaving Ithaca on Sunday. She's got a clerking job lined up for the summer in New York City.''

"Did she say whether she was willing to talk to me?''

"Yes, she said you could call her Friday afternoon at her apartment after two o'clock. She's lukewarm about it, but I get the impression she's been contacted by other journalists trying to get a story. I think maybe she's realizing she won't be left alone until she gives someone an interview. It's like you told Frank, Timothy—all the Greta Garbo routine gets you is more attention.''

Ithaca sits at the southern end of Cayuga Lake, the largest of the Finger Lakes. It's only about thirty miles from my cottage on Seneca Lake as the crow flies, but more than twice that far by land, and the roads that lead there are mostly serpentine two-laners. I had left Mohaca Springs just after eleven Friday morning but, thanks to road reconstruction in Watkins Glen and a caravan of slow campers moving along Route 13, it was half past noon when I arrived.

The city always reminds me of a miniature Boston, only with steep hills and without the rotaries or the Red Sox. It's home to Cornell University, which marks it as not merely a college town, but an Ivy League college town—a place where it's not unusual to see a tie-dye shirt behind the wheel of a Volvo or a pin-striped banker chugging to work on a mountain bike, and where more than a few take their protein from tofu and lentils and condemn red meat as a midwestern conspiracy.

Cornell, like Ithaca itself, was originally designed to handle far fewer people than now inhabit it. Like the city, the campus seems chaotic to the uninitiated, with its narrow, winding streets and restricted parking areas and its compromising mix of the old and the new tucked in cheek-to-jowl amidst the rolling hills. The old buildings are Gothic and imposing, while the newer ones represent a mishmash of architectural styles with a strong emphasis on the utilitarian and the expedient.

Myron Taylor Hall, where the law classes were held, was old school all the way, right down to its ivy-covered walls.

I had parked in a lot around the corner next to Phillips Hall, one of the hard sciences buildings, where many of the students I saw coming and going were Asian. Now, as I sat on a low wall along one end of the broad stone steps that led into the law school, I idly watched the mostly white faces of the attorneys-to-be that streamed in and out. I figured that said a little about cultural influences—and a lot about America's tarnished economic performance.

Martina had told IdaRose that she expected to finish her last exam by one or one thirty. I'd been sitting there outside the buildilng for about twenty mintes when I spotted her coming through the arched portico. She was dressed like a young junior executive out for a little power walking on her lunch hour: neat gray jacket and skirt combination and high-collared white blouse, ankle socks and simple white Keds, a large black bag slung over her shoulder.

I caught up to her on the sidewalk. Her initial surprise at seeing me quickly gave way to a cool appraisal.

"Well, Mr. Sheridan," she said. "Or am I supposed to call you Timothy at this point?"

"I think we already had this conversation, Ms. Wooley. Anyway, most people just call me Sheridan."

"I bet that's not all they call you." She hoisted the leather bag higher on her shoulder. "I thought we were going to do this over the phone."

"And I thought it might be more enjoyable over lunch instead," I said. "The truth is, I'll grab any excuse to get out from behind my desk. Call it cabin fever."

"Call it bullshit." The hazel eyes glittered in the glaring sun. She shifted her weight onto one slender leg and planted a hand on her hip. "You wanted to make sure I couldn't hang up when the questions got tough, right?"

"Am I under oath, Counselor?"

That got me a quick, reluctant smile. "Well, I could use a bite and a drink. Provided you drive and I pick the restaurant."

"I'll even pick up the check."

"That's a given." She caught the wry look on my face. "What's so funny?"

"Oh, nothing," I said. "A favorite line from Shakespeare just came to mind for some reason."

"Uh huh, and I bet I can guess which one. 'The first thing we do—'

I finished it. " '—let's kill all the lawyers.' "

CHAPTER 19

WE ate at a tony little tavern around the corner from the Commons, downtown Ithaca's pedestrian-friendly, open-air shopping district. It was past one thirty when we got to the place, and most of the lunch crowd had already returned to their jobs. Martina led me to a quiet corner booth tucked away in the back, greeting the bartender as she went.

"I worked here for a few months," she explained after we settled into the high-backed booth. "Until I found out I just couldn't handle law school and a part-time job."

"I'm a little surprised you took a job in the first place. I understood your dad and your stepfather were splitting your college expenses."

The vibrant hazel eyes smoldered. "Believe it or not, Sheridan, I like to work. I've had jobs every summer since I was a high school sophomore. It's true that Lou and my father were splitting my expenses, but my father wasn't in a position to start doing that until a couple of years ago while I was a junior at Brown. Before that Lou paid for just about everything." She turned down the glare by a foot-candle or so. "Anyway, I like to have a few dollars of my own to spend as I like."

"So your father wasn't able to contribute to your support until the last few years?"

"I didn't say that. He always made his child-support payments right up until I was eighteen, even though my mother told him he didn't need to. My stepfather owns a commercial laundry service and a liquor distributorship among other things—money has never been a problem."

"But your college expenses? . . . "

"Are very high, as you can imagine. My father sent what he could when he could. Then in 1988 he started sending me a regular monthly check—he insisted on it." She shrugged. "He said they'd given all the retired ballplayers a major cost-of-living adjustment in their pension payments and he didn't need the extra income."

"Nice of him," I mumbled. And damned strange. In the same year Wooley got himself hired and fired as a coach for the Geneva Cubs, he also started mailing a thousand dollars a month to his daughter. I began pulling paraphernalia from the overstressed pockets of my corduroy sport coat—pens, notepad, minirecorder—while Martina went on about her industriousness.

" . . . so I was probably the only girl at school who knew what it was like to flip burgers at McDonald's."

"Is that so," I said, scrambling to catch up. "You went to high school in Saddle River, I take it?"

She shook her head. "Wingate. That's a boarding school for girls—excuse me, young ladies—outside of New Rochelle." She was staring at the tape recorder.

"Does this thing bother you? We don't have to use it, but it's for your protection as well as my own."

She laughed. "That sounds like something my roommate tells her dates."

The laughter looked good on her. Her face lost its controlled high-fashion severity and a softer, gentler beauty emerged. She tossed a shoulder, the copper strains in her hair shimmering in the light of the milk-glass globe that hung high over the booth.

"I'm all for accurate quotes," she said. "Go ahead and tape, if you like. It won't bother me."

The waiter came by with the menus just then and took our drink orders—half a carafe of the house white for Martina, a bottle of Molson's for me. She called him by name—Bobby, an undergrad at Ithaca College, I gathered—and the two of them gabbed for a couple of minutes while I searched the menu for something that resembled lunch.

"No tuna?" I asked.

Bobby shook his head solemnly. "We're boycotting. It's the dolphin thing. People shouldn't support the tuna industry until it stops indiscriminate netting."

I felt guilty for even asking. "I don't eat veal, if that counts for anything."

I could tell by his blank stare that it didn't. Martina ordered chicken-and-walnuts salad stuffed into a slice of pita. I asked for the same, only without the walnuts and the pita and served instead with lettuce on whole wheat toast. The way Bobby was frowning, I was afraid I'd have to go into my Jack Nicholson routine—take the tomato, put it between your knees, etc.—but it turns out he was merely thinking it through.

"The chicken salad already has the walnuts in it," he said. "But I could get you sliced chicken on wheat, with lettuce and mayo."

"That'd be fine, thanks."

I watched the waiter move off toward the kitchen, then tried to pick up the conversation where it had left off.

"So, Ms. Wooley, you were saying you attended . . . "

"You may as well call me Martina. Maybe it'll make this seem less like a cross-examination." She made a face. "Some of the brats at school used to call me Marty, which I hate. I'm not crazy about Martina, for that matter, but my dad named me after Reverend King, so I guess I can't complain too much. At least he didn't name me after Sojourner Truth."

"Not to mention Malcolm X," I said. "I get the impression you weren't crazy about boarding school."

"It was okay. I got a good education out of it—there wasn't much else to do but study," she said with a weary grin. "But if it'd been up to me, I'd just as soon have stayed at home and gone to Darlington High with the kids from the neighborhood."

"Darlington High?"

"That's where we live, in Darlington. It's just outside Saddle River, sort of a suburb of an exurb."

I nodded absently as I made a note in my pad. "So whose idea was it to send you to private school?"

"My mother and stepfather insisted on it—mostly my stepfather Lou, if you ask me." She read the look on my face and shook her head. "No, Sheridan, I'm not going to bore you with a story about the poor little rich girl and her mean, nasty stepfather. Actually, Lou's very nice to me, very generous and all that. It's just that . . . I think he's never been too comfortable introducing his mulatto stepdaughter to his business associates." She frowned. "Which is why I never made too big a stink about the boarding schools."

"And your mother went along with him?" I asked.

"It isn't like that. I mean, Lou's never said or done anything overt. It's just that he's always had little ways to exclude me from the public side of his life." The frown deepened. "Anyway, my mother is . . . I guess you'd say oblivious. About a lot of things. It wouldn't occur to her that Lou was anything but a good provider. If I tried to tell her different, she'd just sort of zone out, start humming show tunes or something. She's not always easy to talk to."

"In more ways than one." I filled her in on my many failed attempts to reach Evie by telephone.

"That's because you're using the published number for the house," Martina explained. "When Lou's gone on business—which is often—my mother always lets the answering machine take those calls. There's an unlisted number that friends and family usually use." She told me the alternate number and then sighed. "Mom's going to be pissed off when she finds out I gave you that, but then, she'll be a lot more pissed off when she hears what else I've told you."

Before I could follow up on that intriguing tease, Bobby arrived with a tray of food and drinks. My chicken sandwich had been made with endive instead of iceberg lettuce, but was fine otherwise. Martina's chicken-and-walnuts salad overflowed the pita pocket like some cross-cultural variation on tacos. I had no doubt that had I attempted one, half would have ended up in my lap. But Martina possessed that peculiarly female knack for nibbling away at messy food without losing a morsel to gravity. Throughout the meal we nursed the conversation along as politely as Martina nursed her wine, neither of us mentioning her father or his death or any of the other things that had brought me there. But by the time she was emptying the last of the wine from the carafe to her glass, and I had managed to cadge a second bottle of Molson's from Bobby, we both knew it was time to get on with the program.

Martina began with a question for me. "Did IdaRose tell you I've been getting a lot of calls from reporters?"

"She mentioned it." I reached over and turned the minirecorder back on.

"They're relentless, some of these guys. Everybody wants the 'big scoop' on my so-called abused childhood with Frank 'Black Sheep' Wooley. Even some little toad from the school paper has been following me around, trying to get an interview. The whole thing gags me."

"But you decided to talk to me."

Her eyes flitted up from the tabletop and held on me. "IdaRose trusts you to be fair, that's one reason we're here now. The other reason is I'm worried about this movement to have my father's election to Cooperstown nullified. IdaRose is, too. She convinced me that if there's anything I can do to clear up at least some of the controversy surrounding my father's life—if I can knock down any of the rumors about him—then I have to do it."

The debate over Frank Wooley and the hall of fame had slowly picked up momentum in the past two weeks. Many of the baseball writers who get to vote on the nominees are columnists, some of them nationally syndicated. Several had written columns about Wooley's impending installation at Cooperstown, with opinion roughly equally divided on whether it was appropriate—or even possible under the rules—to declare his selection null and void.

"For what it's worth, Martina," I said, "there's no precedent for removing a player from the hall once he's been voted in. It's never come up before, as far as I know."

"Yeah, well, there's always a first time. From what I read, the board of governors is already looking at ways to change the rules so Pete Rose's name won't be allowed on the ballot next year—and all he did was get mixed up with a few gamblers and short-change the IRS on his income taxes. Imagine if he'd killed somebody."

I let that go by without comment, partly because I didn't want to interrupt Martina's momentum now that I had her talking and partly because I was still struggling with my own ambivalence over Frank Wooley.

"Anyway, Sheridan, I just want to set the record straight as best I can." She took a deep breath, then let it out slowly.

"I don't know a lot about my father's life over the past seventeen years since he and my mother divorced. I mean, I saw him fairly regularly and all that, but I didn't live with him and I never . . . saw inside him in all that time. But I do remember the man who raised me until I was six years old and I can tell you what I remember from those times, how loving and protective and gentle he was." She pinned me again with those eyes. "Daddy never laid a hand on me in anger, never ever even spanked me, and that's the honest truth."

The tears started to well up right around when "my father" became "daddy." Anguish and loss tinged her words, but so too did conviction. For the first time since I'd begun my search for the Frank Wooley that IdaRose Mack had loved, I had found something solid to contradict the public perception of a man gone irredeemably wrong. He may have done many things, but he had not abused his little girl.

"That day in 1972," I said quietly, "when your father came home after losing the Supreme Court appeal. What really happened, Martina?"

She closed her eyes for a moment and rubbed at her aquiline nose. "This is the hard part."

I waited.

"I was four years old. We were living in Teaneck. I was playing in the kitchen, scooting around the floor on my big wheel." A wan smile came and went. "My mother had accidentally left the door to the basement open and, being a dumb little kid, I rode my trike right through the door and down the stairs. I was knocked out cold, but I guess what happened is that my mother heard the commotion and came running from the living room, only she tripped coming down the stairs herself and fractured her wrist trying to break her fall." Martina shook her head at the memory. "My collarbone was broken, and I had a mild concussion and lots of bruises, but nothing too serious."

"That's all there was to it?" She had mentioned the hard part—I didn't think I'd heard it yet. "The newspaper accounts say your mother had a facial bruises and a split lip when you two checked into the hospital."

"I guess that's true." She looked away, then back at me. "My mother . . . she'd been drinking that afternoon. I suppose she was worried about my father's appeal. Anyway, that's why she forgot to close the basement door when she came up from the laundry room and that's why she was in the living room lying down instead of keeping an eye on me and that's why she fell herself when she came down to get me." She said it in a rush, then in a smaller voice added, "She was drunk."

"And when your father came home. . . ."

"He found mom and me at the bottom of the stairs. I was crying and moaning, I remember, and my mother was trying to help me, but with her broken wrist. . . . Anyway, daddy was so scared for me and so angry at my mother, he slapped her. Hard. And when she screamed at him, he slapped her again. That was it. Daddy carried me to the car, and we all drove to the hospital."

The tears came again, a couple escaping this time and running down either cheek. "It's okay," I told her softly, leaning in over the table. After a long few seconds she suddenly straightened in the booth and took a surreptitious glance back toward the bar, her face changing from a look of abiding sadness to one of mild embarrassment. She touched each cheek with the back of her hand and cleared her throat.

"Well, that was stupid."

"Nonsense," I said. "Everybody needs a good cry once in a while, even an Ivy League lawyer."

She sipped at her wine. "It was a long time ago. It shouldn't bother me so much to discuss it, but it does. It's always been like some dirty little family secret that I wasn't supposed to know about, even though I was there."

A dirty little family secret. Now I knew why, for all those years, Frank had refused to talk about the incident and why, during that last meeting we had out in IdaRose Mack's garage, he had come at me with his fists rather than let me press him for details. It wasn't, as most people believed—as I had believed—a case of a man too small to own up to his own mistakes. It was all about a man whose sense of duty to his family compelled him to accept the condemnation that otherwise would've been directed at his wife.

"Daddy was always the strong one," Martina said, as if reading my mind. "My mother . . . don't get me wrong, I love her, I really do. But she's always been . . . kind of weak, I guess. She reminds me of Blanche from *A Streetcar Named Desire*."

"Dependent on the kindness of strangers?" I said.

"Yes, only in her case it isn't strangers she relies on, but her husbands. First my father, then Lou." Martina shrugged. "I guess she got used to being catered to when she was a showgirl—the flattery, the attention, someone always there to provide for her. It wouldn't occur to her not to let my father cover up for her. She would've taken it for granted, like she takes it for granted that Lou will jet her to Europe every August and pay off her gold card every month no questions asked."

Martina's blunt assessment of her mother brought to mind another fictional character—Norma Desmond from *Sunset Boulevard*, the faded silent-screen star who still believed the world was clamoring for her to make a comeback.

"The funny thing is," Martina continued, "Mom and Lou were made for each other. He spoils her and pampers her and parades her around like she's one of his thoroughbreds, and she loves every bit of it."

"Your stepfather owns race horses?"

"A couple—not that they've ever won anything. They're just another of his little indulgences, like his memorabilia collecting and his antique cars." She allowed herself a small smile. "He's like a sixty-year-old kid himself, in a lot of ways. He can swing a million-dollar business deal, and it doesn't excite him a bit, but let him find out there's a mint-condition Christy Mathews baseball card up for bids someplace, and he goes wild."

It was Mathewson, but I didn't bother to correct her. "He collects baseball memorabilia?"

"Baseball, football, hockey, basketball. As long as it has something to do with a New York team, past or present, Lou Garci has to have it. The basement of our house in Darlington looks like the sports wing at the Smithsonian."

"Interesting," I said as I poured the last of the Molson's into my glass. The ale was room temperature. I checked my watch—we'd been sitting there for two hours.

"Another glass of wine?" I asked Martina.

She shook her head and glanced at her own watch. "Half a carafe is my limit and, anyway, I don't have a lot of time. I've got plans for tonight. . . ."

"A few more questions and I'll let you go. I promise."

I ran a list of names past her—Gimp Smith, Alfie Klem, Harry Lundquist, and Richie Hirshberg. Lundquist got a small rise out of her, but she didn't know any more about her father's relationship with him than I'd been able to learn on my own. Of the other three, only Hirshberg rang any bells. He was an old friend of her parents, she told me. She knew Hirshberg also lived in the Saddle River area, because her mother had talked before about occasionally running into him at the country club, but she didn't know him personally.

Time was up. I paid the check with a credit card and tucked the receipt away in my wallet, then walked Martina out into the late afternoon sunshine. I offered to drive her back to the campus, but she had some shopping to do on the Commons. We chatted briefly—I wished her luck with her summer law-clerking job, she promised to give IdaRose a number where I could reach her in New York if I had any more questions—then I watched her pad off in her no-nonsense Keds, the big black leather bag bouncing against her hip, destroying the line of her designer suit.

CHAPTER 20

NEVER give coincidence the benefit of the doubt.

A grizzled city editor had given me that sage advice when I was a freshman police reporter: Before chalking up anything to chance or kismet or synchronicity, he would harp at me, take a second look at it, and then a third.

Prime example: Frank Wooley and his short-lived coaching job with the Geneva Cubs. Hot-headed former star gets a last shot to return to the game he loves. Two months into the season he bolts into the stands after a heckler—doing no damage—and an hour later he's cleaning out his locker, having resigned before he could be fired. Write it off as just another rash, impassioned act by a man with a reputation for exactly that sort of thing.

Until you begin to examine the coincidences.

First, it happened one day after Wooley got together with his old cronies—Alfie Klem, Gimp Smith, and con man Harry Lundquist—during a baseball memorabilia show.

Second, Wooley's former financial adviser, Richie Hirshberg, showed up shortly after the incident to discuss "business investments"—the same Richie Hirshberg who now acts as agent for one, possibly two, of the old cronies who were with Wooley at the memorabilia show.

Third, Wooley's daughter, Martina, began receiving regularly monthly payments of one thousand dollars two months after her father's brouhaha with the loudmouth in the stands. Money that supposedly came from checks that the pension fund people claim don't exist—the very same pension fund people who employ Gimp Smith.

And that's just for openers. Add that Hirshberg was the only member of the old crowd who had actually visited Wooley at the secluded Mack house, and that it was probably Hirshberg who had told the sportswriter, Mike Delfay, how to find the place. Now factor in the wild cards. Hirshberg lives near Saddle River, New Jersey, same as Wooley's ex-wife and her second husband, Lou Garci, and they all apparently belong to the same country club. And Lou Garci also just happens to be a major collector of baseball memorabilia.

Admittedly the last part may be a bit of a stretch, but forget Garci for a moment. If that crusty editor of mine was still breathing, he'd growl one word at me: extrapolate.

So here goes.

What if Frank Wooley's impetuous leap into the stands during that doubleheader at McDonough field wasn't prompted by a bellowing fan, but was a delayed reaction—pent-up stress—from something that had happened the day before? What if he had seen or participated in something illegal that night at the Stanton—a rigged poker game, maybe. One of Harry Lundquist's cons gone wrong?

And what if Klem and Smith were involved, too? Klem, at least, was a valuable commodity on the old jock circuit—autograph sessions, card shows, old-timers exhibitions. If he were implicated in something shady, wouldn't it be in his interest to pay to keep it quiet? And wouldn't his agent, assuming he were willing, be the logical choice to handle the negotiations for the payoff?

Interesting bit of speculation, the old city editor would say, but you gotta prove it before you can print it.

All right, but at least it's a starting point, a story angle that no one else had looked into—with the possible exception of the late Mike Delfay.

June was starting out right—summer temperatures without the humidity, a soft breeze rippling the lake. Too damned fine a day to waste indoors.

I divided Saturday morning between catching up on my yard

work and sitting out on the deck, sipping iced tea, and brooding about the Wooley assignment. I had a month to go before deadline, plenty of time, I told myself. But I still hadn't spoken with the ex-Mrs. Wooley and I hadn't even tried to contact Alfie Klem or Richie Hirshberg yet; in light of the brush-off I'd gotten from Gimp Smith, I was saving those two until after I'd talked to Harry Lundquist, hoping that he'd provide some leverage I could use on the others. Still, there were plenty of things I could be doing.

Resigned, I forced myself out of the deck chair, poured the iced tea over the railing, and went back inside.

I spent a couple of hours transposing the gist of my luncheon conversation with Martina Wooley from tape and notepad to my computer's hard disk, carefully working the new information into the story file I'd created earlier: Martina's revelations about the so-called domestic incident that had painted her father as an abuser, her memories of him and her mother in happier days, a sketch of Martina's current life as an honors graduate and an Ivy League law student. After weeks of digging into Frank Wooley's past only to come up with more and more dirt, it was a relief finally to write something hopeful, like finding a patch of blue peeking through a bank of thunder clouds. When I finished with the interview notes, I moved on to the tedious task of beginning a rough outline: basically a timeline of the key events in Wooley's life—his major-league debut, his World Series heroics, marriage to Evie, the public scrapes and court challenges and suspensions—here and there making note of a particular anecdote or telling quote that I knew I'd want to use when it came time to write the piece itself.

By mid-afternoon I had assuaged my Irish Catholic version of the Protestant work ethic enough to return with a clear conscience to the sunny deck, where I sipped a bottle of Molson's and paged through the book I'd taken out at the Geneva Public Library—*In Harm's Way; Family Violence and Its Aftermath* written by a pair of Harvard Ph.Ds. Every so often, I'd exchange the book for the cordless telephone and reflexively punch the redial button, letting it ring eight or ten times before turning my attention back to my reading and my beer. I was hoping to gain some insight into Kate Sumner's fragile psyche, but the book proved to be cold and dry and simplistic, nothing like the woman. By late afternoon, I decided to give the phone one more try, then go fishing. It rang only twice before a soft, breathy female voice came on the line.

"Garci residence."

I was so surprised that I'd finally gotten through, I didn't say anything for a split second, then blurted, "Is this Mrs. Garci? Evie Garci?"

"Yes, it is."

"Mrs. Garci, my name's Sheridan."

"Yes?" Not a glimmer of recognition, which meant the numerous messages I'd left on the answering machine at the other number had been forgotten or ignored, or never apprehended.

"I'm researching an article on your former husband, Frank Wooley, for *The Sporting Life*, Mrs. Garci, and I would appreciate a little of your time." I spoke fast but friendly and kept the spiel going, like one of those guys who call up to sell you vinyl replacement windows and don't give you a chance to say no. "I'm sure you must be very busy—I've been trying to reach you for two weeks—but I do need to get your point of view on a few things. Now, if you could begin by giving me . . . "

"Okay, okay, you've got my attention," she interrupted, the cool purr showing mild asperity. "You have your little pencil ready?"

"Uhh." I scrambled for my pad and pen. "All set."

She prefaced things with a lazy sigh, then delivered in an impersonal drone a statement that sounded as if it had been prepared for her by a State Department press secretary.

"Although our marriage ended some seventeen years ago, I'll always have warm memories of those early days with Frank and our dear daughter, Martina, in the little house in Teaneck. Despite the trials and tribulations that eventually drove us apart, the good times far outnumbered the bad. My daughter and I are thrilled that Frank Wooley's accomplishments are finally being recognized by the Baseball Hall of Fame in Cooperstown and we look forward to attending the induction ceremony in July." She took a studied pause before adding, "Did you get that?"

"Yes, I got it," I said, still scribbling. "Now, I have a few questions. You referred to 'the trials and tribulations' of the marriage, Mrs. Garci. I'd like to follow that up. . . . "

"I'm sure you would," she said dryly. "But I have no interest in reopening the public record on my previous marriage—I'm sure you can understand my position. And as for poor Frank's untimely and . . . distressing death, I can only add that I was shocked and saddened when I heard of it. Now, I don't mean to be rude, Mr. . . . whatever your name is, but I do have an engagement later this afternoon and I really have nothing more to say to the press."

I've had enough people hang up on me over the years to know what was coming next, so I quickly fell back on another bit of jaded wisdom provided me by that first city editor of mine: Nothing gets a mule's attention like a two-by-four between the eyes.

"Your daughter told me about falling down the cellar stairs, Mrs. Garci."

My frontal assault was met with a few tense seconds of absolute silence. Then, "I wondered where you got our unlisted number."

"I had lunch with Martina in Ithaca yesterday. . . . "

"She was just a baby when all that happened."

"She was four, Mrs. Garci, old enough to remember a trauma like that distinctly. . . . "

"The latch on the basement door was faulty," she insisted. "I asked Frank to fix it a dozen times, then he takes it out on me when the inevitable happens. I only turned my back on Martina for a minute. . . . "

"That's not how she remembers it, Mrs. Garci."

"She was a baby!" she snapped. "This is all water under the bridge, completely distorted by the newspapers. It was simply an accident—unavoidable—but it so frightened and enraged my husband that he struck out at me." She calmed herself with a slow intake of breath, letting it out dramatically before adding, "You people are always after a juicy quote. Try this. My scars, both physical and emotional, have long since healed and I bear Frank no grudges: He was always a very volatile man—as recent events have shown. Now, that is absolutely all I have to say on the subject, Mr. . . . "

"Sheridan," I said, but I was saying it to a dead phone.

My call to Evie Garci hadn't done much to improve my story or my frame of mind so, rather than sit around the cottage and stew, I decided to look up the man whose allotted fifteen minutes of fame had ended up costing Frank Wooley his coaching job. According to the local papers, the fan who had heckled Wooley three summers earlier was a Dresden man named John Eberling. None of the articles I'd found in the *Daily News* clips file had listed a street address, but the phone directory showed only one Eberling for the small lakeside community.

Dresden is located off Route 14 about eight miles north of Mohaca Springs. Despite the wave of growth that had swept through most of the Finger Lakes in recent years, Dresden had managed to remain largely undiscovered by tourists and developers alike—some would say for good reason. Its most significant landmark is the Greenidge Station power plant, the soaring chimney stacks of which can be seen for miles. The small community is essentially a blue-collar glitch along the west shore of Seneca Lake, a place where trailers and tar-paper shacks stand alongside sturdier homes, and lawn statues of grinning black jockeys persist.

The address I wanted was halfway down a narrow street that dead ended at a small public beach. The house was a modest ranch that had grown a couple of shed-roofed additions along the way. I parked the Bronco in the driveway—two gravel-filled ruts with a strip of weedy grass running between them—and climbed the stoop to the front door.

"Welcome, welcome."

The man who answered my knock was wearing powder-blue sweats, running shoes, and a smarmy grin. "You're not dressed well enough to be a Jehovah's Witness," he said. "Let me guess—either you're selling something or you've got a petition you want me to sign."

CHAPTER 21

No on both counts," I said, forcing a smile. I gave my name and occupation. "I'm looking for John Eberling. I have a few questions for a story I'm working on."

"Well, you've come to the right place, such as it is. I'm John Eberling. But everybody calls me Johnny."

He wasn't what I expected. I'd formed a mental picture of a pot-bellied, middle-aged man whose sole reason for going to a ballgame was to drink too much beer and scream abuse down onto the field. This guy was maybe thirty-two or three, slim and fit, with slicked-back black hair and a set of teeth that looked like they'd glow in the dark.

He cocked his head to one side. "I'll bet you're doing something for the Sunday entertainment section of the *Daily News*, right?"

"Afraid not. I'm doing a piece on Frank Wooley for *The Sporting Life*."

"Ach." His mouth turned down into an exaggerated frown. "I was hoping for a little free publicity for my act." He stepped back from the door and waved me through. "Well, hell, you might as well come on in. I was about to go for a run, but who needs it?"

I followed him into a small living room dominated by a large-screen television. A round coffee table sat between a matched pair of brown loveseats, its surface hidden underneath magazines, empty Chinese take-out cartons, and a half-filled coffee mug.

"Forgive the mess, but I'm between girlfriends at the moment," he said as he dropped onto one of the loveseats. "Which means I don't have anyone to clean up after me, or nag me into doing it myself."

I made the appropriate noises, then settled into the other loveseat. "What sort of act do you have, Johnny?"

"I'm a close-up magician. Cards, coins, foam rubber balls. Part-time, anyway; gigs are hard to find. My straight job is bartending."

We spent a few minutes on Eberling's favorite subjects—prestidigitation and himself. He was currently working behind the bar at the Holiday Inn in Canandaigua, he told me, where, during his breaks, management allowed him to "work the lounge for tips," performing sleight-of-hand tricks for the patrons while the piano trio was between sets.

"Then I do a regular Sunday gig at Laugh Riot, a comedy club in Rochester—no bartending, just magic and patter. That's where it's at these days, the comedy clubs, but you gotta have the shtick to go with the tricks—everybody wants Penn and Teller. So far I've got about twenty minutes worth of decent material, but you need a good forty minutes of A-list stuff if you wanna headline."

I commiserated again, then moved the conversation around to Frank Wooley. "I'm curious about the incident in July of '88."

Eberling smirked. "The infamous battle of the bleachers. Shit, I got more press for that little fiasco than I've had in a dozen years of performing."

"It did get a lot of local play," I said, suddenly wondering if perhaps the whole thing had been a cheap publicity stunt. "Was that your intention?"

"What, you mean . . . geez, give me a break, huh? Christ, when I go out and make an ass of myself it's usually an accident, okay?"

"So what prompted you to do it? You must've been riding Wooley pretty hard to get him to come after you."

Eberling sighed. "To tell you the truth, I don't remember half the junk I yelled at him." An apologetic shrug. "I only went there to give him a piece of my mind, but I had a few beers to psych myself up—big mistake. I found out a couple quarts of brew and the hot sun don't mix too well. You'd think a bartender'd know that."

"What did you have against Wooley?" I asked as I eased a notepad and pen from my jacket.

He glanced at the pad, then leaned back and propped his Reeboks on a worn copy of *People* magazine. "Actually, I'm not supposed to talk about any of this. That was part of the settlement."

"Settlement? I don't remember reading about any lawsuit coming out of this."

"There wasn't. I wasn't even considering one, but, hey. . . . " He threw his hands up. "Somebody wants to hand me fifty-three hundred bucks for a torn shirt, who am I to argue about it, right?"

"Frank Wooley paid you fifty-three hundred dollars?"

"It was paid on his behalf." Eberling shrugged again. "But, like I said, I wasn't supposed to talk about it."

"Did you sign anything to that effect, Johnny?"

"I didn't sign shit. I just said fine by me and took the cash."

"Well, then, I don't see that you're legally obligated," I tried.

He didn't bite, even though I could see he was salivating to talk; he wouldn't have allowed me into the house otherwise. "Maybe I'm not legally obligated," he said, stressing legally. "But I'm not sure I want to see my name tied in with this whole deal again anyway. Like I said, it was kind of embarrassing."

It was my turn to shrug. "The incident will be part of my article, including your name. It's too significant a chapter in Wooley's life not to be included. It's up to you, if you don't want a million readers of *The Sporting Life* to hear your side. . . . "

"Well, you kinda got me there," Eberling said, nodding slowly. "A million readers, huh? Aw, what the hell, the guy's dead now anyway, right?"

To be honest, I'm not sure what the circulation numbers are for *The Sporting Life* but, in any case, it was a lot more people than would ever read about Johnny Eberling in the Sunday entertainment section of the *Finger Lakes Daily News*—a fact that didn't have to be spelled out for my host. For the next twenty minutes he talked nonstop while I scribbled away furiously.

According to Eberling, he had met Frank Wooley at the Stanton the day of the baseball memorabilia show. Eberling was working behind the bar in the taproom when Wooley and two other men came in for drinks following the autograph session. Eberling overheard the three men talking about a card game that was being organized in a suite upstairs and he got himself invited to sit in after his shift ended.

"I know my way around a deck of cards pretty good, but I didn't tell them that—let 'em figure I was just a dumb bartender, right? Not that I planned to cheat or anything. I don't do that, even though I know all the tricks."

"Uh huh," I said, straight faced.

When he got up to the room about an hour later, he saw Wooley standing in a corner, talking with another black man. The two men who had been with Wooley in the bar were involved in a game of stud poker with two other men, one of whom he did recognize: former pitching star Alfie Klem. Eberling bought some chips from the other black man—presumably Gimp Smith—who was acting as house banker for the game.

"Anyway, we played maybe forty-five minutes, the deal went around a few times, and I'm getting hammered. I mean, I'm catching some decent hands, so I stay in, right? But they're never quite good enough. Meantime this goofy-looking guy I'd met downstairs is winning every big pot that comes along and squealing about it like a pig in shit."

Annoyed at being dry-cleaned by a roomful of amateurs, Eberling began paying closer attention as the deck moved around the table. He soon noticed that the squealer's big pots came up whenever his friend from the bar had the deal.

"So I start really concentrating on this other old dude, right? And I couldn't fucking believe it. The guy was a deuce dealer." He read my confusion and leaned forward, elbows on knees. "Dealing seconds, man. The son of a bitch was feeding cards to his buddy. It shouldn't've taken me so long to catch on, but this guy was good—a real mechanic. Not only is he using the old heel peek to check out the top card, he's using a glim to scope out the bottom card, too."

I shook my head. "You're way ahead of me here. The heel peek—that's where you sneak a look at the top card by quickly prying up the edge, right?"

"Yeah. Usually you use the base of the thumb, right here . . . " He held up one of his hands to demonstrate. " . . . to lift the inner corner of the top card, so that your palm is concealing the move from everybody else. If the card looks good, you double deal it to yourself or, in this case, your partner."

"What about a glim? What's that?"

Eberling gave me a look that fell somewhere between pity and scorn. "It's a reflecting surface, like a tiny mirror inserted into the butt end of a cigarette, or a phony ice cube. Only the mechanic in this game was using a cup of black coffee. Very cute."

"You mean he's able to maneuver the deck over a cup of coffee and see the bottom card reflected in it," I said, not trying to hide my skepticism. "And he does this so fast nobody sees him do it?"

"Basic sleight of hand, man. Magicians do it all the time, it just takes practice. Here, I'll show you." He dug a pack of cards out of the drawer in the end table and handed them to me for a shuffle, instructing me to take a look at the bottom card. When I gave the deck back, he had the half-empty cup of coffee positioned on the coffee table near his left hand. Then he began dealing us each five cards, the first—the hole card—dealt face down, the others face up. I had a pair of sevens showing and a king in the hole. Eberling had no pairs showing, ace high.

"You're gonna bet the pair, right?" he asked.

I shrugged. "Sure."

"What was the bottom card?"

"The ace of clubs."

He turned over his hole card—the ace of clubs—then turned on the Pepsodent smile. "I win."

He explained that, had the bottom card been something he couldn't use, he could've snuck a look at the top card in the deck, or he could've simply dealt honestly and folded when he saw he couldn't beat my pair of sevens.

"The point is," Eberling concluded, "you pick up an edge every second or third time you have the deal, see? So you pick your spots and make your play when you can. Working with a partner is the best way to do it because the dealer can give himself a so-so hand and bet it like crazy—which suckers everyone else into seeing his raises. The dealer ends up losing the hand, but his partner ends up winning." He laughed. "I gotta admit, this guy Lester was damn good. He was even double duking—feeding me and Klem and the fifth player decent hands so we'd stay in longer and bump up the pot for his partner."

"The mechanic's name was Lester?"

"Yeah. Hank Lester. The guy was probably pushing sixty but, man, he was slick."

Hank Lester, I wrote in my notepad, also known as Harry Lundquist.

"What was the other guy's name, his partner?" I asked.

"The happy squealer?" Eberling scrunched up his brow. "I don't know—Truman, Truehart? Something like that."

"So the game included five players; Hank Lester and his partner, Truman or whatever. Then there was you, Alfie Klem, and—who was the fifth guy?"

"Don't remember his name, either. He was just some chump from the memorabilia show downstairs. He and Klem were losing almost as bad as I was—and I was down over three hundred bucks before I knew what was happening."

"So what were Frank Wooley and—the other black guy doing while the game was going on?"

"Wooley didn't stick around too long. He and the other black dude went out in the hall together, I remember, but the other one came back alone and just sort of hung around, watching the game, selling chips, like that."

"So Wooley wasn't really a part of the scam."

"C'mon, man. He was the carrot—the celebrity shill. He's the famous ballplayer who attracts the baseball collector nuts up to the room for a friendly party, then Lester and the squealer do their number."

After Eberling realized what was happening, he said, he decided to get his money back by pulling a few tricks of his own. He picked up a couple of pots, but then caught Lester eyeballing him. Lester called a break in the game and he and Smith maneuvered Eberling out into the hallway.

"They called me a hustler and told me to get lost," he said. "So I laughed in their face, told 'em it takes one to know one. Shit, that wasn't too bright. Next thing I know the black guy grabs me and Lester sucker punches me in the gut and they toss me in an elevator." He puffed himself up like a gamecock. "I could've handled a couple of over-the-hill assholes like them, but I gotta be careful of my hands. Anyway, I was working at the

Stanton at the time and I didn't want to make too big a stink and get myself canned."

"So what did you do?" I asked.

"I went home and kicked the furniture around and got more pissed the more I thought about it. I mean, me, a professional card manipulator, getting jacked up like that! So the next day I called the desk at the Stanton and found out everybody had checked out. I didn't know how to find Lester, but I sure as hell knew where his buddy, Frank Wooley, was gonna be later that day. So I went out to McDonough Park, bought myself a seat along the first base line, and sort of vented my frustration at Wooley." He grinned ruefully. "You know the rest."

"Not quite," I said. "What about the fifty-three hundred dollars?"

The grin widened. "That's the silver lining. After the tussle with Wooley—all he did was rip the front of my shirt—I got escorted out by a security guy. Then a sports reporter from the *Daily News* catches up to me in the parking lot and asks a few questions. Well, hell, I was sobering up fast by then, so I tell the reporter I just got carried away and I drive home to sleep it off, right? So about ten o'clock the next morning, I get this phone call—the guy wouldn't give his name, but he's offering me five grand; 'Forgive and forget the whole unfortunate weekend,' is how he put it. So I said what about the three hundred that Wooley and Lester took off me at the Stanton, and the guy says fine, we've got ourselves a gentlemen's agreement—just like that."

The part-time magician raised his hands and twirled his finely manicured fingers in a flourish. "Shazam! Two days later I open my mailbox and find a padded envelope with fifty-three hundred bucks cash stuffed into it."

CHAPTER 22

As it turned out, my interview with Johnny Eberling was the last thing I accomplished on the Wooley story for nearly a week. Monday morning I got a call from the editorial manager of the Bishop Group, which owns a chain of dailies in several small cities in Pennsylvania and New York. Two Elmira teenagers were on trial for murder, kidnapping, and half-a-dozen lesser charges. The pair, a boy and a girl, had allegedly snatched a baby from a day-care center and gone on a shooting spree down Route 15, robbing several convenience stores and leaving one luckless management trainee dead along the way. A veteran reporter had been assigned to cover the proceedings, the managing editor told me, but he had been rear ended that morning and was laid up in the hospital just as the trial was about to go into its final week. The editor needed an experienced replacement pronto and, since I'd done some work for Bishop in the past, he called me first.

I could've begged off, but I didn't. The trial was getting national play thanks to the defense attorney's claim that his clients were influenced by a movie—the papers had already dubbed the case "The *Raising Arizona* Defense"—which meant the assignment was too good to turn down.

The trial ended on Thursday morning when the stony jury returned with a guilty verdict on most counts, including murder and kidnapping on the boy, nineteen, and kidnapping and aiding and abetting on his seventeen-year-old girlfriend. I stayed around long enough to hear the judge set a sentencing date, then I filed my final story and drove home.

I thought about kicking back and forgetting the Wooley assignment for another day, but the mail brought a letter from the warden at Auburn, approving my request to see Harry Lundquist the following week. So I called the prison to sort out the particulars of my visit. And then, since I was already at my desk, I resigned myself to getting a couple of hours in on the first draft before packing it in for an early dinner at Ralph and Kay's.

"You look beat, Sheridan." Ralph Cramer poured me another cup of decaf, then topped off his own mug before returning the orange pot to the warming tray behind the lunch counter. "That Wooley story must be dragging you down. You spoke to Alfie Klem yet?"

"Not yet." I had stopped by the diner for a burger last Saturday, shortly after my interview with Johnny Eberling. As always, Ralph had wanted an update on my current assignments, so I used the opportunity to do a little thinking out loud about the cast of characters I'd been assembling over the previous weeks. "I've been working out of town most of the week."

"Oh, yeah, that *Raising Arizona* case. That's why you're so worn out, huh?"

I nodded. "Long week down in Elmira."

"Mark Twain's buried down there in Elmira, y'know."

"Yeah, I know." I sipped the coffee and, with a silent apology to dolphins everywhere, took another bite of Kay's blue-plate special, tuna casserole.

"Knowing Twain, I'll bet he'd have something clever to say about spendin' time in Elmira." He took a last drag on his Camel before dropping the butt in the trash barrel under the counter. At Ralph and Kay's, the smoking section was wherever Ralph happened to light up—provided Kay wasn't around. "Twain would've said something tart, like 'The coldest winter I ever spent was the summer I spent in San Francisco.' I figured a writer could come up with something more memorable than 'Long week down in Elmira.' "

"Okay. How about, 'All in all, I'd rather be in Philadelphia.' "

"W. C. Fields," he said dismissively. "Your problem is, your mind's on the Wooley thing. You said he finished up with the Phillies, didn't you?"

"His last four years in the bigs," I said. I had no idea where Ralph was going with all this and I wasn't sure I wanted to go along. It had been a busy few days, covering the trial, interviewing family members and attorneys, then going back to the local paper's newsroom each night to hammer out my stories on a Royal manual that should've been retired along with H. L. Mencken. But Ralph was relentless.

"I believe you also said that it was in Philadelphia that Wooley hooked up with Alfie Klem," he said, squinting at me with that leathery, sunbaked face.

"Yeah, so?" I said warily.

"So, I was only gonna say that Batavia's not too far. 'Bout thirty miles west of Rochester, I'd guesstimate."

"And what does Batavia have to do with anything?"

"Funny you should ask." With a move that would do Johnny Eberling proud, Ralph slipped a hand under the counter and brought up a section of newspaper. "Says here Klem's gonna be signing autographs at a party house in Batavia on Saturday, Sheridan. Just thought you ought to know, is all."

Batavia, a city of perhaps ten thousand, squats alongside the state thruway about halfway between Rochester and Buffalo. Local industry includes a turf farm, which harvests rolls of sod for lawns, the Melton Shirt Company, and Batavia Downs, a harness-racing track. It's a hardworking, blue-collar town where men and boys alike wear the colors of their favorite teams—most often the navy and red of the Buffalo Bills—and where professional jocks of any stripe are at once envied and admired. In short, a town where a sports memorabilia promoter could make a small killing. The autograph session was scheduled to begin at one o'clock, but it was closer to two by the time I pulled into the crowded lot at Murella's Party House.

I'd gotten a late start, in part because I'd overslept that morning and in part because I had made another visit to the library in Geneva before continuing the eighty-mile drive to Batavia. There I looked up Klem's record in the *Baseball Encyclopedia* and skimmed a few other sources for background on the colorful pitcher, including an autobiography he'd done a few years before. Alford 'Alfie' Klem had pitched for six teams over a twenty-two year career that began in St. Louis in 1959 and ended with the Toronto Blue Jays in 1980. Once a power pitcher, he had injured his arm early on and had been forced to become a junkballer. His repertoire included a diminished fastball, a big curve, a knuckleball, and—as he openly admitted in his autobiography—"the best spitter in the big leagues." The assortment had proved good enough to win 272 games, the record showed. It also showed that Klem had managed to lose almost as many.

In his good years, he had been very good, but much of his career had been marked by mediocrity. The star status he eventually achieved owed as much to his candor and down-home humor as to his accomplishments on the mound. Widely dismissed as a simple country boy from Pine Bluff, Arkansas, Klem had in fact been the son of a prominent local doctor, and a college man himself, signing with St. Louis after his junior year at Clemson. In the decade since his retirement, he had become a popular speaker on the sports banquet and autograph circuits.

I found a spot for the Bronco at the far end of the lot and joined a short line in the lobby, mostly middle-aged men and adolescent boys. A five-dollar fee got me into the main room—a broad, low-ceilinged banquet hall. Running down the middle of the room were two parallel rows of display tables where baseball cards and other collectibles were on sale. At one end of the hall sat two smaller tables, each sequestered within a maze of velvet ropes like the kind used to channel the clientèle at a bank. These tables were occupied by the affair's featured stars, Alfie Klem to the left and, to the right, former Red Sox slugger Dick Kadinski.

The admission charge bought a chance to browse the baseball memorabilia, where a fan could expect to drop some serious money—I spotted a 1968 Nolan Ryan rookie card on sale for twelve hundred dollars. An autograph by either of the two retired ballplayers was extra, too—in Klem's case, fifteen bucks worth of extra.

A fat guy in a one-size-fits-all Mets cap manned a card table outside the roped-off area, collecting the signing fees. I told him why I was there, then waited while he conferred with Klem, who was signing a ball for a kid whose dad looked a lot more excited than he did. When the fat man came back, he told me to wait for a lull in the action, which came about five minutes later.

"What's *The Sporting Life* doin' way the hell and gone out here?" Klem bellowed as he waved me over to his table. "Don't tell me you're a staff writer—those boys don't never leave Manhattan 'less it's to jet out to the west coast."

"I'm freelance," I said, extending my hand. "T.S.W. Sheridan—Sheridan will do."

"Sheridan will do what?" Klem asked with a wink as he whipped my arm up and down. "Call me Alfie or Alf, or Klem if you want; anything but Alford or daddy." Another wink, followed by a shrewd squint. "Understand you're doin' a spread on my old pard, Frank Wooley. You got a sealed deal there, Sheridan, or you writin' this on speculation?"

"I'm under contract, Mr. . . . Alfie. We're scheduled for the magazine's hall of fame issue next month."

"Good enough." He cocked his head. "Y'know, a lot of Frank's old teammates prob'ly wouldn't wanna talk, given the way Frank went out. But not Alfie Klem. I wasn't raised to turn my back on folks just because they've had some trouble."

Or miss a chance to get his name into a major publication.

"C'mon around and sit awhile. We'll get this done while the kiddies are busy pestering Kadinski—now, don't you go quoting me on that." Wink.

I settled in one of the two ladder-back chairs tucked in behind the signing table, Klem taking the other. He was a tall man with wide, bony shoulders, an ample belly spilling over his western belt buckle, and long bandy legs stuffed into a pair of snakeskin boots. The eyes were a washed-out gray, his thin blond hair blow-dryed and teased into a cotton candy swirl atop his head. His appearance and attitude suited a fading country-western star doing perpetual two-week engagements in a Las Vegas lounge. Only his hands—huge and strong, yet supple—pegged him as a man who had once hurled baseballs for a living.

I started off with a soft toss.

"I understand you and Frank were friends off the field, too. That seems like an odd pairing."

Klem grinned. "You mean the southern redneck and the black militant? Hell, I don't give a damn about a fella's politics. Show me a man likes to have a good time and I'll run with him. We had our share of choir boys back on the Phillies, but Frank wasn't one of 'em. He liked his bourbon after a game, liked the ponies and a friendly game of cards now and again, same as me." He dropped the grin. "God, old Frank. He was one tough little son of a gun. Good hitter, great wheels, and nobody better on turning the double play—a pitcher's best friend. I'll never forget a game in Chicago in 1969. I had a shutout goin' with the wind blowin' out at Wrigley, if you can believe it. . . . "

Klem went on for half an hour, one tale after the other, while I slipped in a question here and there to try and guide him in the right direction.

"Did you know Frank's wife, Evie?"

"Met her in spring trainin' a couple times. Good lookin' woman—and I mean gooood lookin'. Reminds me of my first wife, bless her mercenary little heart. . . . "

"Your agent, Richie Hirshberg, used to be a close friend of Wooley's, too, didn't he?"

"Yeah, I met him through Frank. Used to be a long-haired flag-burnin' fool but, hey, I ain't political. Man knows his business, that's all I need to know. He put me into this beer commercial a few years back. . . . "

"You mentioned that you and Wooley had common interests in horse racing, cards, that sort of thing."

"Hell, pardner, if you don't golf, you gotta do somethin' to pass the time between games. Never forget one time over at Garden State, me and Frank and Bud Molina—our catcher? We teamed up on an exacta. . . . "

"How did you feel when Wooley was suspended for associating with a professional gambler?"

"Aw, that was a load of manure from the git-go. Frank and me were stars, pard. We had people hangin' around us all the time, didn't know who half of 'em were. I remember this time I was havin' dinner at Bookbinder's, this seafood place in Philly. . . . "

"These hangers-on, they included Gimp Smith and Harry Lundquist?"

"Hey, now, old Gimp wasn't no leech. He was a ballplayer himself, y'know, before he blew out his arm. He could really bring it, too—I'm talkin' gas. Sorta wild, though. Why, I remember back in '65 . . . "

"Let's get back to Harry Lundquist, Alfie."

"The sharpy Frank took the fall for with the commissioner? Can't tell you much about him, pard." He put on a puzzled frown and scratched at one of his sideburns. "Like I said, the whole thing was blown out of proportion, you ask me. I mean, Frank wasn't found to be bettin' on ball games or nothin' like that. He just buddied up with the wrong kinda guy. I'll tell you this—this Lundquist wasn't part of our regular crowd, I'm sure of that."

I looked up from my note taking. "Are you saying that you didn't personally associate with Harry Lundquist?"

He looked horrified at the suggestion. "Me? Hell, no! I never met the son of a bitch. Never saw Frank hangin' with him, either, but like I say, there were plenty of groupies and gofers around back then, so maybe I just didn't notice." He heaved his wide shoulders. "Anyhow, me and Frank weren't joined at the hip. Just because we partied on a Saturday night don't mean I knew what he was up to the rest of the week."

I continued to stare at Klem, digesting what he was telling me and comparing it to what I'd already heard from Al Hargis and Johnny Eberling. Was it possible that Klem didn't know that the "Hank Lester" he had played cards with at the Stanton was actually Harry Lundquist? Or was Klem, like most good storytellers, a gifted liar?

"When was the last time you saw Frank Wooley?" I asked.

He scratched at the sideburn again. "Lessee, that'd be about three years back. Frank was still coachin' for that minor-league outfit in Geneva, and I was in town to do an autograph session, as I recall."

"That was the weekend Wooley was fired."

"Well, I guess it was, now I think back. That happened the day after I left, I think. I do so many of these things, you get so you can't keep track." His eyes drifted past me. "I don't mean to rush you, pard, but there's some folks in line for my John Hancock and the promoter's gettin' antsy."

I glanced over my shoulder. Three little boys and a middle-aged man were standing back behind the ropes, impatiently rocking back and forth in their Nikes.

"Maybe we could get together later?" I suggested.

"Wish I could, pard, but I'm doin' that charity banquet thing here right after the show, then me and the promoters are gonna mosey over to take in the trotters at Batavia Downs." He grinned. "Catch me next time, huh?"

"One last thing," I insisted. "That autograph session you did in Geneva. You were involved in a card game upstairs at the hotel afterward."

"I was?"

"I've got a source who says you were."

He tossed up his hands. "Okay, I probably was. Like I say, you're on the road as much as me, you lose track of where you are now, let alone where you were three years ago."

"This game should be more memorable, Alfie. Frank Wooley and Gimp Smith were both there. . . . "

"The three of us been in so many all nighters. . . . "

"There was also a guy calling himself Hank Lester, better known as Harry Lundquist. The game I'm talking about was a setup, Alfie. Lundquist and another guy were cheating—double dealing."

Klem's watery gray eyes opened wide. "You kiddin' me? Hell, that proves my point, don't it? I wouldn't know Lundquist if he was standin' right in front of me. Damn, imagine old Frank Wooley lettin' me walk into a thing like that." He slapped his hands down on his knees and stood to stretch, letting me know the interview was over.

"Anyway, pard, it's water under the bridge. If I had a dime for every dollar somebody cheated me outa, I wouldn't have to work so many of these damn shindigs—but don't you go quotin' me on that," he added with a wink.

CHAPTER 23

Y OU must think I'm a classic bitch."

"No, I don't."

"I just misdirected everything. It was that stupid actor, Allan, that I was furious with."

"I know."

"I feel so embarrassed—the way I snapped at you, like any of this was your fault."

"I could've been a little more understanding myself," I said. I took a long swallow from my glass of lemonade. "It has to be tough, being a single parent—managing the home front and a full-time job."

"You sound like you've been reading *Ms.* magazine, Sheridan. Have you been boning up on how to handle anxiety-ridden women?"

"Of course not," I said, trying to push a certain pair of Harvard professors out of mind. "I'm just a sensitive, nineties kind of a guy."

We were on the cedar deck attached to the back of Kate's house. The rest of the small yard was taken up with a winding gravel path and several planting areas bordered with landscape timbers. Across the back was a high privacy fence. Despite the closeness of the neighboring houses and the traffic noises from busy Lake Avenue a block away, it was a pleasant retreat on an overly warm June night. Or it would have been if the two of us had been able to put aside the scene that had occurred earlier.

After my truncated interview with Alfie Klem, I had hung around Murella's Party House for another hour and a half, hoping to get a few more minutes with the infamous old spitballer before the sports banquet. But small clutches of fathers and sons with items to be signed kept dribbling in all afternoon and, after plunking down fifteen dollars, most of them wanted a story or two from the garrulous Klem to go with the autograph. At four o'clock Klem and Kadinski, surrounded by promoters and gladhanders, headed for a door at the back of the hall. Just then a PA announcement came on, thanking everyone for participating and asking those of us who didn't have dinner tickets to leave so that the tables could be set up for the banquet.

Deciding to give it one last try, I climbed over the velvet ropes and angled toward the same door Klem and his entourage were aiming for.

"Alfie, if you could spare a minute," I called to him, but he continued on, disappearing through the open door without a glance in my direction. Meanwhile a couple of bruisers who looked like a tag team from the World Wrestling Federation formed a wall in front of me.

"Do you have a dinner ticket, sir?" one of them asked.

"I'm a reporter," I tried, holding up my pad as if it were a press pass. "I just want a word with Alfie Klem. . . . "

"Dinner tickets are forty dollars, sir. The money goes to local charities. You wanna buy a ticket, you can stay."

"Look, I don't want to stay for dinner, I . . . "

The polite one nodded to his silent partner, who hooked a giant hand over my shoulder and twisted his wrist, turning me 180 degrees.

"The door you want is that way, sir."

This time, I didn't argue.

By the time I backtracked to Rochester and checked into a motel, it was after five. I tossed my bags onto the bed, took a shower, and changed my clothes, then hurried on to Kate's house. I had called the night before and made arrangements to pick her up at a quarter to six for an early dinner and a movie, followed, I hoped, by a romantic couple of hours back at my room. I was almost forty minutes late arriving, which meant the dinner would have to be rushed a bit if we were going to make our movie at eight. Hardly a major catastrophe—which is why I was so surprised when Kate greeted me at the door with fire in her eyes.

"Sheridan! Where the hell have you been?"

"I got delayed in Batavia. Nice to know you missed me, though." I tried to lighten the mood with a smile and a patronizing wink I must've contracted from Alfie Klem. Big mistake.

Kate stared darts into me. "I hate it when people are late—Michael was always late—it's just so goddamn rude. Shit!" She threw up her hands, one of which, I noticed, was clutching a phone directory. "This is such a mess!"

"Hey, c'mon, Kate, don't go ballistic," I said, borrowing one of her favorite agency phrases. "We can catch a later movie if . . ."

"No we can't," she said, biting off the words. "Because I got a call from Bram Goddard an hour ago. That miserable excuse for an actor I hired to play Packy Penguin quit this afternoon and now Bram informs me that because we have no backup available and because Mohaca Springs Wine Coolers is my goddamn account, I have to spend from seven until nine tonight standing around at a supermarket opening in Newark, acting like a fool and sweating like a pig inside that stupid penguin suit!"

"Why don't you tell Bram to stuff it!" I said, which constituted big mistake number two.

"Because I have a career to think about and responsibilities, that's why," Kate seethed. "Unlike some people, Sheridan, I didn't inherit a house—I have a mortgage to pay."

Maybe that stung a little more than I like to admit, or maybe I was still chafing at the way those two bozos had intimidated me back at the party house. Whatever the reason, I came back with a line I regretted even before it was all the way out of my big mouth.

"Some career, traipsing around in a penguin suit."

My third and final big mistake. The darts suddenly upgraded to nuclear missiles, and she slammed the door in my face. Two minutes of ringing the doorbell brought me little Mandy, who asked me why her mother was in the kitchen crying. Now feeling like a total scumbag, I took Mandy's hand and we walked to the kitchen. Kate was alternately thumbing through the phone book, wiping the back of her hand across her wet eyes, and trying to punch out a number. After apparently getting a busy signal, she groaned and slammed down the handset.

"I'm sorry, Kate," I said.

"Oh, just forget it, okay?" She sighed, the anger draining away, replaced by frustration. "I'm sorry, too. It's just, nothing's gone right today. The babysitter called to cancel twenty minutes ago, so now I don't have anyone to watch Mandy and I'm already late. I'm supposed to pick up the suit at the agency and drive out to Newark."

"I'm a fool when it comes to a lot of things," I said, trying a grin. "But babysitting I'm good at. Call my niece and nephew if you want references."

"Oh, God, that would be great, Sheridan—a life saver. I've got a lasagna made up in the freezer, all you have to do is microwave it."

"Nah." I looked down at Mandy, who was still clutching my hand. "What d'you think, sweetheart? Should we order in a pizza and a liter of coke, or make a run to Burger King?"

"Pizza, pizza, pizza!"

"I feel like I'm going to explode," I told Kate now as we relaxed on the deck.

She frowned ruefully. "From the pizza, you mean, or from my little temper tantrum?"

It was almost ten when Kate made it back from Newark. I was half asleep in front of the television. Mandy had long since gone to bed, losing interest half-way through cable's umpteenth showing of the *Teenage Mutant Ninja Turtles* movie. After a few hugs, Kate and I got out the lemonade and adjourned to the relative coolness of the backyard deck.

"I'm sorry I was such a bitch," she said again as she slumped back against the lawn chair. Her hair was plastered to the side of her head, thanks to two hours in a hot penguin suit, and her expressive brown eyes were downcast, seeming to melt into the mascara that had bled down either cheek. She looked like a Barbie doll left too long at the bottom of her daughter's toy chest.

"Make you a deal," I said. "You stop apologizing for being human and I'll promise not to whine about the frustrations I'm having with this Wooley story."

"Actually, I was wondering how that's going."

"Really?"

"Really."

"Well—okay." I told her what I'd learned about the memorabilia show and the rigged poker game at the Stanton. Then, treading lightly, I brought up my conversations with Martina Wooley and her mother, Evie. She frowned as she listened, running a hand absently threw her thick hair.

"So your instincts were right all along," she said after a moment, a note of concession in her words. "Frank Wooley apparently wasn't the abuser everybody thought."

"He did slap Evie around pretty good after Martina's fall," I said. "But, no, there doesn't seem to have been any pattern of violence, as far as I can tell."

"I'm glad." She sipped her lemonade. "But the rest of what you've learned doesn't sound good. What I don't understand is what Wooley would have to gain by helping Lundquist cheat people? Why would he be foolish enough to get mixed up with that man again?"

"Money, if you believe Wooley was that greedy."

Kate studied me while she rattled the ice cubes in her glass. "But you don't believe he was."

"I don't know. He didn't live like a man who had much money—or needed it." I waved at a passing mosquito, dismissing the thought along with the pest. "Maybe I'm looking at it with my heart instead of my eyes."

"Your heart told you Wooley wasn't the kind of man who'd harm his daughter," Kate reminded me.

"Yeah, well, I've never gotten too far simply by following my heart."

"Mmm, tell me about it."

We sat through a comfortable silence, Kate in the lawn chair, me half sprawled on a big chaise lounge, both of us too weary to wrestle further with the Wooley conundrum. Eventually, she said, "Before I get too vegetative, I wondered if you'd like to see a Little Feat concert down at the Finger Lakes Performing Arts Center next weekend. We got free tickets through the agency; a bunch of us are going down. I thought we could meet in Canandaigua, save you some driving."

"Sounds good," I murmured, my eyes closed. "Maybe we can sort out the details tomorrow, over brunch?"

She groaned. "I'm afraid we might as well forget about doing anything together tomorrow, Sheridan. I've got to put on the bird suit again; ten to two at the Italian Festival downtown. Maybe you're right—I should tell Bram to shove this job."

"What, and give up show business?"

That, at least, got a tiny grin. I made room on the chaise lounge and waved her over. She slumped next to me and laid her head against my shoulder. We stared vacantly out at the tiny yard and breathed in the night air, Kate looping a leg over mine while I gently ran my fingers along the back of her neck.

I'm not sure which of us fell asleep first.

CHAPTER 24

THE main gate at Auburn Correctional Facility is flanked by twin brick towers with Gothic crenelations adorning the top, but that's where the prison's resemblance to Camelot ends. Next to the right tower is a glass guard station, mounted above the twelve-foot iron fence that runs along the front of the prison grounds. Around the corner on the north side, the fence gives way to a higher, solid wall that looms over the public sidewalk and casts a permanent shadow on the lines of people who wait to be checked through the small, heavily secured visitor's gate.

I knew a little of the prison's history from an article I had done for a Rochester paper. In August of 1890, the world's first execution by electric chair had been carried out at Auburn, the grisly honor going to a convicted murderer named William Kemmler. The equipment didn't perform up to expectations; the execution was so badly botched that George Westinghouse, whose newly invented AC dynamos were used to provide the current, reportedly said, "They could have done it better with an axe."

The warden had approved a Wednesday afternoon visit. When I reached the head of the line along the north wall, I was told to sign my name on a sheet, and was then ushered through a gauntlet of metal detectors and clanging doors that eventually led me into a long room, windowless but harshly lighted from fluorescent fixtures suspended from the high ceiling. Unlike the popular image—small booths with glass or wire-mesh dividers—

the center of the room was taken up with rows of trestle tables like those in a factory cafeteria. Molded plastic chairs lined three of the walls.

The room was about a third full, most of the visitors women— middle-aged mothers and young wives, some of them with children in tow. I gave my name to a guard with a clipboard and followed his pointing finger to a table at the far end, where a solitary inmate sat with his hands cupped protectively around a burning cigarette.

"Harry Lundquist?"

He looked up and appraised me, squinting against a curl of tobacco smoke. "The one and only." His voice was a loud rasp, the kind you can hear in a restaurant when you're six tables away. He was a stocky man with thick, wavy gray hair and dark blue eyes. I knew from his rap sheet that Lundquist was in his late fifties, but the deep creases around his eyes and the prison pallor made him appear ten years older.

I introduced myself and sat down opposite him. "Thanks for agreeing to talk to me."

He shrugged. "Beats the shit outa the metal shop."

I took my tape recorder and notepad from the nylon bag I was carrying and laid them out. Then I took out a carton of Kools and pushed it across the Formica. Lundquist acknowledged the cigarettes with a nod, then took a drag on the one cupped in his hand.

"So you wanna know all about me and my old pal, Frank Wooley," he said. "Put a hole in his head, they say—after popping one of your kind."

"The man Wooley supposedly killed was a sportswriter," I said. "I'm an ex-police reporter—I write mostly crime stories." I wanted to establish my bona fides at the outset. Lundquist didn't sound impressed.

" 'Supposedly'? You don't think he did the sports guy?"

"I don't know. The police say he did, but their investigation has turned up a few inconsistencies."

"Yeah? Like what?" His eyes were locked onto mine now, his left hand rubbing the tabletop anxiously.

"Tell you what, Harry. You answer a few of my questions first and maybe I'll answer a few of yours later."

"You think you're a fuckin' D.A. or something? I could go back to my cell right now, tell you to stick it."

He could, but he wouldn't—not if he was like the grifters I'd dealt with in the past. Con men have egos the size of Trump Plaza; it's what pushes them to go after the big score. When you walk into a roomful of marks, you do it convinced that you're better, smarter, than they are. But, like most conceits, it needs constant reinforcement, especially when your plans go wrong and you end up in prison.

"You claim you and Frank were old pals," I said, ignoring his threat. "People I've talked to say that's bullshit, Harry. They say you were just a guy who hung around the fringes when Wooley and his ballplayer friends were out on the town. Just another face in the crowd."

"Yeah, well, that there is pure bullshit." He ground out his cigarette in one of the cheap tin ashtrays that sat on each of the tables. "Back in Philly, I probably spent more nights with Frank holier-than-fuckin'-thou Wooley than he spent with Evie—his old lady. I showed him where all the action was when he first come down from the Yankees. We played cards, drank together, gambled the ponies." He brought out the grin. "These people you say you talked to, did they tell you who ran Wooley's bets for him out at Garden State? So the big man wouldn't be seen laying down a lousy sawbuck at the window? They tell you who showed him where the best games were around town?"

"So you were his favorite gofer."

He pointed his index finger at my face. "I wasn't nobody's errand boy, pal. People like Wooley didn't use me—I used them."

"Used them to front your rigged poker games?"

He leaned back, arms folded, looking like the cat who ate the canary. "I'm a professional gambler, okay? That don't make me a gaffer. That sorta thing's illegal."

"I'm not with the parole board, Harry. You wanna pretend you've turned over a new leaf, fine. All I'm interested in is the old days with Frank Wooley—before you got religion."

He considered that for a moment, then glanced around. "The old days? Yeah, I mighta run a few setups way back when." He held up his hands. "These don't look like much, but they made me a lotta dough—once upon a time."

"Tell me about the setups," I said.

His right shoulder rose and fell. "Like I said, I'm a professional gambler. Most times I could clean out a room of fat cats perfectly legit. But sometimes—" He smiled, warming to the subject. "Sometimes you sorta goose up the odds, give yourself an edge. First you gotta get into the right games—amateurs with a lotta dough, I mean. Like a convention of doctors, just as a for-instance. That's where knowin' the convention promoters and knowin' a guy like Frankie does some good. I mean, you get the promoters to bring him in as a celebrity guest, right? And he's pressin' the flesh over cocktails, introducin' me around. I feel out the room, line up the marks, then we go to a room upstairs—usually me and a partner—and we play some cards. The gynecologist from Harrisburg or whatever, he's half in the bag anyway. He drops a few grand, he figures he shoulda known better. He goes home with a light wallet, never realizin' he got skinned." He paused to fire up a fresh cigarette. "Anyway, that was the old days, like you said. Before I seen the error of my ways."

"And Wooley knew this was going on?"

"He knew. I mean, he didn't play, but he knew why he was there. He liked money, like everybody else."

"He was paid a percentage of your take afterward?"

"Nah, guys like Frank were too cute for that. He'd get his right off the top, through the promoter. We'd buy off the promoter first, see, get him to bring in the celebrity we want. The promoter pays the celebrity or the celebrity's handler what they call an appearance fee."

I frowned. "What you're describing happens all the time—pro athletes getting paid to do conventions, auto shows, autograph sessions. It's perfectly legal."

"Which is why it's such a good cover. The difference is, when you're running a game on somebody, you need a marquee guy who'll cooperate—somebody willin' to introduce me and my partner around like we're a couple of regular guys. So the marks'll buy into the action upstairs without thinkin' anything's queer."

"How'd you get Wooley involved in the first place?"

"I told you, we were pals. He liked to gamble, liked havin' a roll in his pocket. One day I let him in on a little play I got hired for, happened to be a gig at a sales convention down in Atlantic

City. This was before they brought back the casinos, remember, so the only action in town was back-room stuff. . . . "

"Hold it," I cut him off. "You say you were hired. I thought you ran these schemes yourself."

He shook his head. "I'm a freelancer, like you. Sometimes I work for myself and sometimes I hire out. A big game like this Atlantic City deal, it takes a lotta dough and connections to set up. And you gotta be sanctioned, otherwise you might step on the wrong toes."

"Explain sanctioned."

"Sanctioned. An okay from the boys. You know, like approved ahead of time by the powers that be."

"You're talking about the mob?"

"I sure don't mean the Maryknoll Sisters."

"But they don't actually run the setups?"

He waved his cigarette. "Nah, they just wanna know who's doin' what to who, is all. And they want their cut, just like everybody else."

"Who arranged this Atlantic City setup?"

"Friend of a friend. I wouldn't give a name even if I could remember it. Anyway, that's the first time Frank worked with me. 'Stead of his usual five-hundred-buck appearance fee—that was top dollar for jocks back then—I got him two grand for a few hours of hangin' out at a cocktail party, shootin' the shit with office equipment reps and guzzlin' Old Grandad. He was all for it."

"And this was when?"

"Sixty-eight, '69, in there."

"Wooley fronted for you regularly after that?"

"Big plays don't come along every day, pal. We teamed up maybe four or five times over the next couple of years until the baseball commissioner started sniffin' around."

"I want to come back to that," I said as I made some notes. "What's the most Wooley made on one of these deals?"

"Don't know for sure, probably about five, six k. I told you, I was a hired mechanic most of the time. I got my money after the play, he got his up-front, usually paid out through his manager just to keep everything nice and neat."

"This 'manager,' you mean Richie Hirshberg?"

He shrugged. "I don't remember names."

I jotted another note. "Let's go back to Wooley's suspension in '70. What happened there?"

Lundquist's cobalt blue eyes fixed on me. "This is gettin' one-sided. I thought you were gonna tell me about Frankie and the sports guy—did he off him or didn't he."

"What difference does that make to you, Harry?"

He exhaled a plume of smoke. "Nosy, is all. Except for a stabbing every other week, we don't get much excitement in here." He flashed tobacco-stained teeth. "I just like to stay current with what my old pals are up to."

"Yeah, well, I like to take things in chronological order. Frank Wooley's death comes last. Now, how did the baseball commissioner get on to you two?"

"He didn't—not really. All he knew was that Frankie and me were seen hangin' out—out at Garden State, a couple conventions, like I said." He laughed. "I was an unsavory character, Frankie was a pain in the ass as far as the commissioner was concerned. Add 'em up and you get a thirty-day suspension. Big fuckin' deal. Scared the hell outa Wooley, though. He cut me off after that—wouldn't come near me. Broke my poor little heart."

"You didn't hang out together after the suspension?"

"That's what I just said."

"So how is it you turned up with Wooley's lawyer at the Bergen County Civic Center in '72?"

He glanced away, took another long drag on the cigarette. "I drove the lawyer over as a favor, that's all. Nobody figured it'd turn into such a big deal."

"A favor for whom?"

"Somebody I knew who was a friend of Evie and Frank. Somebody who heard about the trouble and wanted to help out."

"What was the lawyer's name?"

"I don't recall—that's the truth. You gotta remember, that was almost twenty years ago."

"What about the guy who hired him?" I pressed. "You remember his name, don't you?"

Another yellow smile. "A friend of a friend, that's all. I might wanna write my memoirs when I get outa here, pal. Can't go givin' away all my stories, can I?"

I made busywork with the tape recorder for a few seconds, both to mask my frustration and to think out my next move. I'd gotten him started by goading him; maybe it would work again.

"Looks like this friend didn't bother to send you a lawyer when you took a fall, Harry," I said as I looked around the room. "Or maybe they just didn't send a very good one. I guess you don't rate the same as a celebrity, huh?"

That sent a momentary rush of blood into his chalky face, but it passed just as quickly. "I told you, that was a long time ago, me and Wooley. By the time this beef came up, I was outa touch with the old crowd. Anyway, with good time I'll be outa here in another year, which I can do with no sweat."

"Are you trying to tell me that you didn't keep in touch with Wooley after 1972?"

"That's right. From what I hear he stayed up around northern Jersey, workin' construction, kickin' around—tryin' to stay close to his daughter, I guess, after Evie gave him the heave-ho. I was down south—Philly, Atlantic City—doin' my thing, makin' a few bucks, livin' right."

"Uh huh." He forgot to mention the eighteen-month stretch he did in a federal prison for tax fraud in the late seventies, but I let it slide. "So I guess you didn't see Frank again until, what, 1988? That weekend when you worked a setup at the Stanton Motor Inn in Geneva."

I was expecting his look of surprise. What I hadn't counted on was the fear that accompanied it.

"I never worked a game—where'd you say?"

"The Stanton in Geneva, a third-floor suite, right after a memorabilia show and autograph session downstairs. You and Frank Wooley and Alfie Klem and Gimp Smith." I laid out the names like I was reading them from a grand-jury indictment. "I've got a source who saw you there, Harry, and another one who knows exactly what kind of play you were running. You used a cup of coffee for a glim. . . ."

"You been talkin' to that asshole magician."

"Ah, your memory is making a comeback."

He drew on the cigarette. "Sure, I remember now. I'm not good with places, but, yeah, I remember a game with Frank and those guys. I was passin' through from Buffalo, on my way back to Atlantic City. I read about the show in the paper, I see Frank is in town, so I stop by. We had a few drinks, a few laughs. Somebody invited us up to their room to play—who am I to turn down a game?'' He shook his head. ''But you got the rest wrong, pal. It was that punk bartender that tried to scam us. I caught onto his moves and we threw him out, that's all there was to it.''

''I don't think so, Harry.''

''Hey, fuck you!'' He pushed himself away from the table and stood. ''I don't need any more of this shit—you're just jerkin' me around here.''

''Sit down, Harry. Relax. Let's talk about the old crowd; Alfie Klem and Gimp. . . . ''

''I got nothin' else to say to you, pal.''

I hurried on. ''We haven't even gotten to Frank and the sportswriter yet, Harry. Don't you wanna hear what happened out there?''

He hesitated, gnawing at his lower lip while he glared down at me. Then he scooped the carton of Kools from the table and hugged it to his prison gray shirt.

''I got nothin' else to say,'' he repeated quietly. He turned around and slowly walked toward an open doorway at the far side of the room, his eyes to the floor as he shuffled past the guard.

CHAPTER 25

I came home from a few errands Friday morning to find a message from Sergeant Leek on my machine. I had tried calling him at the Yates Sheriff's Department several times the day before, only to have an officious functionary repeatedly inform me that the sergeant was "unavailable at present." I was getting the idea that Leek was purposely avoiding me but now, as I listened to the playback on the answering machine, it sounded like he was as eager to talk as I was. Predictably, he wanted to meet away from his office.

"One o'clock, if you're agreeable, at the public playground west of the village," he instructed, sounding a little like a machine himself. "Wear sneakers, please."

When I arrived, I found Leek out on a blacktopped basketball court practicing his jumpshot against a phantom defender. He was outfitted in scarred high tops, gym shorts, and an orange Syracuse University sweatshirt that made him look more like a basketball than a basketball player—a gross misjudgement on my part, as it turned out.

"Glad you could make it, Sheridan," he greeted me, puffing mildly but not missing a dribble. "How about a little one-on-one, just to loosen things up?"

"Basketball isn't my game. Too short."

"You're the same height I am."

"So we're both too short."

He stared at me with what is known in schoolyards everywhere as the are-you-chicken look.

I exhaled and stripped off my jacket. "Okay, Sergeant, the first guy to ten wins."

"You wanna take a few practice shots first?"

"Wouldn't help."

I took the ball back to midcourt and began my dribble, bobbing and juking like the big boys, my back to the basket. Leek shadowed me, hand-checking with his left while waving his right in my face.

"How're you coming with your piece on Wooley?"

"I'm making progress." I faked left and whirled right, driving in for a layup. The ball clanged off the rim. Leek snagged the rebound and dribbled out to midcourt.

"How about you?" I asked, my hand pressing the small of his back as he began his approach. "You and the dogcatcher get anywhere with Sturdevant?"

"We took the dog. One of the deputies has him for the time being. I doubt I could make an animal abuse charge stick, but—" He turned and knocked me back with a forearm, then arched a twenty-foot jumper. All net. "One, zip. I caught Sturdevant with a trailerful of unregistered handguns. That and the obstructing justice threat got him talking."

"That was a foul," I said.

Leek smiled angelically. "I didn't hear a whistle."

I brought up the ball again, the sergeant hounding me.

"You got him to tell you what he saw out there?"

"Uh huh."

I tried another feint left, but Leek stayed with me, so I shot my elbow into his stomach. It bounced off as if he were the Michelin Man. I launched a hookshot. The ball flew over the backboard and rattled off the chain-link backstop.

Leek retrieved it. "You're quick enough, but your technique needs a lot of work."

"That's what my ex said."

He came at me with a frontal assault, moving slow and deliberate. Then he executed a cross-over dribble, driving by me like I was a lamppost and laying it in off the glass.

"Two, zip."

It went on like that for another ten minutes, Leek teasing me both with the ball and with the information on Sturdevant. By the time the score had risen to eight to three, we were both sweating like sumo wrestlers, and my chest had a permanent welt the size and shape of Leek's forearm.

"Tell you what," I huffed, hands on hips. "How about if I concede? Then we can call this off before somebody shows up and starts filming a Dockers commercial."

We adjourned to a nearby bench, the sergeant stretching his stocky white legs out straight.

"You're a changed man when you ditch the bow tie," I said between breaths. "Like Clark Kent without the glasses—except Clark wouldn't flagrantly foul a guy."

"I like to maintain a certain level of professionalism when I'm working," he said. "But everyone has both a public persona and a private self, Mr. Sheridan."

"Yeah, but we're talking Jekyll and Hyde. You even called me Sheridan on the court. Now it's 'Mr. Sheridan.' "

"Sheridan then, if that's what you prefer. And I'm Art, by the way."

"Good. Now tell me what Sturdevant saw, Art."

He pulled in his legs and looked sideward at me. "A large middle-aged man walking along the ridge trail up behind the Mack property. Heading south, away from the house, at about one thirty the afternoon of the shootings."

His sudden candor, like his quickness on the basketball court, caught me off guard.

"Hold it a second. The ridge trail?"

"A hiking path. Part of the Finger Lakes Trail that winds up and down the region. A branch of it runs right along the spine of the hill that parallels Lookout Run."

"So Sturdevant saw a hiker on a public trail," I said. "So what? People must walk that ridge all the time."

"Not that early in the year, after such a wet spring. And Sturdevant claims the man wasn't dressed for hiking."

This was sounding better and better, but the reporter in me couldn't resist the role of devil's advocate. "Sturdevant's place has to be, what, two or three hundred yards away from that hilltop. I'm surprised he could see the guy at all, let alone make out what he was wearing."

"He says he was at his kitchen table cleaning his thirty-aught-six when he heard what may've been two gunshots over at the Mack place—another item he held back when I interviewed him the first time. Anyway, this was around one thirty. A couple minutes later, still working on his rifle, he spotted a man moving south along the ridge trail. He used the rifle's scope to get a better look. He saw a big, middle-aged man in a cowboy hat and a sportcoat.''

"Would he know the guy if he saw him again?"

"He says probably yes, but I have my doubts. By the time I got done with him, he was ready to tell me anything he thought I wanted to hear."

"What'd you do, force him to play basketball with you?"

Leek was as impervious to my humor as he had been to my elbows. He stared out across the playground, his round baby face placid. After a few seconds, he gave me the sidelong appraisal again. "Your story; when do you plan to publish?"

"My editor wants it for the July 15 issue, to coincide with the induction ceremonies in Cooperstown. Which means I have to file no later than July first."

"Roughly three weeks?"

"Good choice of adverb. It's going to be rough, all right, if I don't start putting some meat to the bones I've dug up so far."

"Tell me about the bones."

"After you tell me about IdaRose Mack's freshly vacuumed carpet, and why it intrigued you."

He considered me a moment longer. "All right, Sheridan, a fair exchange. If you assure me this all goes as deep background for the time being."

"For now that's no problem, but I'll have to use your department as an official source when I write the article."

"I'm not sure where I'll be with this in three weeks—or three years." He heaved a sigh. "You were correct; there are indicators that suggest the Wooley case wasn't a homicide-suicide. I've been given tacit permission to look a little closer, so long as I'm discreet. In other words, I'm on a short leash here, Sheridan. I've got suspicions, but no suspects. That's where I'm hoping you may prove helpful."

The disclaimer completed, Leek finally took the plunge.

"When you told me Sturdevant was holding something back, you implied that I hadn't asked all the right questions. You're right, I didn't. But I asked one that I think you missed. When you were interviewing Sturdevant and the other neighbor, Mrs. Karnes, you asked both if they'd seen a white Toyota come through. Did you also ask them what time they'd seen it?"

I frowned. "No, I guess I didn't."

"Mrs. Karnes saw the car at about twelve thirty-five. She knew this to be correct because her children always finish lunch at half past noon. Sturdevant, on the other hand, arrived home from work around one, as always on Saturdays. He says he could be off a little on the time, but no more than five minutes either way. That's a gap of at least twenty minutes for a drive that shouldn't take more than three or four."

I said, "Delfay could have missed the turnoff for the Mack place. By the time he went all the way to the end of Lookout Run and doubled back, he might've used up . . ."

"Ten minutes at most, fifteen if he had stopped to ask directions—which he didn't according to what we learned when we canvassed the other houses. That bothered me, the unaccounted for twenty minutes. In and of itself, it's unimportant, but there were the other inconsistencies to consider. Mrs. Mack's freshly vacuumed carpet, for example. You're familiar with the plush new carpeting in her den?"

"I've seen it."

"The nap in that kind of deep pile tends to set up after a vacuuming, then mat down when it's walked on. Very faint, of course, but you can get an inference of where it's been recently trod. The patterns I saw the day of the shootings indicated the possibility that there had been three sets of feet moving around the room."

"Did I say Jekyll and Hyde? I meant Sherlock Holmes."

"My superiors had a similar reaction," he said. "But there's more. One of the French doors leading onto the patio was slightly ajar, as if someone had entered or left the room that way— exited, if my analysis of the carpet prints is correct. And then there's the missing steno-pad page."

"Possibly containing the directions to the Mack Place?" I asked. "The directions you insisted Delfay didn't have?"

"It was an accurate statement, Sheridan. The steno pads didn't have any directions written in them when we found them. But there were a few paper binder fragments on the carpet, as if a page had been torn out. The missing page probably ended up in the fireplace.''

''There had to be more than directions on the page, otherwise why would anyone feel the need to burn it?''

''Agreed. I'm assuming that the directions included the name of the person Delfay rendezvoused with on Lookout Run.''

''You're a tough nut to crack, Art, but once you get on a roll you're a font of fascinating information. What leads you to believe that Delfay met up with someone out there?''

''The missing twenty minutes. Mrs. Karnes swears Delfay was alone when he passed her place but, from Sturdevant's vantage point, he couldn't tell if there was anyone else in the car. That means Delfay could've picked up a passenger out at the end of Lookout Run and driven him back to Mrs. Mack's house.''

''The two cabins out at the dead end,'' I said, catching on. ''They're rental properties.''

Leek nodded. ''I'm working that angle. One of the cabins was rented the weekend of the shootings—unusual so early in the season. The owner lists the property with an agency in Geneva. They were paid in advance with a postal money order, which I'm trying to trace. But I did get the name of the person who supposedly rented the place.''

The ''supposedly'' was a tip-off. ''Let me guess,'' I said. ''Mike Delfay.''

''Correct. Of course, if Delfay had rented the cabin himself, he wouldn't have had a plane ticket back to Laguardia later in the day. Which leads me to believe that our 'third man' booked the cabin using Delfay's name. But all I really have is a great deal of circumstantial evidence and conjecture. Was there a third man? Did he accompany Delfay to the Mack place? If so, did he kill Delfay, then shoot Wooley following a struggle for the gun?'' He frowned. ''Or is my boss right. Am I searching for a 'grassy knoll' where none exists? If it wasn't a homicide-suicide, then who killed Frank Wooley, and why? You tell me, Sheridan.''

So I did, sort of.

''I think it all ties in with something that happened at the Stanton Motor Inn in Geneva in 1988,'' I began.

For the next half hour, I filled Leek in on what I'd learned. I told him about Wooley's association with Harry Lundquist, and Lundquist's claim that the two of them had started running poker hustles in the late sixties. I told him about Alfie Klem and Gimp Smith and Richie Hirshberg, old friends who ran with Wooley in the Philadelphia days, and I told him about the public circumstances surrounding Wooley's long banishment from baseball and his aborted return with the Geneva Cubs three seasons earlier. Then I went back to the rigged poker game at the Stanton involving Lundquist, Wooley, Klem, and Smith; Wooley's blowup and dismissal as a Cubs coach the next day; Hirshberg's timely arrival soon after to discuss "business arrangements" with Wooley; and the phantom checks Wooley claimed to be receiving from the players' pension fund, which employs Smith.

When I finished, the sergeant sat there nibbling his lower lip while frowning down at his high tops.

"Interesting," he murmured. His head snapped up. "I think I see where you're going, but spell it out for me."

"The way I see it, the memorabilia show at the Stanton was a replay of the Philly days, with Lundquist running a poker scam and the others playing their parts as window dressing. Only something went wrong; the bartender they let into the game, Johnny Eberling, was smart enough to cop to the setup." I paused to organize my thoughts. "Okay. The next day Eberling takes out his anger on Wooley. Wooley foolishly retaliates and, in the process, blows his last chance to get back into organized baseball. Eberling is a concern—the others can't afford to have it get out that they were involved in a gambling scam—so he's paid a tidy sum to make him forget the whole thing, fifty-three hundred dollars. Great. Klem keeps raking in money on the card show circuit, Hirshberg continues to get his ten percent of Klem's action, and Smith keeps his job with the players' pension fund office. But, once again, Frank Wooley is the fall guy—he's out of baseball and poison to promoters. He figures the others owe him, so he decides to seek compensation."

Leek was nodding. "Wooley threatens to expose the others unless he's paid off—a thousand dollars in regular monthly installments."

"Right. In exchange, he agrees to go back underground and stay there. But then, surprisingly, he gets elected to the hall of fame and he's back in the public eye. Reporters are hot to get his story and a venal ghostwriter named Mike Delfay decides to do a biography. This makes the others nervous. What if Wooley has a change of heart? Or what if Delfay was somehow getting close to the truth—something Hirshberg might've found out when Delfay approached him for help in finding Wooley. Somebody—Hirshberg or Klem, probably—decides not to take the risk, so he runs a little setup of his own. He arranges to meet Delfay out at the Mack place, ostensibly to interview Wooley. Then he kills both men, arranging it to look like a murder-suicide.''

Leek did some more nibbling. ''You say Hirshberg was Klem's agent? And he knew where the Mack place is located?''

''He visited the house once. In fact, IdaRose Mack told me Hirshberg got lost on the way down and ended up driving all the way to the end of Lookout Run.''

''Which means he could've taken note of the rental cabins at that time,'' the sergeant said. ''He passes this information on to Klem, who uses it to setup Delfay and Wooley—or Hirshberg does it himself. There is that possibility. Have you interviewed him yet?''

I shook my head. ''But I'm planning to very soon.''

''It's all pretty tenuous,'' the sergeant said, crossing his arms over his barrel chest. ''I wish I could be as certain as you that the key lies with the card game at the Stanton. But I will give the matter my attention, starting with this magician, Johnny Eberling.'' He sighed. ''You know who I feel sorry for, Sheridan? IdaRose Mack. Because whichever way this shakes out—homicide-suicide or double homicide—your article isn't going to rehabilitate the reputation of Frank Wooley.''

CHAPTER 26

WHEN I got back to the cottage I worked the phone, touching base with Lev Ascher at his ad agency in New York before calling Eddie Gentile, a city-government reporter for the *Philadelphia Inquirer*. Lev had found a woman who knew Evie March slightly in her early New York days. She couldn't tell Lev much that I didn't already know, but she gave him the name of an ex-roommate of Evie's who she thought might know more. Lev hadn't yet tracked down the old roommate, but he was eager to stay on it.

Eddie Gentile was the reporter whose byline had appeared in the 1972 *Newark Ledger* story about Frank Wooley's arrest for assaulting his wife and daughter—the story that had featured the infamous photo of Wooley leaving the Bergen County Civic Center with Lundquist and the lawyer. I had tracked down Gentile through his newspaper guild membership, learning that he had left the Newark paper in 1983, moving on to *Newsweek* for five years before landing with the *Inquirer*. After introducing myself and filling him in on my interest in Frank Wooley, I asked him to tell me how his scoop on Wooley's arrest had come about.

"It was a phone tip," Gentile said. "A guy called the city desk at the *Ledger* and said Wooley'd been arrested for assault and was due to be arraigned at two o'clock, so the city editor sent me out with a photographer."

"The lawyer's name didn't appear in your story or the cutline," I said. "Do you remember who he was?"

"Yeah, a guy named Haskell. Warren Haskell, I think. He's with a high-powered firm in Trenton." Gentile named the firm. "As I recall, they used to do a lot of government-related work up at the state capital there; union contracts, political lobbying, things like that. Why they'd be representing a baseball player at an arraignment, I don't know."

After we rang off, I had the operator put me through to directory assistance in Trenton and got the number of Warren Haskell's law firm. It turned out to be a wasted effort; Haskell had died four years ago, I was told, and there was no one there who would be willing to discuss any of his old clients.

Next, I called for assistance again and got the number for Richie Hirshberg's sports agency in New York and dialed it. A haughty woman who called herself Hirshberg's administrative assistant informed me that her boss was out of the office until Monday. I told her I needed to speak to him about an urgent personal matter and asked her for Hirshberg's home number and address. She hung up on me.

Before closing up shop and heading down to the Lakeside Inn for a charbroiled cheeseburger, I made one last call, booking myself on a mid-morning flight to New Jersey.

Martina Wooley had called Darlington a suburb of an exurb; a fair assessment, I thought as I drove past the town's centerpiece, a glittering new shopping mall.

I had landed in Newark at 10:45 on Saturday morning, picking up a rental car at the airport and working my way out of the city to Route 17, my auto-club trip ticket propped on the dashboard. The drive had taken me past the Meadowlands sports complex, then blocks of old factories and warehouses, followed by commercial strips and mile after mile of postwar housing tracts. By the time I exited for the Saddle River area north of Paterson, the landscape had changed. There were more trees and rolling hills and newer residential developments featuring large homes on wide green lots.

The Garci address led me to a winding, woodsy cul-de-sac set a strong three wood away from the Darlington Country Club. The dozen houses on the street came in as many different styles, the common denominator being size—they were all huge. The one I wanted was a white colonial that was perhaps a couple hundred square feet shy of palatial. I parked in a turnaround next to a yellow station wagon bearing the logo of a cleaning service on its sides and trekked up the walk to the front portico's double doors.

"Yes?"

I had seen only gray newspaper photos of Frank Wooley's ex-wife, taken more than twenty years ago, but I instantly recognized the woman who answered my ring. She had to be nearly fifty now, but if she wanted to claim thirty-nine, you wouldn't get an argument from me. In the old news photos her hair had been longer and teased out and, at least in my mind's eye, a brassy shade of blond. Now it was ashy and shorter, just touching her shoulder blades, and the teasing comb had been replaced with a dash of styling mousse at either temple. The nose was aquiline and the lips full, reminding me of her daughter. The eyes were azure blue, a perfect match for her leotard. She stood about five-six in her stocking feet, most of her height attributable to her long, shapely dancer's legs.

"My name's Sheridan, Mrs. Garci. We spoke on the phone a couple of weeks ago," I said, glancing down at the body suit. "I hope I'm not catching you at a bad time."

"I was just about to start my workout, but . . . " She rested a fist on her hip. "Wait a minute, you're a reporter?"

"Afraid so. I called you about a piece I'm doing on Frank Wooley for *The Sporting Life*," I reminded her. "Your daughter Martina . . . "

"She's not here now. She's rooming with a friend in the city for the summer."

Just then a small, dark woman carrying a basket of cleaning tools squeezed past the lady of the house, muttering in a language that sounded middle eastern. At the same time a phone rang somewhere inside.

"Oh, for . . . " Evie Garci threw up her hands. "Well, you might as well come in while I get that."

I followed her into a soaring two-story foyer with a winding staircase that would've looked right at home in the antebellum South. She disappeared through a door behind the staircase, leaving me the option of cooling my heels on the foyer's terra cotta tiles or inviting myself into the formal living room that ran off to my left. I opted for the living room. When she returned two minutes later, I was seated on one of the camelback sofas that flanked the fireplace.

"Well, make yourself at home, Mr. . . . "

"Sheridan."

Her hands fluttered the air. "I'm terrible with names. In one ear, out the other. Lou tells me to try using word associations. Let's see. Sheridan—like Ann Sheridan, the actress. Remember her?"

"Not really. I've probably seen her on the late show."

She sat on the sofa across from me and sighed dramatically. "Here today, forgotten tomorrow. It's a tough life, show business. I was a performer myself once. A Juliet Prowse type, only not so tall—a booking agent told me that."

"You look like you could still be up on a stage somewhere," I said. "You were dancing in clubs, I understand, when you met your first husband."

"What? . . . " She blinked, as if dazzled by the memory of stage lights, then frowned at me. "Oh, Frank. I forgot why you were here for a second."

I suddenly wondered if the spaciness was normal for Evie or if it had been helped along. I hadn't detected the smell of alcohol on her, but she seemed to be running on something besides a bad case of nostalgia.

"Hold on," she said, the frown deepening. "You said Martina. You're the one she gave our private number."

"I interviewed her up at Cornell. We had a nice, long talk over lunch."

"Yes, yes, I remember what you talked about. Martina's a brilliant student, you know, but she tends to make up things about her childhood. Her school psychologist told Lou and me that it was a defense mechanism or something." She leaned forward. "Anyway, I gave you my statement over the phone, didn't I? That's all I have to say on the subject, so if you don't mind. . . . "

"What really puzzles me about the whole overblown incident," I interjected, "is why you pressed charges in the first place, Mrs. Garci."

"I was mad as hell, that's why. Frank could've broken my nose, disfigured me permanently, hitting me like that."

"But you reconsidered," I said. "That's why you sent Warren

Haskell to the civic center." I figured the best way to keep her talking was to keep her off balance with one question after the other. It apparently was working. She blinked twice this time.

"Warren who?"

"The attorney who got the charges dismissed at Frank's arraignment. The one who got his picture taken with Frank and Harry Lundquist."

"I don't know anything about any attorney—Frank must've hired him. Anyway, I dropped the charges, so there wasn't anything for a lawyer to do."

"Maybe Harry Lundquist hired him?"

"Hah!" The shapely legs crossed. "That weasel wouldn't lift a finger to help a friend, even if he had one."

"Richie Hirshberg, then," I suggested. "He was a friend, wasn't he? Frank's unofficial agent at the time? Maybe he sent out the lawyer."

Evie shrugged. "Maybe. I guess he probably did."

"Did you ever ask Hirshberg about it? At the club or anything? I understand he lives right around the corner. Wildwood Lane, isn't it?"

Wildwood Lane was one of the streets I had passed on the way to the Garci place. I was reasonably certain I could find Hirshberg's actual address with a little research at the local post office, but Evie, if she knew, could save me some time. She didn't disappoint.

"Wildwood Lane? Last I knew he had a condo at The Ravine," she said. "Lou would know. He golfs with Richie sometimes."

"You've stayed close with some of the old crowd, I take it? Richie, Alfie Klem. . . . "

"Alfie Klem? I haven't seen that old degenerate in years, unless you count beer commercials." She uncrossed her legs and added conspiratorially, "He has a thing about showgirls. Touchy-feely, you know?" Then she glanced at the long-case clock tucked in the far corner of the living room. "Richie I see to say hello to, at the club or Le Bisque or wherever. Now, if you don't mind, Mr. . . . Sheridan. My husband will be home for lunch any minute, and I have to see that Margarita has everything ready. You have no idea what it takes to run a house this size."

"I guess not," I said as she got to her feet. "I'd love to meet your husband. Martina tells me he's a collector of sports memorabilia."

She rolled the baby blues. "God, is he ever. He'd talk your ear off about that stuff—but I know what you're really interested in, Mr. Reporter, and you can forget it. Lou's very sensitive about Frank and me. People talk when a woman ends up marrying one of her ex's old friends."

I stood up. "Your husband and Frank were friends?"

"Since the New York days. Lou knew a lot of the Yankee players from his collecting." She began walking toward the foyer, leaving me little choice but to follow. "Now, like I told you in my statement, we're all very pleased that Frank made it into the hall of fame. As for the rest, that's a closed chapter in my life."

Just as we stepped out onto the terra cotta, a man came out of the banquet-sized dining room across the foyer. He was about sixty, stocky and muscular, his upper arms packed like sausages into a navy polo shirt. He had close-cropped white hair, a thick nose, and the sort of year-round tan that proves the sun always shines on the wealthy.

"Oh, Lou, I didn't know you were home."

"Yeah, babe, just got in. I was out watching Margarita do the salads." He gave his wife an easy grin, then looked at me. "Lou Garci," he said, extending his arm.

"Sheridan. I'm covering the Wooley story for *The Sporting Life.*"

"Ahh." He let go of my hand and, without losing eye contact with me, asked his wife, "Everything kosher with Mr. Sheridan here, babe?"

"Oh, he's all right. Tired me out a little with all his questions— you know these reporters." She put on a moue. "Where were all these guys back when I was hungry for a little publicity?"

"Speaking of hungry," Garci said, "Margarita says lunch'll be ready in ten minutes. She wants to know what kind of dressing you want."

Evie exhaled as if she'd just been asked to plan the Normandy invasion. "I told her the light Italian."

"Better go tell her again, sweets."

"Yes." Evie looked from her husband to me. "Well, good-bye then, Mr. . . . damn!"

"Sheridan," I prompted her. "Like Ann, the actress?"

CHAPTER 27

WE watched her disappear through the door under the staircase, Garci's gaze filled with possessive pride. When he turned back to me, the eyes were neutral.

"My wife is a fabulous woman, but fragile," he said. "She bruises easily. I try to see that doesn't happen—and if it does, I get very upset."

The best way to deal with a veiled threat, I've found, is to ignore it. "She was just telling me a little about your collection," I said. "I'd love to see it. I used to collect baseball cards when I was a kid, mostly Yankees."

He stared at me for a few seconds more, trying to fathom my intent. Finally the collector in him won and he said, "Don't tell me; your mother threw 'em out while you were away at college, right? I know card traders who make a living off people's mothers."

"Actually, I traded them to my cousin for a used Fender reverb amplifier." I grinned. "Which my mother gave away while I was in the service."

"Women. They never understand about a man's toys." He glanced at his watch. "Well—I've got a few minutes till lunch. C'mon, I'll give you the Cook's tour."

I followed him down into the basement and along a short, wood-paneled corridor to a broad oak door. Mounted next to the jamb was a keypad, a little red light glowing to show that the security system was operating. Garci tossed an apologetic smile over his shoulder, then blocked my view as he punched in a three-digit code. A sedate beep was followed by the metallic sound of a dead bolt withdrawing.

"Can't be too careful," he said as he led me into the room. "I've got thirty years worth of collecting in here."

The room was about fifteen by thirty feet, carpeted with a thick sky-blue pile rug and paneled in the same hardwood veneer as the corridor, judging from what little I could see of it; most of the wall space was taken up with display shelves jammed with sports equipment and Lucite picture frames encasing signed posters, photographs, and a few pencil sketches. Running down the center of the room were three glass display cases like those found at a jeweler's, but instead of diamond rings and necklaces, the cases held autographed baseballs and footballs, hockey sticks, basketball shoes, and plenty more.

I walked to the nearest corner where an old-fashioned green wooden locker housed a mammoth, dark-stained bat and a heavy flannel uniform with GIANTS stitched across the shirt.

"Mel Ott," Garci said. "I picked up the locker when they tore down the Polo Grounds. I already had one of his bats, but it took another fifteen years to find the uniform." He indicated the opposite corner, where a second locker stood, this one containing a dated Giants football uniform.

"Frank Gifford wore that his last game. I got the locker when they remodeled Yankee Stadium. The locker along the wall over there's from Ebbets Field. I got Duke Snider's jersey and glove in there."

"Impressive."

"Yeah, I've got almost two dozen uniforms now; DiMaggio, Mantle, Tittle, Stengel from when he managed the Mets, Walt Frazier. . . ."

"Frank Wooley?"

He hesitated. "I had some of his stuff in here, but I packed it up and gave it to Martina. For a keepsake. Some of it'll probably end up in the hall of fame, along with her old man." He motioned me over to one of the glass display cases. "You should've saved those trading cards, Sheridan. That's where the money is. See that?"

"The Mantle card?" It lay in a place of honor on a strip of

velvet, covered by a glassine envelope, as if the plate glass display case wasn't protection enough.

"1952 Topps, mint condition. I won't say what I paid for mine, but a Mickey Mantle just like that one sold for forty-five grand at Sotheby's three months ago. In the same auction a Honus Wagner went for almost half a million."

"Too bad you're not into Pittsburgh teams."

"Smart collectors stick to some sort of theme. I grew up on the Lower East Side. My father had a wholesale produce business. He taught me how to buy and sell, took me to ball games on Sunday afternoons—all the sports, all the teams. Long as they were New York, we rooted for 'em. Once I went out on my own and had some success, I guess I wanted to get back some of the old days. So I started collecting. But this is nothing compared to some. There's a guy named Halper—owns a piece of the Yankees?—he's got a collection damn near as big as Cooperstown."

I worked my way around to the wall with the framed photographs. Most were black and white, all were signed.

"Your father must've taught you very well," I said as I continued to peruse the photos. "Martina said you were in the laundry business? And you have liquor distributorships, too?"

"My main thing is the laundries. We've got plants up here and down in south Jersey." The business talk obviously bored him. "See that autographed picture of Sam Huff there? I picked that up at garage sale in West Orange for a dollar."

"How do you know it's real?"

"What?"

"The autograph. How do you know it isn't a fake? For that matter, how do you know if any of these are genuine?"

It was like asking a priest—Jesuits excepted—how Noah crammed all those animals on a boat. Garci frowned his disapproval at my sacrilege. "Some I collected firsthand, some I verify by comparing them to authenticated signatures—some, like that one, you just accept on faith. Besides, why would some housewife cheat you for a dollar?"

"Mmm." I pointed to another photo, a grinning, gangly man in a Mets uniform, circa 1964. "There's a face I know." I read the inscription. " 'To my pard Lou, All my best, Alfie Klem.' Your wife said you and Frank Wooley were friends from the New York days. Was Alfie part of that crowd, too?"

"Not really. I got to know Klem a little bit when my company had the laundry contract with the Mets years ago. He calls everybody 'pard.' "

"But you were close to Frank Wooley—and Evie. Back in the Teaneck days?"

The permanent tan developed a sudden sunburn. "I allowed you down here as a courtesy, because I thought you were actually interested in seeing the collection."

"I am," I said. "But I'm also interested in Frank's old friends—the folks who knew him when. What sort of man was he, would you say?"

"I wouldn't. We were friends once, but that ended. He was a great ballplayer. Leave it at that."

"You must've seen him around once in a while," I tried. "He was still close to Martina. I understand you and he were splitting her college expenses."

"What about it?"

"I just wondered how you two worked that out if you weren't on good terms." I lifted my eyebrows, as if inspiration had just struck. "Or did Richie Hirshberg make the arrangements—sort of an intermediary?"

Garci studied my face speculatively. "I don't know what you've got in mind with any of this, Sheridan, and I really don't care. If you want to know if Hirshberg is somebody I met through Frank, the answer is yes. These days we play a little golf together, and sometimes I take advantage of his sports connections to get an autograph or a piece of memorabilia. As for the college thing, Frank and I handled that through Martina. Now, I hope you're out of questions, because I'm out of time."

He put a light grip on my elbow and steered me toward the door, then paused and looked back. "It took me a long time to put all this together, and there's still more to come—there's always more. They talk about great athletes having desire, well, it's the same thing with a successful businessman or a serious collector. You see a prize out there and you go after it until you get it. You can't do anything else."

That last line sounded curiously like an apology, and I wondered, as I followed him along the corridor, if he was referring to the collection in the basement or the mint-condition wife upstairs.

Finding where Richie Hirshberg lived proved to be the easy part. Catching him at home was another story.

The counter girl at Wendy's was able to direct me to The Ravine, a pricey townhouse condominium development located on the border of Darlington and Saddle River. The units were contemporary with red cedar siding and, in back, large decks that cantilevered out into space, giving each homeowner a bird's-eye view of the wooded ravine below. High tech and low maintenance seemed to be the key selling points, although exclusivity probably figured in, too.

I found Hirshberg's house number by checking the mailboxes that were bunched together under a little cedar-shingled roof at the entrance to the development. But he wasn't in at two o'-clock, when I first tried his doorbell, or at four, when I returned to try again after killing a couple of hours walking around the new mall. I drove back out by the interstate and booked a room at a motel, ate dinner at a chain restaurant across the way, and drove back to The Ravine at seven. Still nobody home. I spent the rest of the evening cruising aimlessly around town, stopping once at a Denny's for coffee, checking back at Hirshberg's place every hour. At ten I gave up and went back to my motel.

I was back at Hirshberg's door at ten o'clock Sunday morning, sending up a little prayer on my own behalf as I pressed the buzzer. My return flight was scheduled to leave Newark at three thirty in the afternoon, and I didn't look forward to having to change my reservation, but I also didn't want to miss a chance to talk face-to-face with the man whose name kept turning up wherever the Wooley story led me.

I leaned into the doorbell a second time, letting it ring for several seconds, then dropped my arm as I heard the sound of footsteps inside. A moment later the door opened.

"Yeah?"

Like most any kid who had come of age in the late sixties, I had seen news footage and newspaper photos of activist Richie Hirshberg; the full, flowing mane of wavy brown hair, the tattered jeans and sloganeering sweatshirts, the clenched fist and blazing eyes and flaming rhetoric, most often delivered from the steps of a courthouse or a flatbed sound truck. The dour man who now stared out at me was a generation older, short and small boned, almost delicate. His hair was darker and slicked straight back, the eyes looked damp and unfocused, and the clenched fist gripped a mug of coffee. He was barefoot, wearing a yellow V-neck sweater sans shirt and pleated cotton slacks. If it wasn't for the hawk nose and the thick reddish-brown moustache, I might have taken him for any other fortysomething business executive caught without his wing tips and power tie on a lazy Sunday morning.

"Mr. Hirshberg, my name's Sheridan. I'm a writer, working on a piece for *The Sporting Life*. . . . "

"Oh, yeah?" He perked up. "You doing a profile on one of my clients, are you?"

"A former client. Frank Wooley."

"Oh." He raised the mug and swallowed. "What'd you say your name was again?"

"Sheridan."

"Uh huh." He glanced at his wristwatch, a Rolex that probably cost more than I was getting for the Wooley piece. "This is a little irregular, isn't it, Mr. Sheridan? I mean, I usually handle interviews through my office. . . . "

"I was in the area, interviewing Frank's ex-wife," I said. "When Evie told me you lived nearby, I thought I'd take a chance. I won't take too much of your morning."

"Well . . . sure, come on in."

I followed him along a central hallway that ran past a long, sunny living room-dining room combination, and into a white-on-white kitchen. Hirshberg, his bare feet slapping on the ceramic tiles, kept up a running monologue as we detoured around a cooking island, past a breakfast nook, and into a den with a long wall of glass opening onto the obligatory deck.

"It wasn't really a client-agent relationship between Frank and me. We started out just as friends from the antiwar movement. I began giving him advice on his contract—the owners frowned on agent representation in those days—and pretty soon I was handling most of his finances, taking a small percentage. Word got around that I'd been helping Frank and, by the time free agency came along in the mid-seventies, I already had half a dozen ballplayers signed up for my management services. Today I've got over thirty clients, mostly baseball and football, but a few basketball players and even an ex-coach."

A cream-colored leather loveseat and matching chair were grouped in front of a wall of shelves housing books, pottery pieces, and lots of high end audio/video hardware. Hirshberg stopped reciting his resume long enough to direct me onto the loveseat, then he dropped into the chair and took another hit of caffeine.

"Mmm, I need this. I took the red-eye in from the coast last night, didn't get in till one this morning. I should've stayed in town—I've got a little pied-à-terre near the office—but I hate to give up my weekends out here. At least the coast trip was worthwhile. I lined up a very tasty endorsement package for one of my clients." He dropped the name of a former football star who now appeared in shaving cream ads, then, as an afterthought, he waggled the mug. "Get you anything?"

I declined.

"Anyway, like I was saying, I owe a lot to Frank for letting me work with him in the early days." He smiled. "I wasn't exactly a favorite of the pro sports crowd back then, what with my antiwar involvement and everything. What very few people knew was that, when I wasn't protesting the ROTC in front of the president's office at Columbia, I was completing a graduate degree in financial management."

I had taken out my pad by this time and was scribbling a few quotes. "It's ironic," I said, glancing up. "You've done so well, thanks to the players getting free agency, while Wooley, the guy who was ahead of his time in suing for free agency, ends up losing what was left of his career."

Hirshberg nodded. "It's a shame. Tragic, even. Like Van Gogh never selling a painting and now they go for millions. Frank always had great timing on the field, but off? He was his own worst enemy, sad to say."

"I interviewed him a few times before he died," I said. "He told me you were supportive of his decision to challenge baseball's reserve clause."

"That's true—I supported him one hundred percent on principle. The reserve clause was un-American, no more than a form of well-paid slavery for the players. But I also cautioned him that he might lose and that, even if he won, at his age and with his reputation, chances were he was kissing his career good-bye."

"But he went ahead anyway. Why?" I asked. "Because of his principles?"

"Definitely. The slave analogy really bothered him." Hirshberg shrugged. "The fact that his wife Evie didn't want to move to K. C. was a big part of it, too, of course."

"I wonder what she had against Kansas City?"

"I don't know. I guess she just didn't want to pull up her New Jersey roots and move."

"Wooley told me that most of his old friends, including you, backed away from him after he lost the suit."

Hirshberg shot to the edge of his chair, spilling a few drops of coffee on the leather in the process. "That's not fair at all. We grew apart, true, but it had nothing to do with his losing the suit. It was the ban the commissioner handed down that did it, as much as anything. Frank was railroaded, in my opinion, but still, he did it to himself. I warned him about continuing to hang around with a bad crowd, but he didn't listen."

"By 'bad crowd,'" I said, "you mean Harry Lundquist?"

"Yes. The man was a gambler and an ex-con."

"How well did you know him?"

"I didn't know him." Hirshberg's denial was emphatic, but the eyes were evasive. "I knew of him. When I heard what sort of guy he was, I warned Frank off."

I let that go by for the moment. "Do you know how Wooley got tangled up with Lundquist in the first place?"

"I can guess. Frank liked to gamble—horses, cards. You meet a lot of losers when you go down that road. Anyway, I started putting our relationship into mothballs after the last incident with Lundquist. Frank didn't have much in the way of new earnings for me to handle by then and, well, I had just started to attract feelers from a few other players, wanting me to handle their business. . . . " He let the sentence fall away with another shrug.

"You were afraid of guilt by association?"

"Wouldn't you be?" He gulped down the last of the coffee, then excused himself to go for a refill. I busied myself with my notes while he was gone, settling in my mind where I wanted the next sequence of questions to take us. The former firebrand who had mixed it up with Mayor Daley's cops in Chicago and marched arm in arm with Black Panthers up Pennsylvania Avenue had cut off an old friend because he was bad for business; because Wooley had been in with a bad crowd. Seen through the lens of the disillusionment of the seventies and the cynicism of the eighties, Hirshberg's attitude seemed plausible—but for one thing: Everything I had learned so far suggested that Hirshberg had been a main cog in that bad crowd he was now decrying.

When he returned with his coffee mug replenished, I went straight to the heart of the matter.

"I interviewed Harry Lundquist at Auburn last week," I said. "He claimed that he and Frank Wooley cooperated on several poker scams in the late sixties." Hirshberg's face registered surprise, which grew in proportion as I detailed what Lundquist had told me. When I finished, Hirshberg shook his head.

"I'm shocked," he said.

"Lundquist also suggested that Frank's cut of the action was funneled through you, disguised as 'appearance fees.' And that you knew all about it."

"That is a goddamn lie! Sure, I booked Frank into plenty of conventions and trade shows when he was with the Phillies— and I collected his appearance fees for him. But if you or *The Sporting Life* even hints that I had anything to do with Harry Lundquist and his cons, I'll lay a libel suit on you before the ink dries!" He slammed the coffee mug down on the side table and stood. "This interview is over."

I didn't budge. "You represent Alfie Klem, don't you?"

Wariness mingled with the indignation. "Yeah."

"And Gimp Smith?"

He turned away, gazing out toward the deck. "Not really. I set him up with a few card shows now and then."

"Like the one at the Stanton Motor Inn in Geneva three years ago," I said. "The one where Frank and Smith and Klem got together with Harry Lundquist to relive old times?"

"I have no idea what you're babbling about. I told you this interview was over. . . . "

"How about the name Johnny Eberling? Does that ring any bells?"

He faced me again, his arms crossed, his hands worrying at the elbows of his sweater, like a fearful child hugging himself for protection against unseen demons.

"I've asked you to leave my home," he said, the voice brittle. "If I have to I'll call the police to remove you."

I put away my notepad and pushed up from the loveseat. "We'll save the police for another time," I said.

CHAPTER 28

My plane left Newark an hour late, landing at Rochester at quarter after five. I considered driving across town and dropping in on Kate instead of heading straight down to Mohaca Springs, but I was still focused on my confrontation with Hirshberg and I decided the seventy-mile drive home would give me a chance to sort a few things out. That turned out to be a wise decision, although for an altogether different reason.

The first thing I did when I got home was to dump William's litter box and let him out into the yard. Then I carried my bag to the bedroom, got a cold Molson's from the fridge, and headed up to the loft to check my answering machine. There were two messages, both of them from Kate—and both confirming that I was in serious trouble.

Her first call had come Saturday morning, reminding me when and where we were to meet that night for the Little Feat concert in Canandaigua. As I listened, I put my hands over my eyes and groaned. Her second call must've come around midnight. The gist of it, delivered in a slightly drunken slur, was that I was an inconsiderate bastard, that I had missed a great concert and an equally great bottle of Wagner white, and that I should take my answering machine and shove it where the sun don't shine.

Dreading what was to come, I picked up the phone and dialed. Kate answered on the first ring, as if she'd been sitting there seething since the night before.

"Yes?"

"It's me. Kate, I'm really sorry. . . . "

"Well, that makes me feel sooo much better, Sheridan. Now I don't feel so bad about being stood up with half the office staff on hand to witness it."

"I forgot the concert was this Saturday," I said.

"I gave you all the information last weekend!"

"I know, but I've been distracted by this story I'm working on. I had to fly down to New Jersey yesterday. . . . "

"Well, you can fly back there again next weekend, as far as I'm concerned. I don't need this kind of aggravation, Sheridan, I really don't. But, listen, if you ever manage to get Frank Wooley out of your system once and for all, give me a call. It'll give me another chance to do this!"

She slammed down the receiver. As soon as my eardrum recovered sufficiently, I called back, but she didn't pick up. Several more attempts went unanswered that night until, around ten, having worked up a pretty good dander of my own, I said the hell with it and went to bed.

I spent Monday morning trying to convince myself that I didn't need the aggravation, either. I was already carrying around enough emotional baggage from my own divorce; I couldn't handle Kate Sumner's, too. Besides, she wasn't the only smart, attractive, single woman around—it only seemed that way sometimes.

Just before noon I gave in and called her at the agency.

"We should talk about this, Kate," I said when we'd gotten past the muted hellos. "I've already admitted I'm an oaf, okay? But this isn't just about missing a date, is it."

"It's . . . I'm not even sure what it's about, Sheridan." Her voice was low; whether because of her mood or the potential for eavesdroppers, I wasn't sure. "Respect, maybe. Or self-respect, I guess—I don't know."

"I can drive up—"

"No." She was unequivocal on that. "Maybe I'm wrong, but I'm still too angry to deal with this right now. And I need to figure out why that is."

That was all. After we broke the connection, I spent the early afternoon trying to put Kate aside and get my mind back on the Wooley assignment. I eventually succeeded, thanks to Lev

Ascher. He called to tell me he had tracked down Evie March's former roommate.

"Name's Brenda Gould," he said. "She and Evie were chorus girls in a show back in '65—they roomed together for about a year. She says Evie was a good dancer, but her singing and acting were nowhere."

According to Brenda, Evie was more interested in finding a man than in advancing her show business career anyway. Brenda characterized Evie as a MAP.

"You know," Lev said, chuckling. "A midwestern American princess, looking for Prince Charming to come along and build her an ivory tower out in the suburbs someplace. Apparently she grew up in Missouri. Brenda thinks the town was called Pleasant Hill, if you can believe it. Anyway, I've got Brenda's number if you want to talk to her. She's going out of town with a touring company in a few days though—they're taking *I'm Not Rappaport* to the theater-starved denizens of the Pacific Northwest."

After getting off the phone with Lev, I dug out my Rand McNally atlas and located Pleasant Hill, Missouri, finding it just outside of Kansas City. Interesting. Frank Wooley had refused a trade to Kansas City and had sued baseball for his free agency because, he had told me, his wife didn't want to move there. Maybe Evie subscribed to the theory that you can't go home again.

It was almost noon Tuesday before I was able to reach Brenda Gould at her Manhattan apartment. She couldn't tell me much more. She recalled that Evie's first name was actually Evelyn, which she hated, and that she had shortened her last name to March "from something that sounded sort of slavic, but I don't remember just what it was," Brenda said.

Later in the day I received the first pre-panic call from Pete Calvett.

"Just touching base, Sheridan," he said in that booming voice. "I'm gonna see some Wooley copy any day now, right?"

"I've still got over two weeks till deadline."

"Yeah, if absolutely necessary, but I was hoping to leave a little lead time for the crosscheckers—gotta make sure you dotted all the i's. And we'll have to zoom it past the legal department to be on the safe side."

"That would be a real good idea in this case," I told him. "But I'll still need the two weeks, maybe more."

"More? Are you shitting me? You've been on this for a month already, Sheridan, not counting the time you put in on the original profile."

"You said you wanted a story worthy of the cover, Pete. I may have one for you, but I'm not there yet." I could hear his blood pressure shooting up, so I added quickly, "There's a chance Wooley and Delfay were both murdered."

That silenced him for five seconds, a personal best for Pete Calvett. "This is on the level? I mean, the cops are in on this theory, right?"

"Officially, no. Unofficially, they're looking at it."

"Gimme what you got," he said.

I told him what I knew and what I suspected about Lundquist, Klem, and the others. I also detailed Art Leek's investigation of the Wooley-Delfay case and the questions it raised. When I finished, Calvett was excited but skeptical.

"This could be absolute dynamite, Sheridan, but you've got a lotta holes to fill."

"That's why I may need more time, Pete. I need to figure out what the motive for the whole thing could have been."

"You need more than that," he said pointedly. "You need to get that cop on record—an indictment against somebody, or at least an official statement that Hirshberg and the others are under investigation. Without that to cover our asses, we've got nothing to print. But, Jesus, I love the potential. Is there anything we can do at this end to speed things up?"

I considered the offer for a moment. "I could use some help with a background check on Evie Garci, Wooley's ex."

"What's she got to do with all this?"

"I don't know, probably nothing. But I still want her checked out."

"Well, it's your call," Calvett said. "I've got this kid from Columbia U. I told you about, the summer intern? Gwen's like a pit bull when you sic her on something. Tell me what you need."

I split the next two days between working on my rough draft of the Wooley story and making a series of mostly unproductive calls to old teammates of both Wooley's and Klem's from the New York and Philadelphia years. No one I spoke to told me anything that I didn't already know.

On Thursday I received a couple of calls, the first from J. D. Staub, who wanted to get together over dinner that night. He had something that might interest me, he said, but he didn't have time to go into it over the phone. We agreed to meet at seven at a steakhouse in Geneva.

The second call came from IdaRose Mack. I felt a pang of guilt when I heard her voice; I'd been subconsciously avoiding her, not wanting to have to tell her what I'd learned about her man— that I suspected him of gambling, fraud, and blackmail, at the very least. I knew she could sense my discomfort and, maybe because she didn't want to hear the bad news any more than I wanted to relay it, she never asked where my investigation stood.

"I just thought you'd want to know," she said, her voice rather stiff. "I spoke with a couple of people at the branch bank Frank used. Frank always cashed his first-of-the-month pension checks there, and I assumed he did the same with the second check. They told me he cashed only the one check a month. But—here's the odd part—he did come in regularly around mid-month and purchase a thousand-dollar money order to send to Martina, as I told you. The thing is, he always paid for it in cash—crisp, new hundred-dollar bills every time."

Not so odd, I thought. Klem or Hirshberg or whoever was behind the payoff to Wooley wouldn't want the connection to lead back to them, and what was harder to trace than cash?

"You haven't received any more of these mid-month mailings from the pension office?" I asked her.

"No. Nothing more since Frank . . . died."

I thanked IdaRose for the information and promised her we'd talk again before I sent in my story. Before hanging up, she said, "Be sure, Timothy. That's all I can ask."

Her quiet admonition was still echoing in my head when I met J. D. Staub for dinner at Salter's Restaurant, a clubby little steak and brew tucked away just off Main Street in Geneva's rehabilitated historical district. His rank as county sheriff had garnered him the best table in the place, positioned beside a plant-filled bay window that offered a view of two restored Georgian town houses across the street and, between them, a sliver of Seneca Lake in the distance.

J.D. dominated the conversation through the initial round of beers and the salads, roundly denouncing the county legislature's decision to freeze his department's budget at the previous year's spending levels—a cut of almost 5 percent when inflation is figured in, he told me. I shook my head sympathetically at all the right moments and resisted the temptation to press him for the information he had promised me over the phone. Then, just as the steaks arrived, he asked me how my love life was going; a casual remark, but I told him anyway. When I finished detailing my travails with Kate Sumner, he sighed wistfully.

"This sort of reminds me of old times with your Uncle Charlie," he said as he poured the remainder of his second Twelve Horse into his glass. "Me bitching about the job, and Charlie carrying on about his latest female troubles. You know what he would've told you about this Kate of yours?"

"Yeah. He would've said, 'Timothy, women are like buses— another one comes along every ten minutes.' " I frowned. "Look where that philosophy got him."

"Mm, good point." J.D. popped a piece of charbroiled meat into his mouth and chewed. "On to new business. I got to thinking about you and this Wooley thing the other day—my brain's actually functioning again now that the budget hearings are finally done with. Anyway, Tony reminded me that you were still trying to find out about that request we had awhile back—the one that had something to do with the baseball card show at the Stanton?"

"Yeah?"

"Well, just for the hell of it, I went through the old file reports from the summer of '88 and I found a memo stuck in there." He drew things out with a long swallow of beer. "The long and short of it is, we got a missing persons inquiry from a sheriff's department down in Pennsylvania—Montgomery County. One of their citizens was supposed to be home Sunday evening from attending the baseball memorabilia show at the Stanton. When the fella didn't turn up by Monday, his wife called the local law and they called us. We assigned a man to check it out from our end, but before he could do much, we got another call from the sheriff down there, telling us to forget it. They found the guy."

I realized I had eased forward in my chair, but now I sank back, disappointed. "What happened, he go on a bender somewhere?"

"A fender bender, I guess you could say. They found his car down in a swale along Interstate 81 north of Scranton. He was in it, dead. Apparently he had a heart attack and ran off the road. According to Mrs. Truesdale, he had a history of coronary . . . "

"Wait a second, J.D.," I interrupted. "Mrs. who?"

"Truesdale. The dead guy's wife."

My interview with Johnny Eberling flooded back to me. Harry Lundquist's partner in the setup game—Truman or Truehart or something like that, Eberling said.

"How about another round, J.D.," I said as I waved for the waiter. "On me."

CHAPTER 29

ON Friday morning, I called Johnny Eberling. He wasn't in a chatty mood. Art Leek had paid him a visit since our last meeting to grill him on the events at the Stanton. Eberling didn't like getting mixed up with the police—bad for his image, he said—and he knew I was the one who had given Leek his name. I told him I only had one question; he could either answer it for me or I could pass the question along to the sergeant and let him ask it.

"Does the name Truesdale mean anything to you?"

"Truesdale?" He paused. "No . . . wait a minute, yeah, that was Lester's partner, the one Lester kept feeding winning hands. Bob Truesdale."

It was the name J.D. had given me: Robert Truesdale of North Hills, Pennsylvania, a small town near Philadelphia.

I made a series of calls to the Montgomery County Sheriff's Department before finally being transferred to an accommodating file clerk. She agreed to search her files and call me back, which she did late in the afternoon. She read off the particulars from the original missing-persons report, including the name of Truesdale's wife and her phone number. I began calling the number that evening and kept at it straight through Saturday, but there was no answer. Finally, late Sunday morning, I got through.

"Hello?" Said a pleasant, matronly voice.

"Hello," I responded. "Is this Eleanor Truesdale?"

"Yes, it is."

"Great. Mrs. Truesdale, my name is Sheridan." I told her I was a writer and briefly sketched out my interest in her husband and the baseball memorabilia show he attended in Geneva just prior to his death. I didn't bring up Lundquist or the others; I simply told her I was looking for information on people who had attended that show in 1988.

"Well, if this has anything to do with my husband's collection, Mr. Sheridan, you're too late," she told me. "I sold all Bob's baseball memorabilia long ago. My only hobbies are bingo and gardening."

"No, ma'am, I'm only trying to learn about a few of the people who attended the show at the Stanton," I said. "Your husband was an avid collector?"

"A collector and a trader. It developed into a sideline for him. He had a carpet-cleaning business here in the Philadelphia area. That was his main work, but he loved the baseball trading." She sighed. "I guess you could say I was a baseball widow before I became an actual widow. Bob drove to card shows and the like all over, two or three weekends a month. I didn't mind really—I had my garden to keep me occupied—but I worried about him. He had a weak heart, of course, and he sometimes tended to get carried away when he was off to one of those things, like a salesman at an out-of-town convention."

"Carried away, Mrs. Truesdale?"

"Oh, I don't mean party girls or anything like that," she said, laughing lightly. "Bob was perfectly trustworthy in that way. It's just, he always had quite a bit of money with him, for buying items, and he was susceptible . . . " She paused a moment. "Well, let's just say he liked his cards."

"Trading cards, you mean."

"Those, too," she clucked. "Heaven knows, he collected enough of them. But I meant playing cards, Mr. Sheridan. Bob loved poker, which was fine," she hastened to add, "when he was close to home where I could keep an eye on him. But sometimes when he was on the road, he'd get into a game with people he didn't know and, well, he'd lose too much. I didn't begrudge him the money, you understand—he always provided well for us, thanks to the carpet-cleaning business—but I didn't like to see him get taken. If nothing else, it was bad for his heart."

"Yes, I can understand that," I mumbled. After a few seconds, I said, "Did your husband take any of his collection with him when he made the Geneva trip?"

"Yes, he always packed along a display board of some of his better trading cards—those he wanted to sell or trade. Sometimes he brought home more than he left with."

"About that last weekend, Mrs. Truesdale," I asked, as delicately as I could manage. "When they—located your husband, did he have his display board with him?"

"Yes, everything seemed to be accounted for, as best I could tell. His trading cards, his wallet, about half his traveler's checks; they were all in the car when the police, you know—" she struggled momentarily to find the word "—found Bob down in that ditch off the highway."

"Mmm." I wasn't sure where to go next. According to Johnny Eberling, Bob Truesdale had been one of the bad guys. But Mrs. Truesdale's description was of a man who, if anything, was more likely to be a victim than a victimizer. On the other hand, if he had been found with his money and his collection largely untouched. . . .

"Was there anything else, Mr. Sheridan?" she asked, breaking up my reverie. "I was getting ready for church. . . . "

"I'm sorry, ma'am. Just a couple more questions, if you don't mind." I ran some names past her. She hadn't heard of a Hank Lester or Harry Lundquist, she said. Ditto for Gimp Smith and Richie Hirshberg. Frank Wooley and Alfie Klem she recognized vaguely as "a couple of old Phillies."

While trying to think what to do next, I threw away a line. "So you sold your husband's collection?"

"Along with the business, yes. Bob's brother bought out his half of the carpet-cleaning business. To be honest, I was more worried about selling the baseball collection, I know so little about that sort of thing. But, luckily, an acquaintance of Bob's— another collector—volunteered to have everything appraised and sold off. It brought in a tidy sum, too. Bob had some very desirable trading cards. One went for four thousand dollars."

"It must've been pretty rare."

"A Mickey Mantle card from 1952," she said. "Apparently those are highly prized."

My heart did one of those flip-flops you start worrying about when you're over thirty. "This friend of your husband's who handled the sale of the collection. . . . "

"An acquaintance," Mrs. Truesdale corrected. "They weren't actually friends—oh, I suppose they ran into each other at various card shows, but mostly Bob knew him through work. They both had cleaning contracts with some of the hotels in Philadelphia; Bob handled the carpets, of course, and Lou has a commercial laundry service."

"Lou?"

"That's right. Lou Garci."

In addition to being thorough, polite, and professional, Sergeant Arthur Leek apparently was psychic. He turned up at my cottage door at noon on Monday, just as I gave up trying to reach him at his office.

"I hope I'm not interrupting anything," he said, his navy bow tie bobbing with each syllable.

"I was just . . . " I hesitated. No sense giving up an advantage needlessly. " . . . about to have a sandwich. Would you like one?"

"No, thank you."

I had him sit on a stool on the other side of the kitchen's pass-through counter while I made my lunch—liverwurst with hot mustard on pumpernickel and a bottle of Molson's. He surprised me by accepting a beer.

I ate standing at the counter. "So what brings you out of your jurisdiction on a gray Monday, Art?"

"I thought it was time we compared notes again. I assume you're still interested in the Wooley case?"

"A correct assumption. You've made some progress?"

"Some." He fussed with the cuffs of his tan summer-weight suit. "Since we last spoke, I've talked to a few people about that alleged poker scam at the Stanton."

"Johnny Eberling, for one."

"Yes. I see you've been doing some follow-up." When I didn't offer a reply, Leek continued. "I've also done phone interviews with Alfie Klem and Randell Smith—Gimp Smith, as he's called.

What I've come up with is a standoff. Eberling described the game as a setup, with the man he knew as Hank Lester feeding cards to his accomplice, which supports your theory of a conspiracy. But both Klem and Smith deny any knowledge. They insist they didn't know that Lester was really Harry Lundquist. Both claim that Frank Wooley invited them up to the suite for a friendly game."

"Of course that's what they'd say. How do they explain the fact that Wooley didn't participate in the game? And that Smith acted as the house banker?"

"They say Johnny Eberling is a liar and a cheater himself, which is why he was thrown out of the game. It's their word against his."

I bit off a chunk of the sandwich and chewed awhile. "So who do you believe, Art?"

"I believe Eberling," he said simply. "But it doesn't matter what I believe if I can't prove it."

I muttered a curse and began absently tapping my fingers on the counter. "We need to show that Klem or Smith—preferably both—knew Harry Lundquist back in Philadelphia when he and Wooley were running around together. That would prove they were lying about not recognizing 'Hank Lester' at the Stanton." I stuck out my index finger. "You should go see Lundquist at Auburn."

"I thought of that," Leek said. "But not soon enough."

I frowned at him. "What's that mean?"

"Harry Lundquist is dead, Sheridan. As of last Wednesday." His boyish face was expressionless. "One of his fellow inmates cut his throat in the showers. No witnesses, needless to say."

"Jesus." I remembered something Lundquist had said when I interviewed him at the prison. "Except for a stabbing every other week, we don't get much excitement in here." Journalists love colorful quotes like that and I had written it down, hoping to find a way to work it into my story. Now that I had a legitimate use for the line, the prospect left me feeling hollow. What little I knew of Lundquist I didn't like. Still, I couldn't help but feel sorry for his death—and a little guilty.

"They got to him," I said grimly. "I was getting too close, so they paid some lifer to eliminate Lundquist. Now I know why he seemed scared when I told him Wooley may not've killed

Delfay or himself. He was afraid the others may've gotten rid of Wooley, and he knew he could be next."

"Perhaps," Leek conceded. "But, again, it might be impossible to prove. Unless I can turn one of the conspirators against the others—which is how these things usually get resolved. Somebody cuts a deal and informs on his confederates." He brooded for a moment. "I also need a better handle on motive. The scenario you presented was intriguing—that all this resulted from a poker scam gone wrong—but it lacks a strong motive or, for that matter, a victim. We have Johnny Eberling, of course, but he's perfectly happy with the so-called settlement he received. Who else lost anything that night at the Stanton?"

I smiled. "I've been refining that scenario since last we met."

"Oh?"

I let Leek fidget while I savored my beer; payback for the way he'd sprung Lundquist's death on me.

"This is a little convoluted, but trust me," I said as I set down the bottle. "Lundquist—the card mechanic—was hired by a third party—Mr. X, we'll call him—to run a scam after the memorabilia show at the Stanton. Klem, Smith, and Wooley were recruited to act as window dressing to lure the mark into the game. The mark was a baseball card trader who was known by Mr. X to have a weakness for poker. The idea was to have Lundquist set up the mark by feeding him good cards, letting him win until he was convinced he was riding a once-in-a-lifetime winning streak. This is the point where Johnny Eberling, who wasn't supposed to be in the game in the first place, catches on to Lundquist's moves—only Eberling thinks the mark is actually Lundquist's partner and that the two of them are trying to rip off everybody else. So Eberling starts cheating, too, and gets thrown out of the game. You with me?"

Leek nodded curtly. "Go on."

"Well, once they get Eberling out of the game, Lundquist lets the mark win a few more hands. Then the others gradually up the ante, complaining that they need a chance to get even. The mark goes along—he can't lose, right? Only he does lose, and he loses big. So big, in fact, that he's in danger of having to cover his bets by putting up his card collection for collateral—at least, that's how Mr. X, who arranged the whole thing, had it planned. But there was a wild card no one had counted on."

Leek's brows arched, but he said nothing.

"The mark had a heart condition. When he started losing—or maybe even when he was winning big—he got too excited." I shrugged. "He had a coronary and died. The others decided things had gotten too hot, so they packed the dead guy into his car, drove him halfway back home, ran his car off the highway, and left him behind the wheel. When the police investigated, they concluded the obvious."

Leek was peering at me. "Who was the mark?"

"A guy from Pennsylvania named Bob Truesdale."

"And the guy who set up the whole thing—Mr. X? That would be Richie Hirshberg?"

"No, I think Hirshberg was brought in later, to help clean things up." I smiled at Leek's puzzled expression. "I did warn you this was convoluted, Art. Maybe I should have said Byzantine."

I told him about my trip to New Jersey, particularly the stuff on Lou Garci—his connections to Frank Wooley and Klem and Hirshberg, his commercial laundry business, his obsession with sports memorabilia. Then I explained how J. D. Staub had led me to Eleanor Truesdale, who in turn had led me straight back to Lou Garci.

"As I see it, Garci was after certain items that Truesdale didn't want to sell—maybe just the 1952 Mantle card, but probably other pieces, as well. He thought he could either cause Truesdale to lose the collection outright, or force him to have to sell it off later to repay his debt. Truesdale's heart attack actually made things easier. All Garci had to do then was go to Mrs. Truesdale and offer to help her out in her time of need. He sold off the collection, buying for himself the Mantle card and whatever else interested him."

The sergeant was nodding his head very slowly. "This is good. Yes, I might even be able to take this to the DA."

"Great," I said. "Because I've got a story to file in ten days and I need you guys on the record. . . . "

Leek started backpedaling. "Let's not get hasty, now. I still need to turn one of the principals against the others. Now, I'm working a lead that might possibly connect Gimp Smith to Harry Lundquist—"

"Yeah? What sort of a lead?"

"A very tenuous one, at the moment. I'll brief you if and when it proves out, not before." He sipped his beer. "If I can turn Smith, or possibly Hirshberg. . . . "

"Smith was just a bit player in all this," I protested. "Why concentrate on him?"

"Because, as I indicated, I may have leverage to use on him," Leek explained pedantically. "And because it's always smart to follow the money. Smith was the conduit through which Wooley received his phony pension checks—which was Wooley's price for keeping quiet about what happened."

"Look, I've got a story to do and I'm running out of time. Maybe if you tell me what you've got, I could . . . "

He held up his hand. "I want you to stay away from Gimp Smith, Sheridan. In fact, I'd appreciate it if you'd stay away from the others, too, at this point. I can't risk having you muddy the waters. You've done a fine job of investigative reporting—now let me do my job. As far as going on record for your story, I'm still a long way from making a case here, and I'm afraid you'll just have to wait until I do."

I stared at him, incredulous. "After practically handing you this thing on a platter, you're telling me to back off? Because I might screw things up? You've got to be kidding me."

"I thought you knew me by now, Sheridan," he said, shaking his head. "I never kid."

CHAPTER 30

TUESDAY morning I ran into Allison Humbert and Kate on the sidewalk outside the Mohaca Springs town offices. Each was carrying a slim portfolio under her left arm, leaving the right free to slice the air, puncuating the animated conversation that flowed between them. They were too involved to notice me at first, giving me a moment to envy their easy camaraderie and to appreciate the colorful summer print dress Kate was wearing, the way her thick auburn hair caught the sun. Then she glanced up and saw me there, her expression flickering from surprise to pleasure to embarrassment before settling into an inscrutable smile.

"Sheridan!" She reached out, put her hand on my sleeve, then dropped it back to her side. "I was thinking about calling you, but I'm only in town for the day and we have so many meetings planned. . . ."

"I've been a little backed up, too," I said, letting her off the hook. Trying to wiggle off myself. "Still trying to put together the Wooley piece mostly."

Allison looked at us in turn. "Busy, busy," she said.

Allison was part of the problem—just her being there, grinning like a deranged pixie. But it was more than that. There was too much to say, so we said almost nothing at all.

"Maybe in a couple of weeks," Kate offered, "after we wrap up this promotions' schedule—"

"And I finish up with *The Sporting Life*," I said.

"Yes. I wish . . . " The thought drifted into a sigh. "Well, I guess we'd better leave it at that for now."

She leaned in, brushed my cheek with her lips, then stepped back. I watched her walk away with Allison, two pairs of sensible pumps clicking purposefully down the sidewalk. Then I turned in the opposite direction and headed for home.

I spent the next few days stomping around the cottage, muttering curses into the silence, kicking the furniture, snarling at William's feline indifference. I was angry at Art Leek for painting me into a corner on the Wooley story and angry at Kate Sumner, for destroying my ability to focus on work. And, when I bothered to analyze it, I was angriest of all with Frank Wooley for making me give a damn in the first place.

In between the tantrums, I forced myself to tinker half-heartedly with my rough draft, rewriting a paragraph here, making a phone call there, hoping to find a way to fill in the holes. No such luck. Finally, on Thursday, with only a week left until deadline, I knew I had to call Pete Calvett at *The Sporting Life*.

"Shit," he said when I brought him up to date on my investigation and told him about Leek's refusal to go public. "I've got a hole slotted for the Wooley piece for July 15, Sheridan. I've even got the cover art in the works. Damn!" He grumbled a moment, considering his options. "That cop's got us by the short hairs. I'd say screw it, we publish what we've got and use the sergeant's name as a source whether he likes it or not—but if it ends up he doesn't ever make a case, he's apt to stonewall us and then we're wide open for libel. I know damn well Klem and Hirshberg would sue and Garci doesn't sound like the type who'd roll over, either."

"He isn't."

"Well," he said reluctantly, "I hate to lose the slot—the hall of fame tie-in is perfect—but it's too damn good a story to do it half way. Unless we can somehow get the cops on record by next week, we'll have to hold the piece until they make up their minds."

I knew he was right, but I didn't want to hear it. I wanted that cover and I also wanted to be done with Frank Wooley, the sooner the better.

"Maybe I can find a way to force things," I said, thinking it out as I went along. "I'd like to get another chance at Alfie Klem. He's the one who best fits the description of the guy seen walking behind the Mack place after the shootings."

"So if he was the shooter, he's got the most to lose," Calvett argued. "He's not going to cooperate while you try to fit him for a double homicide."

"Maybe not, but I think this was Garci's deal all the way. He used money or influence or whatever to get Klem and the others to pull the original scam at the Stanton. Then, when Delfay became a problem, he sent the troops in again to do his dirty work. Now Lundquist is dead, and I'd bet my house that Garci was behind it. Klem isn't stupid, Pete. He sees Garci slowly getting rid of his problems—first Delfay and Wooley, now Lundquist. If I could plant the seed in his mind—that Garci might come after him next—maybe Klem would panic, decide it was time to cut a deal for himself."

"Personally I wouldn't go near the guy," Calvett said. "But if you're up for it, Sheridan, I can almost guarantee where Klem'll be next week—due south of here in Oceanside, over on the Jersey shore. There's a huge baseball memorabilia show held down there every year the last week in June. If Hirshberg didn't book his client in there, he ain't earning his ten percent."

"Sounds like my best chance." I asked Pete to verify that Klem would be appearing at the show and, if he was, to have my name put on the press list. Then I asked if Gwen, his summer intern, had turned up anything on Evie March.

"Not that I know of—I've been keeping her jumping lately, fact checking the hall of fame stuff we're putting together on Palmer and Morgan," Pete said. "Anyway, I still don't think Wooley's ex matters, Sheridan. Your story is the gambling connection, and what we think went down in Geneva in '88. Evie divorced Wooley years ago."

"And married Lou Garci," I reminded him. "The guy I figure is responsible for the Stanton setup and everything that's happened since. Evie's right in the middle of this thing—I'm just not sure how."

"Tell you what I think," Pete said. "You're still trying to find someone to dump all this on besides Frank Wooley himself—his ex made him do it, his old friends took advantage. You've got a great story working here, Sheridan, but you've got to keep it in perspective. So concentrate on breaking down Klem—and don't waste what little time you have left trying to resuscitate a dead hero.''

The following Tuesday I took my second flight to Newark in two weeks, picked up a rented Ford Taurus and drove forty miles southeast to Oceanside. In the preceding few days, I had worked on my draft of the Wooley piece, refining the prose and going as far as I dared with the story angle. But Leek hadn't returned any of my calls and, without him or his department to back me up, the article, as Pete Calvett had said, was a lawsuit waiting to happen. On Monday I sent the manuscript off to New York by express delivery so that Pete would have something to work with when and if I was able to make any progress with Alfie Klem.

The Oceanside Convention Center and Exhibition Hall was an aging dome-shaped building that filled up a whole block on Atlantic Boulevard, across from the public beach and boardwalk. Judging from all the promotional signs and banners I spotted as I cruised down the main drag, Calvett hadn't been exaggerating about the size of the baseball card and memorabilia show. It was an annual extravagaza in the resort town, the kickoff to summer at the shore. In addition to the main attraction—the card show at the convention center—the week-long festivities included dozens of autograph sessions with former star players, seminars and luncheons and dinners featuring many of the same stars as guest speakers, pitching and batting cages where frustrated jocks could play out their fantasies, and an old-timers' exhibition game at the local high school field.

I found a parking slot at a ramp garage down the street and backtracked to the convention center. A security guard pointed me to the publicity office, where I picked up a press packet and pass, along with directions to the lower level exhibition rooms. It was almost two o'clock and, according to the schedule I'd been given, Alfie Klem and a trio of other celebrities should've just been wrapping up a seminar titled "Baseball: When the Grass Was Real.''

The room was long and narrow and low. Several dozen folding chairs had been set up in rows, only about a third of them occupied. The big crowds were expected later in the week, I'd been told, when the hitting and pitching exhibitions and the old-timers game were scheduled. At the far end of the room, a dais had been set up for the four guest speakers—Alfie Klem and former Oakland outfielder Max Underwood, a retired broadcaster named Red Kelso, and Jim Fedders, a play-by-play man with ESPN.

I took an aisle seat and listened as the four men fielded a few questions from the audience. Most were of the why-aren't-players-as-good-as-they-used-to-be variety. The answers from the dais alternately savaged artificial turf, the designated hitter, long-term contracts, and major-league expansion. When the call came for one last question, I jumped up and waved my hand.

"I have a question for Alfie Klem," I said. "As an old teammate of Frank Wooley's, do you think the current controversy surrounding his induction into Cooperstown is justified?"

Klem peered out at me for a moment, puzzled. Then recognition set in and he frowned.

"That's a ways off the topic, pard. But since you asked, I think a man earns his way into the hall based on the numbers and that's how it oughta be. Anyway," he added, "who knows what drove Frank to do what he did? We'll probably never know what really happened out there. . . . "

"Don't bet on it, Alfie."

That sent a murmur through the sparse crowd and caused a few heads to turn in my direction. Klem broke off staring at me and mumbled something to the old radio announcer, Red Kelso, who then slowly rose from his chair and thanked everyone for coming. As the audience began to leave, I moved against the flow, cornering Klem and Kelso behind the dais.

"T.S.W. Sheridan," I said, for Kelso's benefit. I waved my press credential. "On assignment for *The Sporting Life*. I've got some follow-up on Frank Wooley, Alfie. Where can we talk?"

Klem glanced at Kelso, then began fidgeting with the clasp on his string tie. "Well, I'm real sorry, pard," he said. "But I've got twenty minutes till I'm due at an autograph session and I sorta need to visit the little boys' room first, if you catch my drift."

"Later then. I've got all day and all night."

"Too bad I don't. The promoters got me booked solid right through a banquet at the Lions Club tonight. . . . "

"I'll meet you afterward for dessert—can't take no for an answer, pard." I smiled at Kelso, who looked as if he were about to dress me down. "We go back a long way, me and Alf here. He ever tell you about the time he hiked the Finger Lakes Trail? . . . "

"Tell you what let's do, Sheridan," Klem said, regaining a bit of his usual bluster. He hooked an arm around the little broadcaster. "Me and Red here gotta run, but I'll make some time for you after the banquet tonight. No dessert, though. I'm pitchin' in the old-timers game Thursday—gotta watch the calories."

"Okay," I said. "Where and when?"

"Let's say eleven, over to the Grand Slam."

"What's that, a bar?"

"Nah, it's an indoor batting range, around the corner on First Street. The owner's lettin' me use one of the cages to get in my throwin', stretch my arm out for the game. I can use you to catch me while we chew the fat, huh?"

"All right," I said, a little wary.

"Good enough." Klem began moving away, taking Red Kelso with him. "See you at eleven o'clock?"

"I'll be there."

The Grand Slam was laid out similar to a bowling alley, only instead of lanes, there were perhaps a dozen batting cages lined up side by side. Each was about seventy-five feet long, segregated from its neighbor and the accessway by a high chain-link fence. A heavy cord net covered the top and hung down across the back wall like a stage curtain, its purpose to absorb and deaden the baseballs rocketed into it by the batters. While most of the cages featured coin-operated pitching machines—Iron Mikes, as they're known—the two cages at the far end had dirt pitching mounds for live throwing.

About half of the cages were in use when I arrived, teenage boys and young men frowning in concentration and grunting as their bats made contact. Alfie Klem, dressed in a plain gray sweatsuit and wearing baseball cleats, was waiting for me outside the last cage in the row.

"Well, you're a persistent little sumbitch, I'll give you that," he said, smiling coldly. "I seen you bird-doggin' me at the hotel."

I shrugged. "I just didn't want you to forget about me." After finding a motel room for the night, I had hurried back to the convention center to make sure that Klem showed up for his autograph session. Afterward, I tailed him back to his hotel and hung around until almost six, waiting for him to come back down to the lobby. When he did, I followed him and a couple of other men down the street to the Lions hall, where the banquet was being held. Satisfied that he wasn't planning to skip town on me, I went back to my room to shower and change, then went out for dinner myself.

"Well, you might's well make yourself useful." He reached into his gym bag and brought out a well-worn glove and a catcher's mitt. "Warm me up awhile," he said, tossing me the mitt. "Give you somethin' to brag on to your kids."

I followed him into the cage and stood behind home plate. Klem ambled out to the mound and began pawing through the ball bag that was lying there. When he found one he liked, I got down into a catcher's squat.

"Now, I'm gonna lob a few, just to stretch my arm out," he said. He took a slow windup and threw, the ball floating to the plate in a gentle arc.

I tossed it back. "Let's talk about Frank Wooley and the others, Alfie."

He lobbed another pitch. "I ain't loose yet. Can't talk if I ain't loose, pard."

I kept quiet for half a dozen more pitches, each one an easy lob over the heart of the plate; what the players call batting practice fastballs. On Klem's ninth toss, he speeded up his windup a bit, kicked his leg higher, and put a little more on the ball. It came in high and wide, glancing off my mitt and sailing to the backstop. I scrambled up and turned to chase it down—then I stopped.

Standing outside the gate staring at me was a tall, skinny middle-aged black man. He was wearing a warmup suit, a red windbreaker, and sneakers. Resting across his right shoulder was a baseball bat.

"Hey, 'bout time you got your lazy ass down here," Klem called out. "Sheridan, meet an old pard of mine, Gimp Smith."

CHAPTER 31

SMITH didn't look any happier to see me than I was to see him. He stared balefully for a moment longer, then turned his attention to Klem.

"Got bottlenecked in the Holland Tunnel comin' down," he said, his syrupy southern drawl diffident. "Some fool run into some other fool, I guess."

"Y'ask me, you're all fools for livin' in that city," Klem said. "Well, hell, Gimper, you're here now. Get on in here and stand in, take a few rips."

I looked from Klem to Smith, who was letting himself into the cage, moving with the slow, lopsided gait that had earned him his nickname. "I'm not catching with a batter up there," I said. "Not without a mask and chest protector. I think I'll just wait outside."

"Gawd, listen to the pussy," Klem said, then spit. "Gimp's just gonna take half-swings, give me a frame of reference like. I need a catcher to give me my target."

"I didn't come here to play games, Alfie."

"Well, I did, and you're on my time, boy." He cocked his head to the side, the lacquer on his thinning blond hair gleaming in the overhead lights. "Tell you what, you stand in and take some cuts and Gimp'll catch. That okay, Gimper? This boy don't figure to make much contact anyhow."

"Don't matter to me."

I didn't like that idea much, either, but at least it got the bat out of Smith's hands and into mine. I glanced behind me, relieved to see that a few of the cages farther down the row were still occupied by baseball wannabes taking their cuts.

"All right," I said. "Provided you both agree to sit down and talk to me afterward—there's a coffee shop right across the street. We can go there."

"Fair enough," Klem agreed—all too readily, I should've realized. "Now stand in and we'll get this show on the road."

I handed the mitt to Smith and held out my hand for the bat. He gave it up without a word, just continued to stare ominously at me. I hefted the wooden bat, took a few practice swings, and stepped into the box from the right side. Smith hunkered down a few feet behind me and pounded his fist into the catcher's mitt.

"Don't go tryin' to murder the ball now, Sheridan," Klem warned, flashing one of his corn-pone grins. "I don't have no practice screen and I'm too damned old to duck."

The first pitch, a lob, came in over the middle of the plate but high. I let it go. The second was as slow as the first, but in the strike zone. I slid my right hand up the bat and bunted the ball to the left side.

"I didn't say you had to bunt," Klem said. He took another ball from the bag at his feet and went into his windup. The pitch came in straight, but much faster than the others. By the time I swung, it was past me and into Smith's mitt. Klem was chuckling.

"That there was my everyday fastball—hell of a lot slower than you'd see in the majors," he said. "Try her again."

He threw the same pitch, spotting it out over the plate at the belt. Klem was right—it was a less-than-mediocre fastball by professional standards, but still plenty quick for a Babe Ruth League hacker like me. I swung under the ball and fouled it back.

He cackled as he rubbed up another ball. "Ain't as easy as it looks from the press box, is it, Sheridan. Wait'll I put a little bend into the old horsehide."

He went into his easy motion again, kicking the leg high and snapping off a near sidearm delivery. The ball seemed to be speeding straight for my head. My knees buckled involuntarily and I stumbled back, just as the pitch suddenly bit the air and darted down and away, passing over the center of the plate. Even Smith got a laugh out of that one.

"Strike two," he drawled as he tossed the ball back.

"Know what I hate about these damn sportswriters, Gimper," Klem said. "They got no respect. Always writin' trash about ballplayers, puttin' us down in the papers for blowin' a lead or strikin' out with the bases loaded. Like any one of 'em would have the stones to stand in against a Nolan Ryan heater and do anythin' but piss in their pants."

"I'm not a sportswriter," I reminded him, returning his glare. "I'm a reporter. Most of the people I write about don't deserve any respect, Alfie—guys like Harry Lundquist." I stood outside the batter's box, waggling the bat as I looked down at Smith. "You remember Lundquist, Gimp. Also known as Hank Lester? Hell of a card mechanic. He's run his last setup game, though— somebody stuck a knife into him a couple weeks ago."

Smith gazed up stoically. "That so?"

"Oh, now, you're supposed to get all flustered, Gimp," Klem called out mockingly. "Sheridan here's the one I told you about—the boy's tryin' to make out like you and me was mixed up with that Lester fella and Frank. Bet you dollars to biscuits he's the one been talkin' to the county cop up there, bendin' his ear 'bout what a couple of card sharks we are." He scratched at the mound with his right cleat, like an old rodeo bull making ready to charge the clown in the barrel. "Even had the gall to come down here today and try to embarrass me in public."

I glanced back toward the other cages again. Only two were still occupied, halfway down the row: a pair of gangly young men in jeans and softball jerseys, chattering to each other through the chain link as they packed their gear away in gym bags.

"It's getting late," I said. "Why don't we take this conversation over to the coffee shop. . . . "

Klem cut me off. "I already told you, boy, you're on my time now. That coffee shop ain't goin' nowhere and neither are we— not till I get my throwin' done. Now, you gonna swing that lumber or you gonna put on a dress and start singin' soprano?"

I told myself I was too old and too smart to let Klem's school-yard taunts get to me. Then I thought about how pleasing it would be to nail just one pitch and send it straight back at his sneering face. Once again, testosterone triumphed over intelligence.

I stepped back into the batter's box and dug in. Klem waited until I was set, then rocked into his motion and threw. The ball seemed to flutter up to the plate like a butterfly. I took a big cut—and missed.

"Strike three," Smith said laconically.

"That there was the knuckler," Klem informed me. "You're lucky I don't load one up on you, Sheridan. You'd screw yourself into the ground trying to hit my spitter."

I shook my head, mumbled a curse, and reset myself.

Klem's next offering was the batting practice fastball. I managed to get a piece of it, grounding it to what would've been shortstop if we were out on a diamond. No one spoke as we settled into a rhythm, Klem sending up a full assortment of pitches—slow curveball, straight change, good fastball, knuckler, good fastball again. I fouled off a couple of the breaking pitches and got good wood on the second fastball, lining it just to the right of the pitcher's mound. I backed out to adjust my grip and wipe the perspiration off my eyelids, hoping the others wouldn't notice the sweat or the tiny grin I was trying to suppress.

"Little late gettin' around, but not too bad," Klem conceded. "You shoulda seen me in the days when I could pop a prime heater whenever I wanted. Can still bring the gas every so often, but the old arm won't allow me but one or two a day without achin' for a week after." He waved me back into the batter's box. "Six more pitches and you can stick a fork in me, I'll be done."

I placed my feet back into the two depressions I'd dug in the box and took a few measured practice strokes. Klem missed the strike zone with his next two pitches, a knuckler in the dirt and a fastball, high and wide. He was beginning to tire, I assured myself. He aimed the next pitch, a fastball again, and got it out over the plate. I swung and lofted it over his head, into the netting and down the back wall.

Klem watched it until it stopped rolling, then swiped at the sheen on his forehead and reached into the bag for another ball. He rocked, kicked, and fired. In the split second it took the pitch to complete its short journey, my brain registered the three-quarter arm delivery and ordered me to hold my ground and wait for the curve to break. But the message was too late to get to my knees. They buckled again and I bailed out as the ball suddenly changed course and plunged across the plate for a strike.

"Lookit the jelly leg, Gimper," Klem crowed. "Likes the fastball, can't handle the hook. One more time, boy!"

I heaved a sigh and set my feet and stared out. He went into his windup, whipped the arm around again at three quarters. Wait for the break, wait for the break, my brain screamed as the ball came at me—but there was no break this time. Only an explosion of terror and pain as Klem's Sunday-best fastball collided with the side of my head.

" . . . mighta killed him."

"Too bad it didn't. Save me the effort."

"You crazy, Alfie? What you expect all this gonna get you? Anythin' this fella knows, others gonna find out. . . . "

"The whole fuckin' thing woulda stayed dead and buried if this piece of shit didn't come pokin' around! Now it's gonna get buried again, and him along with it."

I couldn't move.

I could hear the voices faintly, drifting down from the blackness, but I couldn't move, couldn't muster the strength to lift my throbbing head, couldn't even tell if my eyes were open or shut.

"You can't go killin' a man like you was throwin' away an old newspaper. It don't make any sense. . . . "

"It makes sense to me, goddamn it! I been takin' shit from sportswriters for thirty-five years, Gimp. I sat around bare ass for hours in stinkin' locker rooms, passin' out quotes, doin' right by these bastards—and what'd it get me? Fourteen lousy votes for the hall of fame last year, that's what it got me. I'd shoot every last one of 'em if I had the chance."

"You're crazy, man. . . . "

"You gonna keep callin' me that or you gonna grab his legs, help me get him to the car?"

"You think that little girl out front ain't gonna say nothin', she sees us haulin' a body through the lobby?"

"She's not gonna see nothin', she's too busy cashin' out for the night, and she knows her boss give me the run of this place.

Anyway, the car's in back by the fire door—we won't be goin' near the lobby.''

I could feel a coarseness on the palm of my left hand. The batting cage's artificial surface, I remembered now—and I could feel it! Could rub my fingers gently against it. Wiggle the toes now; good, good.

"Then what you gonna do, Alfie? How you gonna get rid of the body, you think of that?''

"I'll put him in the trunk, drive down to south Jersey someplace . . . I could bury him in the Pine Barrens, throw his ass in the Atlantic Ocean, what d'you care. All you gotta do is help get him to the fuckin' car. Now grab his legs.''

"Jesus, Alfie, you done that other sportswriter, too, didn't you? Killed him and Frank both and tried to make out like Frank did it hisself.''

"Wooley was an accident—he jumped me, almost screwed up everything. What the hell difference does it make now?''

"What the man gonna say about all this? He know you runnin' around killin' folks?''

"What's with you, Gimp? Used to be you didn't wanna know nothin', now you can't shut up. For chrissake, I got no time—will you just grab his fuckin' legs!''

I tried turning my head to the left, felt an earthquake rattle my skull, felt my throat constrict. Somewhere in the blackness there was a moan.

"Hear that? He's comin' around, Alfie. His eyes are blinkin' at me.''

"Not for long. Gimme that goddamn ball bat.''

The blackness came and went, came and went. Then a gray haze, brightening too fast. My eyes welled with tears, the tears ran off down my temples. A blur hung above me like a full moon. A face—Klem's face, grimacing. Klem's face and shoulders, and the bat.

Someone giggled madly—what's it all about, Alfie?

"I'll shut you up, you stupid son of a bitch.''

"*Freeze!* . . .''

CHAPTER 32

THE sergeant came by the cottage on Thursday. I was out on the deck with pad and pen in front of me, nursing a glass of ginger ale and watching the boats cruise the lake.

"How's the head?" he asked.

My hand moved involuntarily to the lump above my left ear. "Bent but unbroken." I held up my glass. "Get you something? A beer?"

"No, thank you." Leek sat in the deck chair opposite mine, a round redwood table between us. "You got back this morning, I understand?"

"Caught the businessman's special out of Newark."

The doctors at St. Margaret's Hospital in Oceanside had made me stick around for twenty-four hours—just to be on the safe side, they said. The damage was limited to a minor concussion, but it was the second time in nine months that I'd been knocked senseless, so I didn't put up an argument.

"You'll be pleased to hear that Alford Klem is in the Oceanside city jail on an aggravated assault charge," Leek said. "Although we may bargain that away to expedite his extradition to New York for murder."

"That was timely, the way you and the local cops stormed in at the last minute. Did I thank you for saving my life? I don't remember all the details."

"You were, uh, quite disoriented, understandably. You remember the part about the wire?"

I nodded gingerly and picked up the pen. "How'd you manage that anyway?"

"As luck would have it, I was in Manhattan Tuesday to meet with Mr. Smith and his attorney and a representative from the baseball commissioner's office. We were all in a conference room at the pension fund offices, discussing Smith's situation, when Klem phoned him around two thirty, demanding that he drive down to Oceanside. It was an opportunity too good to pass up, so we called the Oceanside PD and arranged the wire."

"How'd you get Smith to go along in the first place?"

Leek smiled serenely. "You recall the leverage I spoke of last week? Well, when I started looking into Klem and Smith, I checked the state computers for any arrest records on the two. I found that in 1975 Randell Smith had been convicted of a drunk-driving charge resulting from an accident in Queens. No one was badly injured, and Smith got off with a suspended license. The interesting part was the passenger who was with Smith at the time of the accident; Harry Lundquist."

I did the ah-hah bit with my eyebrows. "Proving that Gimp did know Lundquist, so he would've recognized him at the Stanton in 1988."

"He tried to claim otherwise at first, until I dropped the other shoe."

My pen stopped in mid-stroke. "Namely?"

"The car he was driving at the time of the accident, a Cadillac, wasn't his. It was registered to Louis Garci."

"Nice symmetry."

"I pointed that out to Mr. Smith, with an assist from the commissioner's aide. We convinced him it would be in his interest to cooperate with my investigation. Once he had his immunity assured, he had quite a lot to say."

According to Gimp, he and Klem had known Lou Garci since their days with the Mets in the early sixties, when Garci's company had the team's laundry contract. A symbiotic relationship developed. Garci's connections in the business community brought Klem lucrative speaking engagements and appearance fees at chamber of commerce luncheons, trade shows, conventions, and so forth. In return, Klem—and his shadow, Smith—got Garci into locker rooms and team parties, where he was able to indulge his passion for collecting autographs and memorabilia.

The relationship continued after Klem was traded to Philadelphia, thanks to Garci's business interests in that city and throughout southern New Jersey. When Frank Wooley joined the Phillies in 1967, Smith said, he already knew Lou Garci from New York. The four men—Garci, Klem, Wooley, and Smith, who had since been released by the Mets—formed their own little rat pack, getting together to bet the horses at Garden State or to play cards or just to sit around a bar.

"Here's the part you won't like," Leek said. "Smith says it was Frank Wooley who introduced Harry Lundquist to the others."

I glanced out at the water. "I can't figure the man. Did Smith know how Wooley and Lundquist hooked up?"

"No, only that it was Wooley who brought Lundquist along on an excursion to the race track one afternoon. After that, he became something of a fixture, I take it."

"Did the others know Lundquist's history?"

"They found out soon enough. Lundquist liked to brag about his abilities with a deck of cards. Garci got the idea to put those skills to work at a banquet he was helping to organize—a Democratic fund raiser. This was around 1969. It seems one of the guests was a New Jersey state legislator that Garci didn't like. He knew the man was an inveterate poker player, so he arranged a game after the banquet and brought in Lundquist as a ringer. Smith says the politician left owing Garci a lot of money—which Garci later took out in trade, so to speak, in the form of political favors.

"After that, Garci had Lundquist pull the same scam several other times; business rivals, union bosses, politicians. He collected a lot of IOUs. As you suspected, Wooley and Klem were employed as window dressing, to impress the marks and lend an air of legitimacy to Lundquist."

I brought my notes up to date, then asked, "Where does Richie Hirshberg come into the picture?"

"He was Frank Wooley's friend, too. As Smith tells it, Hirshberg handled Wooley's money, including the appearance fees that Garci arranged, most of them legitimate—Garci had a lot of pull with trade show and convention organizers at various hotels in Atlantic City and Philadelphia. Eventually Hirshberg started managing Klem's finances, too, the first steps toward building the sports agency he owns today. Smith claims that Hirshberg knew some of the money was dirty—payoffs for participating in Lundquist's and Garci's scams. Hirshberg denies it. He told me yesterday that he was completely unaware of the gambling cons until after the Stanton incident in '88.''

Leek said he had spent the last day and a half questioning, in turn, Alfie Klem, Gimp Smith, Richie Hirshberg, and Lou Garci. Garci had stonewalled, but the others had been more forthcoming. By piecing together what each man told him, Leek was able to decipher the big picture.

The setup game at the Stanton had been arranged by Lou Garci. In the long years that Frank Wooley had spent in exile, Garci and Klem had remained friends, occasionally getting together again with Lundquist whenever Garci had need of his services. In the spring of 1988, Garci had planned to buy several pieces for his baseball collection from an upcoming estate sale in Camden. He inadvertently mentioned this fact to a business acquaintance and fellow collector—Bob Truesdale. But Truesdale aced him out by going to the heirs before the sale and arranging to buy up the collection. Furious, Garci decided to get even. He knew that Truesdale was a poker player; he also knew Truesdale would be in Geneva for the memorabilia show. The rest was easy. Garci arranged for Richie Hirshberg to book Klem and Smith into the show. He also contacted Harry Lundquist, paying him a set amount to meet the others in Geneva and run a setup game on Truesdale.

"It had worked flawlessly many times in the past," the sergeant said. "But this time, their luck ran out. The first mistake was letting Johnny Eberling into the game—himself a ringer. Then Truesdale became suspicious when his losses began mounting. He launched into a tirade against Lundquist, began pounding his fist on the table. Before anyone knew what was happening, he turned beet red and pitched over onto the floor, dead.''

"Back up a minute, Art," I said. "You say Garci had Klem and Smith booked into the autograph session at the show. What about Wooley?''

"He'd been recruited for the show locally. Klem says that

when Lundquist saw Wooley was there, he decided his old buddy deserved a piece of the action." Leek frowned. "I get the impression from Smith, though, that Wooley wasn't happy about being there. In fact, Smith and Klem both say that Lundquist and Wooley had always made an odd pairing. They were supposed to be friends, yet they didn't seem to like each other." He shrugged. "Greed makes strange bedfellows, I suppose."

"Mmm." I gnawed the tip of my pen. "What about the monthly payoff to Wooley? How'd that come about?"

"According to the others, Wooley had left the setup game before Truesdale suffered his fatal heart attack. Lundquist phoned him at his apartment and insisted he come back and help them get rid of the body—apparently wanting to make sure that everyone was equally culpable. But Wooley refused to come back. Klem says the payoff was later suggested by Garci, with the details worked out by Richie Hirshberg. Garci sent the money by messenger to Smith's apartment on Saturdays, mid-month—always ten crisp one-hundred dollar bills. Smith would bring it into work on Monday morning and post it inside a pension fund envelope."

"What did Garci have to say about the money?"

"It's the one thing he admitted to—paying Wooley the thousand dollars a month. But he claims it had nothing to do with any poker scam or cover-up. He says it was merely a favor he was doing for a former friend: a face-saving device he set up so that Wooley could appear to be contributing to his daughter's education. Garci said he would've just had to give Martina the money himself, so it wasn't costing him anything to do it this way."

"Sure." I made a notation on my pad and circled it. "What about the shootings out at the Mack place?"

Leek allowed a self-satisfied smile. "Mr. Klem caved quite nicely after I confronted him with the evidence."

"You've got evidence?" I said, surprised.

"There's the recording we took from the wire, assuming it's ruled admissible. More important, we found his prints in one of the rental cabins out on Lookout Run and we have a positive ID from Sturdevant that Klem was the man he saw out on that ridge. We've also established a possible motive, aside from the Truesdale affair. It turns out that Mike Delfay was the ghost writer who worked with Klem on his autobiography a few years ago. Apparently Delfay insisted that Klem admit in the book that he had regularly thrown a spitball as part of his pitching repertoire. Klem believes—irrationally, I'm sure—that this admission cost him precious votes for the hall of fame."

"So Klem killed Delfay in revenge for that?"

"He claims not—that his hatred for Delfay merely made him an easy mark when Garci suggested that the nosy sportswriter was becoming a problem. Klem says Delfay, in researching his book on Wooley, had found out about the Garci-Lundquist-Klem connection. Garci decided Delfay had to go and that it would be best if Wooley went right along with him. But Klem claims he didn't plan to kill Wooley, only Delfay. He thought he could force Wooley's cooperation."

I said, "He kills Delfay, assuming Wooley will help him dispose of the body. But Wooley goes for the gun instead and ends up dead himself."

"That's the scenario." Leek exhaled wearily. "Klem's lawyer is trying to bargain us down to manslaughter on Delfay, which won't happen. We present our case to the grand jury next week, and I'm fairly confident we'll get a murder-two indictment on Klem. Smith and Hirshberg have accepted immunity in exchange for their testimony; neither one had prior knowledge of the Delfay hit. The problem is Lou Garci. I believe Klem's version—that it was Garci who planned the murder—and I have no doubt that it was Garci who arranged the hit on Lundquist at Auburn; among his many connections, Garci is reputed to have ties to organized crime. I'm just not confident we can prove any of it in court."

I thumbed back a page in my notebook. "So Garci was just sending Wooley the money as a good samaritan, right? He knew nothing about Delfay and the rest of it?"

"So he claims."

"Did the messenger bring Gimp Smith the regular mid-month payoff that Saturday?"

He frowned. "I don't know."

"Maybe you should find out. Because Wooley should've received it three days after the shootings. It never came."

Leek jumped as if I'd poked him with a cattle prod. "Of course! Garci didn't send it because he knew ahead of time that Wooley wouldn't be alive to spend it."

I leaned back. "Sounds right to me—not that I want to muddy up your investigation or anything."

Leek's pink moon face went mauve. "I guess I deserve that, Sheridan."

I waved it away. "Ignore me, Art. I'm just in one of those moods."

He turned and stared out at the lake. "Well, anyway, everything's official now. For better or worse, you've got the Frank Wooley story nailed down."

"Yeah," I said, following his gaze. "So it would seem."

CHAPTER 33

Juuly came in hot and muggy. School was out, Independence Day was in the offing, and the lake was growing crowded with fair-weather fishermen and Sunday sailors and drunks on power skis.

I worked through the holiday weekend to update and polish the article, then sent it off to New York by express delivery on Tuesday morning. That night I called IdaRose Mack and, with little preamble, read to her what I had written about the man she loved. She listened without speaking a word. When I finished there was a short silence on the line. Then, gently, she hung up the phone.

On the following Tuesday, the grand jury handed down indictments on Alfie Klem and Lou Garci for second-degree murder and conspiracy to commit. The daily press jumped all over the story and hit the ground running, but they had too little and they had it too late. That Friday *The Sporting Life* exploded onto the newsstands with an old photo of Klem and Frank Wooley on the cover, arm in arm in their Phillies uniforms and mugging for the camera.

The revelations about the Stanton incident and the subsequent murders of Mike Delfay and Wooley effectively put a halt to the move to rescind Wooley's induction into Cooperstown. As one sports columnist put it, sure the guy made some big mistakes, but at least he didn't kill anybody. I suppose it was as good an epitaph as any.

My phone started ringing the same afternoon the magazine article appeared. Congratulations from old friends, a crank call or two, a few fellow journalists trying to flesh out stories for their papers or their newscasts. I answered each call politely the first day, then retreated to my boat and the relative peace of the lake to wet a line and brood; about boyhood heroes and angry women and sad little girls and a dozen other things I could do nothing about. It was purely serendipitous that I happened to be in the kitchen Monday afternoon, getting some ice for the cooler I keep in the skiff, when Eddie Gentile phoned from the noisy newsroom of the *Philadelphia Inquirer*.

"Great piece in *The Sporting Life*," he told me. "Got me thinking about that conversation we had last month when you called about that infamous *Newark Ledger* story of mine in '72. I noticed your article didn't mention that lawyer I told you about—Warren Haskell."

"I hit a dead end there," I confessed. "Haskell died a few years ago and nobody at his firm wanted to talk. I was hoping to find out how and why he showed up that day with Harry Lundquist, but it didn't pan out."

"Yeah, well, if you'd told me at the time that Lou Garci was involved, I might've been able to steer you in the right direction, Sheridan. Garci's name is fairly well-known amongst reporters and political insiders down here. He's got laundry and liquor service contracts with half a dozen joints in Atlantic City and, believe me, you don't land those without kowtowing to both the pols and the wise guys."

I said, "I heard recently that he's supposedly mixed up with organized crime."

"He's got ties to just about every power base in New Jersey— the mob, the Democratic party, the unions. You remember I told you Warren Haskell's firm did a lot of union lobbying up in Trenton?"

"Yeah?"

"Well, I don't know if you're still interested," Gentile said. "But I'm planning to follow up on this myself and I figured I owed you a piece of it. Haskell's clientèle included the Teamsters. Garci's laundry and liquor delivery trucks are driven by Teamsters and, because of that, Garci maintains a very cosy relationship with the union's bosses. Course, it could be just coincidence that the union's attorney showed up that day to represent Frank Wooley, but I'm not real big on coincidences myself. Anyway, I just thought you oughta know.''

I thanked him for calling. Then I took the ice out to the boat and putted out to the center of the lake and thought about Lou Garci and Evie. An hour later, I went in and phoned Pete Calvett.

''You just can't let go of Frank Wooley, can you,'' he said after I told him what I'd learned from Eddie Gentile. ''The story's done, Sheridan, and you did a great job. Hell, we doubled our pressrun for the issue, and it's almost sold out already. You should be basking in the glory, man, not fretting about doing a follow-up. Let the daily media clean up the loose ends, if there are any. We've got the pennant races and NFL training camps to focus on now. We're a sports publication, remember?''

''But I'm not a sportswriter, Pete, I'm an investigative reporter. And I don't like leaving part of my story for some other reporter to finish. Look, you hired me to find out everything there was to know about the tragic life and death of Frank Wooley—your words, Peter. I found out plenty, but I didn't answer the key question: Why? Why did Wooley hook up with a lowlife like Harry Lundquist in the first place? Why did he risk all that he had—all that he was—on a small-time grifter and a few penny-ante con games?''

''Wooley got in with a bad crowd and let his greed and ego overrule his judgment. That's the why of it.''

''Maybe, but I think there's more to it,'' I insisted. ''Look, if you're not interested, that's fine—I can take what I come up with to another publication or the wire services. . . . ''

''Whoa, I didn't say I wasn't interested—if you actually come up with something new.'' Calvett let go a frustrated sigh. ''Jesus, I dunno who's more persistent—you or my intern, Gwen. She's been bugging me about the background info on Evie March you wanted. I told her it was moot at this point, but . . . hang on a minute. I'll let her tell you what she's got, for what it's worth.''

Two minutes later a soft, tentative voice came on the line. ''Mr. Sheridan? Gwen Sterling.''

''Hi, Gwen. Pete tells me you came up with some history on Evie March for me?''

''I'm sorry it took so long. They keep me jumping down here, and I haven't had much time to spend on it, but I think I may've tracked down her real name and a few details."

"I appreciate your work, Gwen. Let's hear what you've come up with."

"Well, you thought her hometown was Pleasant Hill, Missouri, right? I found out there was an Evelyn Marchabroda who grew up there back in the fifties—she was the high school prom queen, star of the school plays, all that. It sounds like a profile that would fit Evie March."

"To a tee," I said. "You have anything else?"

"Not much. It appears she left Pleasant Hill after graduating high school in the early sixties and never came back. I spoke to Evelyn's mother—she sounded like a lush, frankly. Anyway, the mother says she disowned her daughter after she left her to move to 'the big city.' "

"New York," I said.

Gwen giggled. "No, she meant Kansas City, if you can believe it."

Louella Marchabroda did indeed sound like a woman lost inside a whiskey bottle. Her voice, when, it wasn't breaking up with a smoker's cough, was alternately a low, self-pitying whine or a loud, grating rasp.

"I don't have a daughter no more, Mister. I ain't heard a word from the little tramp in twenty years—closer to thirty, you wanna know the truth." I pulled the phone away from my ear while she worked a catarrh from her throat. "She run out on me, just like her old man . . . prob'ly as dead as he is by now, for all I know—or care. Two of a kind. . . . "

"I understand she moved to Kansas City after high school," I said. "That's very near to Pleasant Hill, Mrs. Marchabroda. She didn't keep in touch? . . . "

"I told you, I dis . . . disowned the girl!" she barked at me. "Oh, she come home once, wantin' to show off her fancy man, like that worthless son of a bitch was anything to brag on." Another violent hack. "I can spot 'em a mile away, the smooth talkin' liars. I told her, he'll end up doin' you just like your old man done me. Oh, no, she says to me, not my Harry."

* * *

I spent another day and a half on the phone to government agencies in Kansas City and the surrounding counties of Clay and Wyandotte. By Wednesday morning, I was ready to brace Pete Calvett again.

"I think I can put the 'why' into the Wooley story now, Pete," I said. "All I need from you is a press credential for this weekend's hall of fame ceremonies and, if you can swing it, a motel room for Saturday night in Cooperstown."

Calvett mumbled for a moment. "That little burg's jammed for the induction festivities, but I can double you in with our staff guy, Mel Kaiser—he's covering for us. The credential shouldn't be a problem." He paused. "But first you gotta convince me you've got something."

"Try this. In 1963, in a civil ceremony at the city hall in Kansas City, Evelyn Marchabroda—that's Evie March to you, Pete—married Harry Lundquist."

"Hmm, that is very interesting, Sheridan."

"Now comes the kicker," I said. "According to the Clay County Department of Vital Records, Evelyn Marchabroda later had the marriage certificate amended to reflect her divorce from Lundquist."

"What's surprising about that?"

"The date, Peter—the amendment was filed in 1973."

"Oooh," Calvett murmured, "I like it."

CHAPTER 34

A writer once wrote that if baseball wasn't actually invented in Cooperstown, it should've been.

The little village of twenty-five hundred people sits in a green bowl surrounded by steep, undulating hills at the southern end of Otsego Lake, the Glimmerglass of James Fenimore Cooper's novels. It's a place of stone walls and white picket fences and fine Victorian houses, every third one seemingly an antique shop or a bed and breakfast; a place out of a gentler time, where handsome women stroll Main Street in long, loose skirts and old men disdain aluminum walkers for sturdy hickory canes, and where there are no fast-food franchises to be found anywhere. Above all, it's a place of abiding American myth. The shining nine-mile lake and birch forests recall the noble savages and selfless pioneers of the Cooper sagas; the Farmers Museum houses in its displays the Cardiff Giant, an anthropological hoax concocted by an upstate farmer more than a century ago. And then there's the Baseball Hall of Fame, where the greatest heroes of the game live on in perpetual triumph, never striking out with the bases loaded or getting raucously drunk on the long train ride to St. Louis.

I left Mohaca Springs early Saturday morning, completing the 160-mile drive in just over 3 hours. It was ten thirty by the time I checked into the motel room I was to share with Mel Kaiser, *The Sporting Life's* staff writer. He was a young man with an old man's taste for big cigars and loud sports coats. He greeted me cautiously—I was an interloper, after all, come to horn in on one of the sporting year's nicest perks—then hurried out to do a breakfast interview with the president of the National League.

As always on the weekend of the induction festivities, Cooperstown was overflowing with people and cars. I left the Bronco in the motel parking lot and walked the mile into the village center. According to the itinerary Kaiser had handed me along with my press pass, the inductees and their relatives were scheduled for a private tour of the baseball museum that morning, followed by a closed luncheon. In the afternoon, the guests and dignitaries would attend an exhibition game between the Baltimore Orioles and the Montreal Expos at Doubleday Field, a cosy brick ball yard tucked away just off Main Street.

The guest list for Frank Wooley's posthumous induction was short—his ex-wife Evie and their daughter Martina, who was scheduled to deliver a speech on her father's behalf at the formal ceremonies the next day on the steps of the National Baseball Library. There was to be a formal press conference prior to the ceremony, but that wouldn't suit my purpose; I wanted Evie one-on-one.

I spent the better part of the day trying to ambush her as she and Martina and the other guests were ushered from place to place. I almost caught up to them outside the museum around noon, but they were whisked away in a limo before I could get close. Later, during the exhibition game at Doubleday Field, I had a good view of mother and daughter seated together in one of the VIP boxes along the first base line, but I was penned up in the press overflow area a hundred feet away. It wasn't a total waste of time, however; one of the sportswriters sharing the space told me that most of the guest families were staying over at the Otesaga Hotel.

After the game, I returned to the motel room to change into a fresh shirt and a blazer, then walked over to the Otesaga. Built after the turn of the century, the summer resort hotel managed to mimic the conspicuously overdone dimensions of earlier Victorian-era buildings without capturing any of their whimsy or grace. It was a massive, somber redbrick structure with a three-story colonnaded portico hanging off the front facade. Add in the groups of garishly clad men and women who ferried back and forth from the adjacent Leatherstocking Golf Course and the overall impression was of an insane asylum for well-heeled duffers.

The lobby was crowded with guests, about equally divided between excited, chattering baseball fans in town for the ceremonies and the more sedate regular clientèle, on hand for the golf and the boating and the Glimmerglass Opera. The harried desk clerk wouldn't give me Evie's room number, but he did call to see if she was in. She wasn't.

I decided to cruise the hotel, hoping I'd run across her in one of its many public areas. I started with the clubby Hawkeye Bar on the ground floor and, down the corridor from it, the anachronous ladies' lounge. No luck. I took the stairs back to the first floor, loitered awhile near the grand piano in the lobby, then resumed my wandering. I eventually found them both, Evie and Martina, sitting in a shady corner of the rear terrace, quietly sipping drinks and staring out at the pool and the lake.

Martina noticed me first and frowned. "If you're looking for another story, Sheridan, you've picked the wrong time and the wrong place."

Evie glanced up. "God, not you again. Haven't you done enough to this family already?"

I kept my eyes on her daughter. "I apologize for the timing, but I'm not looking for another story—I just want to finish the one I started."

"What's that supposed to mean?"

"It means I'd like to talk to your mother for a few minutes. Alone."

Evie slammed her glass down onto the wrought-iron sidetable. "Oh, you would, would you? You can go to hell, is what you can do. My husband is facing a murder charge because of you and that slimy rag you write for—you're goddamn lucky if we don't sue you all for slander!"

"It's libel, mother," Martina said. "Slander is . . ."

"I don't care what it is—and I don't need to hear anymore from you either, Martina. Maybe if you hadn't gone making up stories for this man, your stepfather wouldn't be in such a mess."

"And maybe my father wouldn't be going into the hall of fame," Martina countered. She looked from her mother to me, unsure which of us she was angriest with. "What's this all about, Sheridan?"

"Something I owe to IdaRose," I said. "Give me twenty minutes."

She considered me a moment longer, then slowly rose, glass in hand. "Twenty minutes. Then I want some answers."

"Wait a minute, Martina!" Evie uncrossed her long, graceful legs. "You're not leaving me with this man!"

Martina ignored her and walked off toward the French doors leading into the hotel. Evie began to get up, but I held up my hand and said, "Let's talk about Pleasant Hill for a minute, Evelyn."

She dropped back into her chair and blinked at me. Then she frowned and picked up her glass. "I told you, I have nothing to say to you."

"Okay," I said, as I sat down. "You can listen while I talk."

I recited what I'd learned about Evelyn Marchabroda: the broken home in Pleasant Hill, the move to Kansas City, the marriage to Harry Lundquist and, ten years later, the divorce decree. Evie took turns staring out at the lake, frowning at me, rolling her eyes and shaking her head, bored with it all.

"It doesn't take much imagination to speculate on the rest of it," I said. "Ambition—yours and Harry's both—led you to New York, where things began to fall apart. In 1965, Harry was sent to prison for two years on a check-fraud conviction. While he was gone, you continued to try and make it in show business, landing a job at a nightclub. You met Frank Wooley—a real celebrity—and when he fell in love with you and asked you to marry him, you said yes. Conveniently forgetting to tell him about the husband you already had."

Evie couldn't hold it in any longer. "Husband?" she snapped. "Some husband Harry was! He left me first, Mister—six months before he got himself arrested. Was I supposed to worry about what happened to that bastard?"

"No, but you might've at least told Frank about him. You could've filed for a divorce then. . . ."

"You know what it took to get a divorce in 1966? How much time?" She shook her head. "You think I was going to risk losing Frank Wooley because of Harry Lundquist? I'm supposed to blow everything by telling him I've got a convict husband sitting up in Sing Sing?"

She turned away again, her lips compressed into a grim line. "I've had enough of this."

"Not yet," I said. "We're just getting to the important stuff. Lundquist read about the marriage while he was in prison. Meanwhile, Frank was traded to Philadelphia and Harry figures, what the hell, maybe Philly would be a good town to work. So after he gets out, he pays you a visit at the house in Teaneck and tells you what he's got on his mind. You're supposed to introduce him to Frank—an old friend from the midwest, is that how it worked, Evie?"

"I was pregnant by then. Frank was gone most of the time— what was I supposed to do?" She teared up, doing the damsel in distress bit for her audience of one. "Harry blackmailed me into telling Frank he was my cousin. He wanted an in with the high rollers who hang around with the ballplayers. What choice did I have?"

"So you went along and Frank bought it. He liked the track and a friendly card game, and so did Harry. But Harry was too greedy. After a while, Frank caught on to him—how Harry was using him to set up his friends and cheat them at cards. He tried to cut his ties to Harry, but Harry played his ace. He told Frank what he had on you."

She laughed bitterly. "I was relieved when he told him—I thought, one way or the other, I was finally done with Lundquist. But Frank was so old-fashioned—he was afraid Harry would follow through on his threat to tell the world that Frank and I weren't legally married, that Martina was supposedly 'illegitimate,' as if anybody really cared about that sort of thing anymore." She rolled the eyes again.

"So Frank went along with Harry and let him continue to use him," I said. "Until the commissioner's office got wind of what was going on and ordered Frank to disassociate himself from Lundquist."

Evie nodded. "Frank knew he had to end it then. Harry refused to give me an uncontested divorce—he wasn't ready to give up his edge. But he let Frank pay him ten thousand dollars to go away and that was that—or so we thought."

"Until 1972, when Lundquist turned up with the lawyer at

the Bergen County Civic Center," I said. "We'll come back to that in a minute. First, tell me about the trade to Kansas City, Evie."

"You seem to have all the answers—you tell me."

"All right. When the Phillies tried to trade Frank to the Royals after the 1970 season, you both got worried. Someone in Kansas City was bound to figure out that Evie March was once Evelyn Marchabroda. Rather than risk the questions that would raise, Frank decided to refuse the trade and challenge baseball's reserve clause."

She shrugged and went back into her bored mode. "It's all water under the bridge now. After Frank lost the suit and we had—the accident with Martina—things got too bad to salvage. We split up and I started seeing Lou. He was good for me—I needed him."

"And Lou needed you," I said. "In fact, he'd been in love with you for years, ever since he first met you and Frank back in New York."

"Yes, Lou had a thing for me from the beginning—but he was a gentleman. He never made a pass, never came on to me at all. Until it was over between me and Frank."

"Uh huh. But maybe he found a way to help things along."

"What're you talking about?"

"The incident with Harry and the lawyer." I told her about Warren Haskell, his connections to the Teamsters and, through the union, to Lou Garci. Then I told her about the "friend of Evie's and Frank's" who called Harry Lundquist and had him drive Haskell to the arraignment, and about the anonymous phone tip to Eddie Gentile at the newsroom of the *Newark Ledger.*

"Garci wanted you, Evie, and he knew you wouldn't last long with Frank once he stopped being a star." She began a protest, but I cut her off. "So he decided to help things along by setting Frank up—getting him tied to Harry Lundquist again."

"That's crazy. In the first place, why would Harry go along. . . ."

"Because he got paid. And because he was afraid of Lou. Harry needed mob approval to run his biggest scams in Atlantic City and Philadelphia. Lou had ties to organized crime in both places.

One word from him and Harry was out of business—maybe worse.''

"I don't—that's ridiculous."

"Ask yourself this, Evie. Why did Harry finally agree to give you an uncontested divorce in 1973, after refusing for all those years? Because Lou ordered him to, that's why. He was about to propose to you himself and he wanted everything nice and legal."

She leaned back into her chair and closed her eyes for a few moments. When she opened them again, her stare was stone cold.

"Men have used me my whole life—I guess I should be used to it by now. Maybe I should thank you, Sheridan. You've filled in a few blanks for my story, too."

"Your story?"

"A publishing house in New York wants me to write an autobiography, and I'm considering their offer. They're very excited about its potential." She turned toward the lake and smiled. "Imagine that, little old Evelyn Marchabroda—a star at last."

Martina was waiting in the lobby.

"Let's take a walk," I said.

Council Rock sits at the southern end of Otsego Lake, four blocks south of the hotel. It's where the Susquehanna River begins and where, according to the historical marker, the Indians and the first settlers used to powwow. There's a concrete quay there and a few park benches. It was the dinner hour by then and the place was empty. We sat on the bench closest to the water, Martina and I, and I told her about her father. When I finished, her soft hazel eyes were glistening, but she didn't cry—it wouldn't do for a future attorney to cry.

"My mother was right about one thing, you know," she said. "It doesn't really matter—the illegitimacy stuff. I mean, who cares anymore?"

"Frank did. He remembered the taunts from his own childhood—he didn't want that for you."

She bowed her head, nodded. "I just wish . . . I always loved him, I think he knew that. But I wanted to be proud of him, too—that was the hardest part."

"For him, too, I'm sure," I said quietly. "Do you remember your Sophocles? In classic Greek literature, the hero always had a fatal flaw. And yet, he always faced up to it and did what he thought was right, even when he knew it meant his own destruction."

She looked at me. "I was worried about tomorrow—what I was going to say up there on the induction stand. The people here have been . . . polite but distant, y'know? I'm glad I know the truth now, and I want them to know. Mother can leave early if she wants—she doesn't belong here."

The tears came then and Martina wiped them away with the back of her hand. "I just wish I'd given him more of a chance, Sheridan. I mean, if I'd worked at knowing him a little harder, forced him to let me in. . . . " She shrugged. "I guess it's always easier just to walk away from someone else's problems."

We went back to the hotel then and said our goodbyes under the yawning portico. I made my way across the village to my motel and packed my bag. I had planned to stay the night and watch the induction ceremonies, maybe even go into the hall of fame gallery afterward to visit the niche where Frank Wooley's shining bronze plaque would be mounted. But I decided to save that moment for a quieter time.

When I got home to the cottage it was after ten. I stroked William's head a bit, replenished his water dish, and tumbled into bed. The next morning, I called IdaRose. We talked for an hour—a good talk.

I showered, refilled the coffee maker, and went out onto the deck while it brewed. The lake was placid, the sun bright. Summertime, and the living was easy.

Too damned easy.

There's often a momentary depression when a story runs its course; when the adrenalin of the pursuit subsides and you're down in the valley again, staring up at the next peak. But this was something else.

"It's always easier to just walk away from someone else's problems."

I thought about Martina's parting words. Then I thought about Kate Sumner. Spring blizzards and warm fires.

I was back inside the cottage, rummaging for the cordless phone, when the sizzle of tires on loose gravel drew me to the front door. A gray Honda Civic was pulled up next to the Bronco, Kate just then coming out from behind the wheel. I met her on the stoop, took her hand.

"I could use a friendly ear," she said, smiling faintly. "And a cup of coffee."

"I just put on a fresh pot."

The smile widened. "You're a mind reader."

"Must be going around," I said.

Wilcox   5-92
Wilcox, Stephen F.
All the dead heroes /
33172000530079 HQ